Downtown *and* Dirty

Downtown and Dirty

Bryan E Patrick

DOUBLE DOG PUBLISHING

The characters and events in this book are fictitious. Any similarity to real persons, living or dead, is coincidental and not intended by the author.

Double Dog Publishing
214 Pelican Street
Magnolia, Texas 77355

www.DoubleDogPublishing.com

ISBN-13: 978-0615581194
ISBN-10: 0615581196

Dedicated to my wife, Melinda

CHAPTER **1**

Bradley Marshall leaned back in the chair and smiled until a painful ring from his phone snapped his attention away from his computer screen. He reached for the phone in his front pocket.

"Brad? It's Renee. I think I'm in trouble. I may have seen something I wasn't supposed to see."

"What? Renee, where are you?"

"I'm at Richard's. I . . ." The connection went dead.

Brad stared at the phone in his hand. He saw on the display she had called from her cell phone. With the press of a couple of buttons he called her back. The phone rang several times before she answered.

"Renee, it's Brad. Are you alright?"

"I'm fine Brad. I'm sorry to have bothered you. It's nothing, really."

"But you said you were in trouble."

"I was mistaken. Again, I'm sorry I bothered you. Goodbye Brad."

The phone went silent again. How strange. With the divorce almost final, she was not in the habit of calling. Then again, if she was really in trouble, she might have called instinctively. They were, after all, still married and had been married for over six years.

Brad rubbed at the tension in the back of his neck. Damn it. It's not my problem even if it feels like it is.

What was I doing? Whatever is was I'm thirsty now.

Brad went into the kitchen and poured himself a glass of apple juice from the refrigerator. Sipping from the glass he drifted back toward the den. Damn it. Sitting around worrying about those phone calls was not an attractive plan. He looked at his watch. It was about eleven this Thursday evening. Jack should be down at the Red Lion Bar & Grill. Better to walk down there and complain to my friend. Who knows, after the walk, perhaps the phone calls will be less bothersome.

Brad left the alarm system off in case Renee came by later while he was out, and left the house which was located in a part of Houston called Mandel Place. He and Renee had shared the house before she moved out. He started down the sidewalk toward the Red Lion.

It was a perfect night to be out. The crisp air of early October was the combination of a hint of autumn and the smell of grass still being mowed. He watched the shadows dart across the sidewalk whenever a breeze blew through the elms lining the street.

He tried to get his mind off the calls from Renee and back on his novel. He was more than half way through the first draft and satisfied with his progress. When it was finished, he would of course, look for a publisher. But he didn't need the money. A couple of years earlier he had sold his computer software security company for several million dollars.   Even after splitting the money with Renee, which was being accomplished quite amicably, he would be more than comfortable.   Publishing the book would be for bragging rights, more than anything else.

He reached the Red Lion in a few minutes.

Scanning the inside of the bar, he saw most of the tables and booths to his left were occupied. He recognized the sound of Michael McDonald singing 'What a Fool Believes' from the jukebox. In front of him he noticed the stocky frame and crew cut of his friend, Jack Wilkerson, hunched over the bar.

"Jack, I keep wondering why Rusty doesn't charge you rent."

"You obviously haven't seen my beer tab. Have a seat and I'll buy you one of those fizzy waters you drink. That is if you're still drinking fizzy water." Jack said.

"I am and you can. Rusty, bring me a club soda." Brad sat next to Jack.

"Your trouble was you never learned to pace yourself. That's the trouble with most younger people these days. They want everything too fast. Instant oatmeal, instant rich, instant drunk."

Brad wrinkled his nose. "I never much cared for oatmeal."

Jack chuckled. "I expected a bigger argument. How long has it been for you now, since you've had a drink?"

"It will be a year soon. I never told you, but you helped me make the decision to quit."

"Me? How so?"

"You had rented a movie and was raving about it. *Shawshank Redemption*."

"I remember that movie. Good flick. When people look at old movies and say 'They don't make 'em like that anymore' you can point to something like *Shawshank* and say 'See here, they do too,' " Jack said.

3

"You were especially taken with a line from the movie, 'You better get busy living or get busy dying.' You asked me one night which I was doing. I couldn't shake that question out of my head. I kept asking myself whether I was busy living or dying and I didn't like the answer. Drinking was interfering with my living and the next day I quit. I'd like to think I've been busy living ever since."

"That's a hell of a story. Almost brings a tear to my eye. Almost. Not quite. Maybe if you told   it better."

Brad laughed. "I have another story for you."

"Is it going to pull on my heart strings some more? There's only so much I can take in one night." Jack said.

"No, I don't think so." Brad relayed to Jack the tale of the phone calls from Renee.

"So we've gone from old movies to old wives. Can we go back to movies?"

Brad chuckled. "She's barely a wife."

"Isn't your divorce about final?" Jack asked.

"It will be in a couple of weeks."

"Odd that she would call you at all. I would expect most of your correspondence these days is through attorneys."

"It is," Brad said.

"Except that if she was really in trouble, you are after all, still her husband."

"I thought of that."

"And you have no idea who this Richard might be?"

"None at all."

"Then my advice is to put it out of your mind. You

may never know what was going on when she called. She may not ever tell you. I know it's not easy, but there's nothing you can do so forget about it," Jack said.

"She just sounded so frantic at first."

"I could offer up an indelicate hypothesis concerning what it may have been about Richard that frightened her so, what with her being more accustomed to you. Since you might find the suggestion insulting, and you are my friend, I'll keep my mouth shut."

Brad smiled and shook his head. "Oh, I do appreciate that."

"You're welcome. Again, nothing you can do. And besides, she's practically your ex-wife. There are different rules for ex-wives, or so I've heard."

"I guess you're right. Hell, I know you're right, I've been telling myself the same thing," Brad said.

A short while later Brad left the bar for the walk home. The banter with Jack had lifted his spirits and his thoughts turned again to his novel. The next chapter would introduce the reader to a surprise. He considered the best way to approach it. He arrived at his house and pulled his keys from his pocket. Inserting the key in the lock he found the door was unlocked. He froze for an instant. He was sure he had locked it on the way out.

He pushed the door open and eased into the house. There in front of him was Renee lying in a pool of blood.

CHAPTER 2

Brad moved to Renee and knelt beside her. His hand crept out to her wrist and felt for a pulse. It was a useless gesture. She was dead. He had seen death before as a Marine in Desert Storm. Not a lot of it, but enough. She looked dead. She was dead.

He scanned the room around him, listening for any sound. The house seemed empty. He snuck into the study, alert to any movement in the room. He reached into his desk and removed a nine-millimeter handgun. He stood for a minute, listening. Satisfied that all was still quiet, he broke the silence by chambering a round in the weapon. He moved out into the living area past Renee's body and into the kitchen. No one was there. He slid upstairs and checked both bedrooms. Satisfied the house was empty, he took a deep breath and went back downstairs. He tucked the weapon in his belt and turned his attention back to Renee.

Looking over her body, he saw that she had been shot in the back and in the back of the head. Her purse lay beside her, along with a .38 revolver. The handle and trigger of the revolver were covered with black tape.

Brad leaned over her body. He pulled the hair back slightly from her face. His jaw tightened. Renee didn't deserve this. She was wife for six years, mother of the child they had lost to cancer when she was three. If only he hadn't gone out. If only he had been here.

He rose and turned away from the body, his shoulders slumped under the weight of the guilt he felt. He was ashamed he didn't wait for her after her call and wasn't there when she arrived at the house. He was ashamed he wasn't there for her after the death of their daughter. That he chose instead to hide in a bottle of whiskey.

For a long time he had been absent when Renee needed him and now when she needed him most he failed her.

He put his hands in his pockets and turned to look at the lifeless body. No, he didn't cause this. He wasn't responsible. He clung to the truth that he didn't cause her death, hoping that the thought would take root and grow to erase some of the guilt he felt.

He shook his head to clear it, his mind racing. She is here, dead. And why? Why here? The phone calls. Where was it she said she was? At Richard's. Richard who?

Brad looked at her purse. The answer might be in there. He peeked inside her purse and found her smart phone, a Christmas present from him to her. It was a powerful computer, but she only used it to hold shopping lists and make calls. He pulled up the address book and sorted it by first name. There were two Richards: a Richard Hackford and Richard Pierce. Pulling his own smart phone from his pocket, he turned it on and then beamed all of Renee's address book entries from her phone to his own. He would contact her friends later and ask about the Richards. He replaced the phones.

He went over to the phone and dialed 9-1-1. He gave the operator his name and address and told her he had come home to find his wife shot dead in his house. He replaced the receiver and noticed he had left the front door open. Going to the front door to close it, he stopped. The sensation of being shut up in the house with Renee's body made him open the door wide. He turned on the porch light for the police. He moved stiffly to a chair and sat staring at Renee's body sprawled across the floor. He waited for the police to arrive. He looked at Renee. He looked at the door. He looked back at Renee.

The room felt emptier than ever before. Brad half expected a huge chasm to open up in the floor as if from some science fiction yarn and swallow them up. With the divorce, he had been getting used to living without her, but not like this. He never called her, but he knew in the back of his mind they still shared a past and if he really needed to talk to her he could. She would be there. Now that was gone. Not as the result of choices made as in a divorce, but through a brutal and senseless act.

Pangs of rage welled up within him. Renee deserved so much better than to be treated this way. Nothing so vibrant and beautiful should be destroyed and discarded without regard. How dare they! How dare they shoot her like this? They should be made to pay. They must be made to pay.

Brad paced around the room as if he were looking for a way out. He looked at Renee, and then at the walls and ceiling, and then back at Renee. Finding no escape, he settled back in the chair with his hands clenched together into a big fist. He sat hunched over and his shoulders shook slightly.

Why? This was not right. His breathing became deep and labored, his jaw like granite. He was jealous of everything right and orderly with the world. He searched the room for a suitable symbol on which to heap obscenities.

His eyes grew wet and a lump came up in his throat. He thought of their wedding and how beautiful she was. He thought of the birth of their daughter and how proud they both were.

Brad started to sob. He thought of the dreams they had once shared and how they had crumbled, mostly with him taking her for granted after Amy died. She had needed someone to lean on, and not getting that from Brad, she turned elsewhere. Brad had been furious at first, but in the end he blamed only himself.

I didn't want the divorce, he thought. But I wanted you to have the life you wanted. Now you have no life at all. I wasn't there for you when Amy died. And I wasn't here for you tonight. Brad shook his head, his teeth grinding. He threw back his head and roared, "No!" He looked at the body of Renee with eyes glazed. I will not let this be on me. Whoever killed her is responsible and they will be made to pay for it. I will make sure of that.

Brad saw blue and red lights flashing outside the open front door, adding a circus quality to the surreal atmosphere. He put the gun from his belt on the chair and walked to the door. A patrol car was parked at the curb in front of his house. He could see movement inside the car. He stood for a while waiting. Another patrol car arrived. Finally, a door opened and a police officer got out. The officer stood until the officer from the other car met him on the sidewalk and they slowly made their way to Brad standing on the porch.

"I'm officer Martinez. This is officer Becker. You called for the police?"

"Yes. My wife is inside. I came home to find her shot. She's dead."

"I see. Can we go inside?"

"Sure." Brad turned to step back into the house.

"No. We need you to stay out here. One of us will go inside. Is anyone in the house?"

"No. I checked. It's empty."

Officer Martinez went through the open front door, pulling plastic gloves on over his hands. He leaned over Renee and studied her body for a minute. He touched her neck, searching for signs of life.

The officer stood up and reached for the radio on his shoulder. "N-8-3-7, request C.S.U. at 1726 Kipling Street. Female gunshot victim, deceased, approximate age 30. You might as well notify homicide. The victim was shot in the back."

Officer Martinez came back out. Turning to Brad he said, "I just called for the Crime Scene Unit. They'll be here in a minute. You say there is no one else in the house?"

"No." Brad said. "I checked it out after I found her. There's no one here."

"Okay. Let's just wait here until C.S.U. gets here."

Brad stood waiting, wondering if he should say anything else. The policemen moved a couple of feet away and started talking in voices low enough that Brad couldn't hear. Undoubtedly the policemen on the way would be the one's that actually investigated the crime. He shifted his weight from one foot to the other.

After another six or seven minutes, a man and woman arrived, wearing business suits. Brad started toward them, but Martinez reached them first and they exchanged a few words that Brad didn't hear. Brad stopped to allow them their conversation. Both took notebooks out of their pockets and started scribbling. They went into the house. After three or four minutes the man came out and approached Brad.

"Hi. I'm Sergeant McNair. My partner in there is Sergeant Woods. What is your name?"

"Marshall. Bradley Marshall."

"Okay Mr. Marshall, suppose you tell me what happened."

"Renee called me at about eleven o'clock. She seemed really upset. She said had seen something she wasn't supposed to see. I asked where she was. She said she was at Richard's. Then the phone went dead. I called her back. She said everything was alright, but she didn't sound alright. I was worried, but there didn't seem to be anything I could do. So I walked down to the Red Lion Bar & Grill. I spent half of an hour down there and then I walked home. When I got here, I found Renee lying inside, dead. I checked the house to make sure whoever did this wasn't still in the house and then I called you."

"I see." Sergeant McNair scribbled furiously. "How

old is Renee?"

"She's twenty-nine."

"And how do you know her?"

"We've been married for about six years, although we were getting a divorce."

"And how was that going?"

"The divorce? It was almost final. No major disagreements. We just grew apart, that's all."

Brad noticed more officers arriving. Some went into the house. Others stood and talked on the lawn.

"You said you were at the Red Lion. Have you had anything to drink?"

"No."

"So you live here. Where did Renee live? Here with you?"

"No. She lived in a townhome over on Memorial Drive."

"How did she come to be here?"

"I have no idea."

"You didn't expect her?"

"No. We hardly see each other. We communicate mostly through our attorneys. Although after those disturbing phone calls I did leave the alarm system off on the odd chance that she would come by. She has a key, but I wasn't sure whether she would remember the alarm codes."

"So she did have a key to the house?"

"Yes. No reason for her not to, as I said, the divorce was quite amicable. We weren't fighting over anything. I just never got around to asking for the key back. I guess it's a part of the separation I was putting off."

"Is that your gun beside Renee?"

"No!"

"Do you own a gun?"

"Yes, a nine-millimeter."

"Where is it now?"

"In the living room. In the chair."

Sergeant McNair moved over to the other officers and said something to him. The other officer went into the house.

"Have you ever seen the gun beside Renee before?" McNair asked.

"No I haven't."

"Have you fired a gun this evening?"

"No."

"Do you mind if we do a gunshot residue test of your hands to verify that?"

"No, I suppose that would be fine, if you feel like you need to."

"It would help move things along."

Brad looked around at the officers standing in his yard and going in and out of the house. The place seemed crowded.

"Mr. Marshall, you said when she called she mentioned a name. Here it is, Richard. Who is that?"

"I have no idea. There are two Richards in her phone. A Richard Hackford and a Richard Pierce."

Sergeant McNair stopped scribbling and jerked his head up, glaring at Brad. He paused. "You don't know either of these gentlemen?"

"No, I don't."

"Who might know of their relationship with Renee? Did she have any friends you were aware of?"

"I can think of two off hand. There's Dianne Parks. She owns Parks Antiques over on Westheimer at Dunlavy. Then there is Lisa Davis. Just a second." Brad pulled his phone from his pocket, retrieved Lisa's address and phone number, and gave it to the Sergeant, along with the contact information for Dianne.

"What sort of business are you in Mr. Marshall?"

"I used to be in computer security software. I sold my company just over a year ago. The last few months I've been working on a novel. I haven't been doing much in the software business, although I do have an office downtown."

"Your business address and telephone number?"

Brad took a business card from his wallet and gave it to the Sergeant.

"What about Ms. Marshall? Did she have an occupation?"

"She was an interior decorator. I don't think I have a card for her." Brad searched his wallet. "Yes, here's one." Brad removed another card from his wallet and gave it to Sergeant McNair.

"How about next of kin, other than you. Parents, brothers, sisters?"

"She has parents here in town. I'd like to be the one to call them if I might."

"Sure. Mr. Marshall, we'd like you to come down to the station and make a formal statement. It's just routine, if you would. It would help us a lot."

"Sure. Anything I can do to help."

"Come with me, please." The Sergeant escorted Brad to one of the many patrol cars parked along the street. He opened a back door and Brad got in the car.

14

After a couple of minutes Sergeant Woods appeared from the house. She and Sergeant McNair got into the front seat of the car. After some positioning and talking on the radio they started moving.

At the police station Brad was led to a small gray room with a plain metal table and four chairs. There was nothing on the walls. He sat in one of the chairs and waited.

An officer came in with a small case and placed in on the table in front of Brad. The officer opened up the case and took out a vial from which he removed two swabs. He instructed Brad to hold his hands out in front of him, swabbed his hands, and then placed the swabs into another vial from the case, which he marked with a pen. He packed everything up and left.

Brad waited for what seemed like a half of an hour. He started to get up and look for someone to see if he had been forgotten when the two detectives came into the room and immediately began asking him questions.

"You say she called you from Richard's. How did that make you feel?"

"How did that make me feel? I didn't care where she was calling from. I don't know Richard. I was just concerned because she sounded frightened." Brad shook his head a little to clear it. Was this making any sense?

"Did you argue about anything over the phone?"

"No. We lost connection. There was nothing to argue about. I called her back and she said not to worry, that everything was fine."

"Did you argue when she came over?"

"I wasn't there when she came to the house. When I

15

got there she was already dead. Hey, what is this about?"

They wanted to know more about the divorce. They wanted to know more about the state of his business and his finances. They asked about children, and upon hearing about Amy wanted to know the details of her illness and death. They asked to whom he had spoken to at the Red Lion and asked him repeatedly if he had been drinking.

It seemed as if he told the story of her phone calls, his trip to the Red Lion, and returning to find Renee a dozen times. After each time, they wanted to hear it again.

Several times they asked him if it was his gun found beside Renee. Several times they asked him if he had fired a gun. They asked if he had removed anything from her purse.

Brad was getting quite frustrated with their questions and twice threatened to call his attorney. Each time he mentioned his lawyer they seemed to back off from their adversarial stance a little, only to pick it up again later. Occasionally one of them would leave the room for a few minutes while the other continued the questions.

Finally, after more than a couple of hours, Brad had enough. "Am I free to go?"

There was a pause. The detectives looked at each other. "Sure. I guess we have enough. We may need to get in contact with you again."

"That's fine. If you call my office and I'm not there, Ms. Abernathy will know how to get in touch with me."

"You'll need to find somewhere else to stay until the

crime scene unit is through with your house. Do you know where you might stay?"

"I'm not sure I would be comfortable there tonight anyway," Brad said. "I'll probably get a room downtown, close to my office. Probably the Hyatt Regency if they have room."

"We'll give you a ride back to your house if you'd like."

"I'd appreciate that." Brad grimaced with some disgust at them. He rose from his chair, his legs stiff, and waited.

The man reached into his shirt pocket. "Again, I'm Sergeant McNair and this is Sergeant Woods." He held a business card out to Brad. "I'd appreciate it if you would get in touch with us if you remember anything else."

"I will do that." Brad took the card. He also received a card from the female officer. "But I've told you all I know."

On the way home he thought about what had transpired at the station. They had seemed more interested in his business than finding Renee's killers. He didn't have a good feeling about this. It was hard to have much confidence in them. But surely they were just doing their job. Surely they would find who did this. He had to believe that whoever did this would be brought to justice. Brad's jaw tightened. Justice has to come out of this.

CHAPTER **3**

Brad sensed that he was not in his own bed and immediately wondered what city he was in and how long he had until his speech. Then it hit him. No, this was not a hotel engaged for the purpose of some seminar where he was to give a tired old presentation on computer security. He was in Houston this Friday morning, at the Hyatt Regency downtown. And Renee was dead.

What time was it? He searched for and found the clock on the nightstand. It was almost nine o'clock. Not much more than four hours sleep. Well, it would have to do for now. He arose from the bed and went to throw some cold water on his face. He could get a shower and shave later at the gym. These clothes would have to do until he got to his office. He kept some spare clothes in a closet there. He was hungry, and rushed to go downstairs for breakfast.

He found the restaurant and made his way behind the hostess to a table. As soon as the waiter arrived, he ordered coffee and a standard breakfast of bacon and eggs. Watching the waiter depart, Brad went over the events of the night before. What was that at the police station? Is that the way they treat all of their witnesses? I wasn't even a witness as such; I just came home to find her dead. A lump came up in his throat at the thought of Renee lying there on his floor. He tried not to think of her last moments alive.

"Hi there."

Bradley looked up to see an attractive woman with a large bag over her shoulder, a bright blouse and dark pants, auburn hair to her shoulders and a huge smile, standing next to his table.

"Excuse me?" Brad replied.

"Aren't you Bradley Marshall?" She stuck out her hand to shake hands. "I recognized you from your photographs in our paper. I'm Jennifer Hart, with the Houston Chronicle."

She's very pretty, he thought. I like the way her hair cascades around her face. Brad rose slightly and shook hands. "Glad to meet you."

Jennifer took the chair opposite Brad before he could respond. "May I join you?"

"Well, I . . ." Brad's brow furrowed. "Be my guest."

Jennifer removed a small notebook from her bag which she opened and placed on the table to her right. She smiled at Brad.

"What's that for?" He asked.

"Oh this? I just make notes everywhere I go. It's just a habit. Part of my profession."

"Which is?"

"Oh, didn't I mention? I'm a reporter. Mr. Marshall, I want to tell you how sorry I was to hear about your wife."

"I see. I'm starting to understand now. How did you find me?"

"Well, it wasn't that easy. Although it wasn't that

hard either. You weren't in your office yet, but then there was no guarantee you would be in today. If you had been at a friend's I would have been out of luck. But I started calling the nicer hotels and I think this one was the fourth one I called. You didn't answer from your room, so I took a chance and came over here from the office."

"I see." Damn. My first breakfast with a beautiful woman in months and it has to be like this. "Ms.?"

"Hart. Jennifer Hart."

"Ms. Hart. I'm not sure what it is I can do for you."

"Oh call me Jennifer. What I'd like more than anything is an interview. But if you don't feel up to it, and I can certainly understand, then I'd settle for just a little something to eat. I'm starving." She smiled sweetly.

The waiter appeared with Brad's breakfast. Jennifer raised her hand at him. "I'll just have toast and some coffee."

Brad looked at his breakfast. He looked up. "I'm not accustomed to having the privacy of my breakfast intruded on by a beautiful woman."

"Well thank you! I really don't mean to intrude."

"Yes. As a matter of fact you do. And I don't really feel like giving any interviews right now. I haven't had much sleep."

"Well forget the interview then. Pretend we just met for the first time."

"We did just meet for the first time."

"Then it should be easy! I searched for your name in our database and you came up a lot. You used to have a company here in Houston. You sold it. What was it called?"

"Datasafe International."

"Yeah, that's it. Why did you sell it?"

"I didn't want to run it anymore. This is starting to feel like the interview that I didn't want to give."

"I'm sorry. I'm just naturally inquisitive. Why don't you ask me a question?" Jennifer sat with her chin in her hands and batted her eyelashes a couple of times.

Brad sat for a moment. Do I really want this to go any further? Is it really so bad to be in the company of a woman again? "Okay. I'll bite. Where are you from?"

"San Diego originally."

"Your parents?" Bradley started on his breakfast.

"They still live there," she replied.

"Let me guess. You got a degree in journalism from UCSD?"

"Very good!"

The waiter appeared at the table with Jennifer's toast and coffee. They sat for a few minutes in silence, eating.

"The police didn't say much about last night. Just that your wife had been shot. Did you see it happen?"

"No. I came home to find her. She was dead when I arrived home." Brad noticed that his comment led to her writing something down. He frowned.

"That must have been very hard. You must have loved her very much."

"Actually we were getting divorced," he said. Why did I say that? "Ms. Hart, my private life is none of your business."

"I'm sorry. I was just making conversation, and your wife's death is like the elephant in the room."

"Waiter." Bradley signaled for his check. "Let me buy you breakfast. It's the least that I could do. Since I really didn't intend to talk to the press, our conversation is evidence that you've been an extremely charming companion. So it's on me."

"I didn't mean to offend you, Mr. Marshall."

"You haven't. And I am sure you were just doing your job." Bradley signed the check. "Good luck at the Chronicle." Bradley turned and walked from the table.

What a gorgeous woman. Too bad meeting her was based on last night. Bradley's stomach was queasy. Is it right to think about a beautiful woman the day after Renee's death? After all, he and Renee had been split for over six months now. It was time to move on anyway. I was just going to shower and shave at the gym. Maybe I should work out as well.

This is also a warning. The press is evidently already alerted. It might take some doing to avoid them. Well, avoid them I will. Renee's memory should be allowed some dignity, and the press may not see it that way.

Bradley reached for the door of his office. He had been to his gym for a quick workout, shower and shave. Opening the door he was greeted with the familiar and welcome face of his longtime assistant, Ms. Rose Abernathy.

"Hello Rose."

"Hello Mr. Marshall. I heard about Ms. Marshall. The press has been calling all morning."

"Continue to tell them that I'm not in, Rose."

"Will do."

Bradley crossed over to his private office and closed the door behind him. He selected a polo shirt and slacks from the closet and changed into them, putting the clothes he was wearing into a bag and placing the bag at the bottom of the closet.

He opened the door to his office. "Rose, I'm going to be out for a little while. I'm going to get some lunch and try to meet with one of Renee's friends. I'll be back this afternoon."

"Mr. Marshall, I didn't get to tell you how sorry I was to hear about Ms. Marshall."

"I know, Rose. Thank you for saying that though. I'm sorry that you have to deal with all of those phone calls."

"It's okay, Mr. Marshall. You have a nice lunch."

Brad headed for the elevator. It was comforting to have Rose Abernathy around at a time like this. The woman seemed able to handle anything, and exuded strength of character. Before lunch he would head out to Dianne Parks' antique shop and see if he could catch her there. Maybe she knew the Richards in Renee's address book.

Down in the parking garage, Bradley considered putting the top down on the car. This was the kind of beautiful day he had in mind when he bought the car, but today he didn't really feel like it.

Pulling out onto the street, he wondered if he were doing the right thing. The police should be the ones investigating and talking to Renee's friends, but after last night, who knows if or when they will get around to it. They didn't seem that interested in learning the names of who might be able to identify the Richards in Renee's life. Going back over the questioning at the police station in his mind, his hands tightened on the steering wheel. In any case, I can't just wait around and do nothing. I've got to find out what I can, and if I learn something, I've got the numbers of the detectives on the case.

Brad turned up Fannin Street in order to avoid some construction downtown. It seemed like most of the streets and sewers downtown were being torn up and remade. Avoiding the mess was not always easy.

Soon he was zipping down Westhiemer approaching the string of antique shops at Dunlavy. Dianne Parks and her husband had one of the better shops there. Several of them were not much more than junkyards. As usual, the street in front of the shops didn't yield any parking so he passed by them to park in a small parking lot about a block away.

Walking down the sidewalk in front of the antique shops, Bradley was greeted by an assortment of furniture and accessories practically tumbling from the open bays of the stores in rows and stacks. A path was left between the merchandise, end tables and dining room chairs in rows. Lamps and candlestick holders were arrayed on cabinets. In the windows of the front of the shops were paintings and stained glass, all in brilliant colors. Signs denoting merchants, bargains and sales competed for attention.

Making his way between the collections of treasure

and junk, Brad found the entrance to Parks' Antiques. The entrance was set back from the sidewalk a little bit and down a narrow path. It was a freshly painted structure in white with blue trim. The Parks didn't believe it necessary to haul examples of their wares outside onto the sidewalk, as did some of their competition.

Closing the front door behind him, Brad turned to see Dianne approaching him. "Hello Dianne."

"Brad! Great to see you! What brings you out this way? I don't suppose you need a new coffee table?"

"No Dianne. I'm afraid I have some bad news. Is there someplace we can talk?"

"Sure, honey. Let's go back to the office. We'll run Larry out of there." Dianne turned and started walking toward the back down a narrow path between rows of bookcases in oak and cherry. Reaching a small office, she spoke to Larry who was sitting at the desk inside. "Larry dear, will you watch the front for a minute?"

"Sure thing. Hello Brad. How're things?"

"They could be better, Larry."

Larry left the two of them alone in the office.

"Now, what's up?" Dianne asked.

"I don't know of any way to tell you except just to tell you straight out. Renee's been murdered, Dianne."

"Oh my God. Oh my God." Dianne reached for a tissue from a box on the desk. She started crying into the tissue.

Brad sat for a moment. Damn. I never know what to do at a time like this. He moved over next to Dianne and put an arm around her shoulder.

After a few moments, Dianne wiped her eyes and

cleared her throat. "Do they know who did it?"

Brad took his arm away and put his hands in his lap. "No. That's part of the reason I'm here. Before she was killed she called me. She said she was at Richard's, but she didn't say Richard who. I was hoping you might have some idea who she was talking about."

"Oh dear. No, I'm pretty sure I don't know. I've not been seeing Renee as much lately as I used to. Oh, she still came by from time to time, and she bought a piece from me just last week. But lately we haven't talked like we used to. She's been going out more at night with that Lisa. That's a wild one, that Lisa. She tends to mash her foot down on the gas pedal of life. It feels strange, me telling you this. But then I guess it doesn't matter so much now." Dianne dabbed at her eyes. "This is horrible. Not Renee."

"I know. I'm sorry to have to ask you these questions, but I really want to find out who did this. Dianne, there were two Richards in her address book. A Richard Hackford and a Richard Pierce. Do you know them? Would either of them be mixed up in this?"

"Let's see. Richard Hackford I believe was a client. Yes, now I'm sure of it. I can't believe he would be mixed up in any murder. As I recall he is an attorney downtown. Renee decorated his office. She bought a couple of lamps from me for that job. That was a couple of months ago. If she had anything else to do with him I certainly didn't hear anything about it."

"What about the other one, Richard Pierce?"

"The name is familiar, but I just don't know. Lisa would probably know. Like I said, the last few weeks her and Renee have been pretty well burning up the town." Dianne said.

"Well, thanks Dianne. It sounds like it probably wasn't Hackford."

"No, I wouldn't think he would have anything to do with murder, but then who would? This is just so horrible. Renee, of all people."

Brad told her about the phone calls, his trip to the Red Lion, and coming home to find Renee's body. At the part about finding Renee, his jaw tightened.

"Oh dear. Brad, I don't know what to say. That must have been awful, finding her like that. I had always hoped that since you had gotten your life back together that you and her would somehow work things out."

"There was just too much water under the bridge as they say for that, Dianne. But I did want the best for her, not this."

"Yes of course, I know you did, Brad. Well, like I said, Lisa will probably know more. Do you know how to get hold of her?"

"Yes. Thanks again, Dianne."

Brad left the shop. That wasn't as much as he had hoped to learn, but it was something. She did seem sure that Lisa would know something.

Sitting in his car, he retrieved Lisa's number and called from his cell phone. He got her answering machine. He didn't leave a message. He didn't think she would call him back anyway, not the soon-to-be ex of her party partner. She probably doesn't know about Renee and I don't want to tell her over the phone. I'll go back to the office and keep trying to contact her.

CHAPTER **4**

Jennifer Hart bounced into the wide-open offices on her floor at the Houston Chronicle and headed for her cubicle. She tried to get by the office of her boss, Bill Caruthers, without being noticed.

"Jennifer."

"Hi, Boss."

"What have you been doing lately to justify us paying you?"

"I just had breakfast with Bradley Marshall, husband of that woman that was killed last night."

"Good work! Write it up. I want to see it yesterday. Did Bobby get any shots?"

"I had Bobby stay back out of the way on this one. I didn't want to spook him with a photographer. He did get shots of the house, but I doubt any of that is usable. Besides, we have stock in the archives on Marshall."

"Well it probably doesn't have him looking sufficiently haggard and distraught, but it will have to do. Go write it up."

Jennifer continued to her cubicle and dropped her bag next to her chair. I shouldn't be feeling this good about it. Sure, I had breakfast with the guy, but I practically ran him off with the first couple of questions. I did find out that he came home to find his wife dead. That should be enough to fill a few inches of the article. And there is stuff in the archives about who he is.

Jennifer peered over the cubicle wall. "Hi Jerry."

"Hello yourself. Did I just overhear that you've been chasing the husband of a murdered woman?"

"I didn't just chase him. I caught him."

"You know, I'd make a much better bedtime companion than a police scanner."

"I've got a bedtime companion. And actually, I got a call on this one. One of the officers with the Crime Scene Unit is a buddy."

"Oh sure, just a buddy. I'm sure he gives you these juicy calls because you're a buddy. Why don't you do for me what you do for him?"

"You want me to feed your dog when you go skiing? I'll be glad to, Jerry."

Jennifer sat down at her computer and logged in. She pulled out her notes. Damn. There wasn't much to go on.

She pulled up a page on the computer to search the archives of past Chronicle articles and typed in the name of Bradley Marshall. Several titles appeared on the screen. Damn. There is the one about the pending divorce. Why didn't I see that earlier this morning?

If I had realized they were getting a divorce, I wouldn't have made that comment about his loving her. Still, he's obviously a sensitive guy. I'll bet he still loved her. I wonder if the divorce was his idea or hers? Probably hers, judging by the way he spat out those words about it. Still, I can't write that.

She typed in the name of Renee Marshall for a search. A couple of the same articles appeared, most notably the one about the divorce. Well, my contact said she was an interior designer.

What can I write? Jennifer squirmed in her chair. I'll start with the facts I got at the scene.

Jennifer lost herself in writing the story for almost an hour and a half. While she had not been allowed into the house, she did get some description from her friend with the Crime Scene Unit. She started with that, pulled in some facts about Renee and Bradley from the archives, and finished with her impressions over breakfast. She read over the article. Satisfied, she hit the button to submit it for review.

Jennifer leaned back in her chair and closed her eyes. She had gotten an early start this morning. Too early, and the day was not done yet. It would be a good idea to try to catch up with Marshall again and try to smooth things over. I'm going to want more from him. I can't leave things where they were at the restaurant. Jennifer smiled at the prospect of meeting with Brad again.

"Ms. Hart! Get in here."

Jennifer jerked open her eyes. She must have drifted off. She got up from her chair and moved toward the direction of the booming voice of her boss that had awakened her.

"I'm coming."

Wiping her eyes, she entered Caruthers' office.

"What are you, in love with this guy?"

"Pardon me?"

"This guy's wife has been murdered. Statistically speaking he killed her."

"But he said he came home to find her dead."

"And we just take his word for that? It's alright to say that's his story but you seem to say it's a fact. Where did he say he was before he came home to find the body?"

Jennifer bit her lower lip. "I don't know."

"Great. I can't believe you missed that."

"He was pretty testy. I felt lucky to get what little I did."

"Say he came home from an undisclosed location. Maybe when he reads that he'll talk to you again to clear it up. We do know he was getting a divorce. He saved a bundle what with his wife going into a coffin. You should drop a hint or two. It'll add drama."

"I got up too early, I guess. I'm sorry. I'll rewrite it."

"No excuses. The first part of this is fine. But in the end you wind up gushing all over this guy. I'm tempted to have Jerry handle the description of Marshall. At least I know he won't fall in love with him."

"No, don't bother Jerry. I can do it. Like I said, it's been a long day, and I just lost focus. You know I can do it, Bill. Let me handle it."

"Well hurry. I don't have to remind you we have deadlines around here."

Jennifer went back to her desk and slumped in her chair. Was it that bad? She didn't want to look at it. Sure, this Marshall guy was good-looking and rich and had a sweet way about him. But that's no excuse for letting it affect my work. Caruthers is right; the guy could be a murderer.

Brad a murderer? There is absolutely no way I

could ever believe it. My instincts are never that wrong. Still, he's not someone to be gushed over as Caruthers put it. I have a boyfriend for that. Maybe I'm just suffering from a little boyfriend withdrawal from working too much. That's probably it.

I'll redo the end of the article. Then I'll see if I can patch up things with Brad, no, this Marshall fellow. I still need to try to get an interview with him. I'll try to remember he might be a murderer even though I know he's not. I can still do that and turn on the charm, I hope.

Tonight I'll take care of the time with the boyfriend issue. He isn't playing tonight, so he should be home. I'll cook something special and spend some quality time with my hunny, Kevin. That should get things all straightened out.

––––––––––––––––––

Brad entered his office Friday afternoon, back from his visit with Dianne Parks. He saw Rose was replacing the phone on the receiver.

"All manner of television and newspaper have been calling, Mr. Marshall."

"You just keep telling them I'm not here, Rose, and I'm sorry they're such a bother."

"It's not your fault. I just wished I could do more. Can I get you anything?"

"No. Thanks Rose."

Brad went into his office and slumped down into his chair. He had made that difficult call to Renee's parents, the Sheridans, first thing this morning. He didn't want them hearing anything on the news first. It would probably be a good idea to call my parents as well. I'll try Lisa again first. Brad dialed the number for Lisa.

"Lisa. It's Brad."

"Well! Hello Bradley. What's up with you?"

"I wonder if I might meet you somewhere? I have a couple of things I want to talk to you about."

"I never turn down an invitation from the rich and handsome. I was planning on being at the Skybar tonight. How about meeting me there, about eight?"

"Scott Gertner's Skybar, on Montrose?"

"That's the one."

"I'll see you at eight."

Brad dialed his parents. His mother answered and he broke the news of Renee's death to her. As with Renee's parents he told them about coming home to find her but left out the details of her phone calls. He didn't see the need in bothering them with any more of the story than necessary. That would lead them to worry over useless speculation. When there was more he would tell them.

"Are you sure there's nothing we can do?" His mother asked.

"There's nothing, Mom. I'm fine."

"What about your brother? Somebody ought to tell him. You want us to do it?"

"Would you, Mom? It's been pretty hectic around here and you talk to him more than I do anyway," Brad said.

"We'll be glad to, son. You take care of yourself."

"You too, Mom."

Brad hung up and leaned back in his chair. He

33

needed a nap. Instead he was greeted with the buzz of his intercom. He punched the lit button on the phone.

"Yes, Rose?"

"Mr. Marshall I hate to bother you, but there is a young woman out here to see you. She says she knows you from breakfast. A Ms. Hart?"

Crap. Well at least she can't get to me in here. He opened his mouth and heard himself say "That's okay, Rose. Show her in." His brow furrowed. Why did I do that? Well it's too late now. You are about to be visited by a beautiful woman; you might as well try to make the best of it. Just be careful of the questions. She's a pro.

Rose opened the door and held it as Ms. Hart entered the room. Brad tried to gauge the reaction on Rose's face but couldn't. Not surprising. That woman was unflappable.

"Mr. Marshall." Jennifer held out her hand.

"Ms. Hart." Brad shook her hand. "Have a seat."

"Thank you. I really didn't think you would see me, after the way we left things this morning."

"I really didn't think I would either, Ms. Hart."

"Well I'm certainly glad you decided in my favor. Please, call me Jennifer." Jennifer took a seat in one of the two chairs facing Brad's desk. "I wanted to apologize again for this morning. I was a little off base. My research on you was a little incomplete before we met." Jennifer took out her notebook and started flipping through the pages.

"Let's come to an understanding on a few things up front, Jennifer. First, you don't owe me an apology.

And second, while I agreed to talk to you I'd appreciate it if you would indulge me by putting that notebook away."

Jennifer looked up from the notebook. She smiled and adjusted herself in the chair. "It's only so that I don't misquote you." She batted her eyelashes.

"Ms. Hart."

"Jennifer."

"Ms. Hart. If you put away the notebook we'll go back to Jennifer. I didn't say that I would grant you an interview. I said that you could come in."

"I see." Looking chastened, Jennifer eased the notebook back into her satchel. "I didn't mean to misunderstand."

"Yes, you did. I don't mind, really. It's part of your charm."

Jennifer looked up with a slight smile. "So an interview is out of the question?"

"It is for now, but you may persuade me to grant you one later." He studied her face. With a coy smile like that she may persuade me of anything. He shifted in his chair. "How long have you been in Houston?"

"Six years."

"Coming from California it must have been a bit of a shock. You like it here?"

"Oh, I love it. The humidity took some getting used to, but other than that I just love it. Houston is so very multicultural. My friends in San Diego thought I was crazy to come here. They thought it would be full of cowboys. Sure, there are a few, but mostly there are people from all over the world. I like that."

"I've found that people from California often have a

very distorted view of Texas. I'm sure you've seen this before, but come over here." He led her to the large windows behind his desk. "Looking down toward the west, what color do you see?"

"Green."

"That's right. The tops of trees. It's the same out of my other windows to the south. Try that in another major city."

They stood next to each other. Brad became aware of her perfume. Feeling awkward, he motioned her back to her seat.

"Am I allowed to ask you questions, Mr. Marshall?"

Brad chuckled. "It's Brad. And sure, ask whatever you want."

"You sold your company over a year ago. What have you been doing since?"

"Oh, this and that. I do a little consulting, if I think the job is interesting. I do some speaking engagements. Lately I've been spending most of my time writing a novel. That part is strictly off of the record." Brad cringed a little inside. *Perhaps he shouldn't have mentioned that. I hope I can trust her. So what, it's not like it's a big secret.*

"A novel! What genre?"

"Science Fiction."

"I'm afraid I haven't read much Science Fiction since the Bradbury and Arthur C. Clarke I read as a kid."

"That's a good start. I would think since you're in the writing business you've entertained the idea of writing a book yourself."

"Well, yeah. I have. Probably a biography though.

I like to tell a person's story. I'd like to be able to take one person who is interesting and really give them the treatment they deserve instead of just a few column inches in the paper. I get tired of jumping from story to story."

"I could see that. I wanted to write a book for years. I finally realized the only way it would get written is if I actually sat down and wrote it. So one day I got started on it. Perhaps one day you'll do the same."

"It would be hard right now. This newspaper job keeps me pretty busy. Also my writing style is so flat and just straight facts these days because of the demands of my job. I try to keep it as interesting as I can, but it's not easy."

"Don't your readers want just the facts?"

"The facts can be written and colored in different ways. Take last night. I can take the same facts and present you as a loving husband who didn't want the divorce and came home to find his wife murdered. Or I can present you as a monster who couldn't wait for the divorce and killed her to save yourself a settlement. These two views can be done with a different presentation of the same facts."

"Which one of those am I?" Brad gripped the arms of his chair, waiting for the answer.

"As far as the newspaper is concerned you are neither. You are somewhere in the middle and we don't know yet."

"And you? Which one of those am I to you?" Brad searched her face.

"Much closer to the first. I know you didn't kill her."

"And how do you know that?"

"I just know. My instincts are too good, and I trust them. You didn't kill your wife, Brad."

Brad folded his hands in his lap. "You're right. I didn't. And you're saying all of the right things."

"The right things for what?"

"For me to grant you an interview. Just give me a couple of days to take care of some things. Set something up with Rose on the way out." Brad rose from his chair. "I've enjoyed talking with you."

"I've enjoyed it, too. You asked most of the questions, though. That's not right."

"Didn't letting me ask the questions move you toward the interview that you wanted when you came here?"

"I guess it did. Thanks so much for your time."

"Don't mention it." Brad escorted her to the door. "Rose, Ms. Hart will be interviewing me for the paper. Set something up with her for a couple of days from now, will you?"

After Jennifer left, Brad returned to his seat. *Am I doing the right thing? I really didn't want an interview. I wanted a date. That's silly. She's probably involved, anyhow.*

Brad closed his eyes and took a deep breath. *The lingering smell of her perfume is going to screw up my nap.* After a couple minutes he jerked his eyes open. *This is not working. I can't relax with the smell of her* in the room. He reached for his computer. I'll work on my novel.

Better yet, I'll log onto the Houston Chronicle website. They have archives of their older articles.
 I'll read some of this Jennifer Hart's stuff. What kind of reporter is she?

CHAPTER **5**

Richard Pierce opened his eyes and wondered what day it was. Friday. Good. The start of a weekend. That can only mean good things. Of course any day is a good day when you've got looks and money.

He looked at the clock. After noon. I need to check with those two meatballs for brains and make sure they didn't screw up last night. He reached over and got his cell phone from the nightstand. He punched a couple of numbers and waited.

"Duane, you and Reggie meet me in an hour. You know where." That settled, he got up from the bed to get dressed.

He picked one of several black shirts from the closet along with some black slacks. Stopping by the nightstand to retrieve his phone, he noticed something else.

"What's this?" There was a ring and necklace lying on the nightstand. "That bitch, Renee." He smiled as he remembered her bent over on her knees, naked and squirming in front of him last night. Too bad. I'm gonna miss her. She was plenty hot. Anyway, she's not going to be needing these anymore. He swept the jewelry into a drawer.

He moved to the living room and picked up a canvas tote bag from beside the couch. Carrying it to the dining room table, he opened it to reveal bundles of one hundred dollar bills.

Richard smiled. I need to tally this up and move it out for distribution. He went over to his desk nearby and got two envelopes. Back at the table he put a bundle of bills in each of the envelopes and put the envelopes in his pocket. Closing the bag he took it to his closet. The distribution could wait until later this afternoon. I don't want to be running around town with all that cash any more than I have to. From another bag in the closet, he removed one of several .38 revolvers and tucked it in his belt at his back.

Right now I need to check with Duane and Reggie to make sure they cleaned up our little problem last night. What dumb fucking luck, those two clowns coming in here spouting our business so she could hear it. And then her getting on her damn phone to hubby! Fuck! Well, she couldn't have said much. She didn't have the time. Besides, she didn't know much; just enough so I couldn't let her spread that shit around town. Her and hubby better not be a problem any more.

A few minutes later Richard left his loft apartment at the old Rice Hotel in downtown Houston. He headed south on Main toward Hermann Park. More than once he had to honk at some friggin' asshole to get out of his way. What are Sunday drivers doing out on a Friday afternoon? Reaching the statue of Sam Houston on his horse, he veered to the right and parked in a small parking lot. He noticed Duane's ride. Good. They're already here. He got out of the car and walked over to a clearing just past the train tracks for the little train that circled the park. Standing near some small pines were

Duane and Reggie.

"Hello, my men. Tell me good news about last night."

"Well there's good news and bad news, Rick." Duane said.

"What do you mean, bad news?"

"Well, we did her like you said. But the husband wasn't there."

"You checked good?"

"Yeah. But we couldn't stick around too long. There was some kind of alarm, and it didn't look like it was set. But we couldn't be sure there wasn't some kind of silent alarm thing, you know."

"I see. It was the right address? The one on her driver's license?"

"Yeah Rick. She said she didn't live there anymore. But one of her keys worked the lock. She said her husband lived there."

"Well it's the address on her license, so she did live there not long ago. You're sure she's dead?"

"Oh yeah. And we left the piece, just like with the security guard. But Rick, I hate to keep burning perfectly good guns," Duane said.

"You just keep burning 'em if you have to. I don't want two jobs traced to the same gun. Drop it as soon as you use it. They can't trace it back to you if they don't catch you with it. I don't want either of you forgetting to get rid of a used weapon, so drop it after you shoot it. Always."

"We got it. We use it, we drop it." Duane said.

"That reminds me, I brought one to replace those from last night. I'll get you another. I forgot you needed two." Richard took the gun from behind his back at his belt and handed it to Duane. "Tell this big joker not to get so jumpy at security guards and maybe you won't have to lose so many."

"It wasn't his fault, Rick. The guard made us. He must have thought we were drug dealers or something. He was going for his radio. You would have done the same thing if you had been there, like you were supposed to be."

Richard put his finger at Duane's chest. "Hey, I say where I'm supposed to be. Not you, okay? And I don't care what happened. You still shouldn't have come busting in over at my place. Never come to my place." Richard turned his back to the small train full of passengers passing a short distance away.

"Sorry Rick, but I just didn't know what else to do. We had all of that money from the drop and we didn't know what to do with it. I wasn't going to be responsible for it. We tried to call you on your cell but you didn't answer."

"I'd left it in my jacket. I guess I couldn't hear it over that bitch's moans. She must have been having some kind of religious experience the way she was hollering to God."

The three of them snickered. "Well fuck it. What's done is done." Richard took the two envelopes out of his pocket and handed them to the two men. "You guys did alright. Don't worry about the husband. I'll take care of him. Hang loose until I need you again."

Richard turned his back to the men and headed to his car. This may take some doing to make sure it gets cleaned up nice and tidy. Fuck. Why couldn't that husband have been home waiting for wifey so everything could have been wrapped up already? I just assumed she called him at home. She must have called his cell. Or else he just stepped out. What a bunch of crap. I hate having to worry about that sonofabitch.

I shouldn't have forgotten about that money drop. I let my mind get distracted by that bitch, Renee. Damn cunt. I am gonna miss her though. Richard grinned. If hubby had made her ass thrash around like it was twitching for me last night, she wouldn't have been stepping out on him. Oh well. She was gettin' used up anyway. Besides, there is plenty more where that came from.

Brad parked his car on the second floor of the parking garage. He was surprised he could find parking so close to the ground on a Friday night, but then it was not quite eight o'clock. By ten, most of the garage will be full.

He walked to the stairs leading to the ground floor lobby of the Skybar and pushed the button for the elevator. Standing there, he remembered that the two elevators were not only slow, but usually only one worked at a time. The dingy plaster walls and yellowed linoleum always made him feel like he was part of something forgotten from the fifties. Finally the doors opened and he stepped inside. Pushing the button for the top floor, he settled back for the slow ride. The doors opened and he took four steps to the entrance to the bar.

"Ten dollars, please."

Brad paid the man and went inside. It hadn't changed since he and Renee had been there for a jazz concert over a year ago. To his left was a bar. In front of him were small tables, and behind them a bandstand. It was too early for the band, but dance music blared, and the dance floor was empty. Behind the bandstand were windows where a short distance away the setting sun gleamed from the skyscrapers downtown. There was a good crowd, but it wasn't elbow to elbow as it would be later. Brad scanned the people in the bar looking for Lisa. He didn't see her.

Moving around to his left he went up to the bar and ordered a club soda. Watching the bartender make his drink he noticed Lisa sitting at the other leg of the "L" shaped bar. After he got his drink and paid for it, he went around the edge of the bar to where Lisa was sitting.

"Lisa."

"Brad! I see you already have a drink. Mine's empty," Lisa said with a pout.

Brad motioned to the bartender to refill Lisa's drink. "We can fix that."

"How have you been? Renee doesn't talk about you much anymore, what with things the way they are. I've been dying to know how you've been getting along." Lisa smiled at Brad as her drink appeared. "Thanks for the drink."

"It's okay. Lisa, can we go outside? I need to talk to you for a minute."

"Yeah, sure." Lisa picked up her drink and headed toward the back of the bar. She practically writhed in her tight blue dress. Lisa could be quite a flirt.

Passing through a doorway they came to the outside deck of the Skybar and stood overlooking the city from ten stories high.

The air was fresh and crisp with a slight breeze and smelled faintly of salt. It must be coming from the Gulf, fifty miles to the south. Latin music was being piped outside from the dance floor.

The sun was almost gone. Soon it would be twilight, then nighttime would find the city below illuminated in all colors of lights. The air, music, the emerging lights, and Lisa's bright blue dress gave the atmosphere a hint of something tropical. The festive, but tranquil setting spoke of carefree leisure, not the somber business at hand.

Brad motioned them to a table away from the doorway and they took chairs next to each other.

"Lisa, I don't know how to tell you this, other than to just come right out and say it. Renee has been murdered. She was shot."

Lisa's face went blank. "You're not kidding are you?" Lisa sat there for a moment, staring at Brad. Her eyes began to tear. "When? Where? Who killed her?" She wiped at her eyes. She reached inside the small purse at her side and took out a tissue.

"I don't know who killed her, Lisa. I was hoping you could help me."

"I'll help you any way I can, Brad. This is horrible." Lisa sniffled and dabbed at her eyes.

"Lisa, she called me last night. She said she was at Richard's. Do you know what Richard she may have been talking about?"

"Sure. Richard Pierce." Lisa said, her head down.

"You're sure?"

"Of course I'm sure. I saw them last night. They were here. She left with him. This is where she met him as a matter of fact, just over a week ago I think it was. But he couldn't have had anything to do with it."

"Why is that, Lisa?"

"Don't you know who Richard Pierce is?" Lisa looked up at Brad. Her eyes were red and wet.

Brad shrugged. He shook his head. "The name sounds familiar."

"Well it should. He's the mayor's son."

The blood left Brad's face. He sat back in his chair and gripped at the arms. "Are you sure?"

"Of course I am, silly."

"Mayor Stuart Pierce? His son?"

Lisa sniffled. "That's the one."

Brad shook his head slowly. This can't be. He can't be the one behind Renee's murder. Can he?

CHAPTER **6**

It was five o'clock Friday afternoon when Jack Wilkerson put down the western he was reading in the living room of his apartment. He turned on the television to watch the news. He was barely paying attention until he heard the name of Renee Marshall, and then the name of his friend Brad.

Brad must have found her dead at his house after he walked home last night. Those phone calls were a lot more trouble than they seemed. Crap.

Jack turned the television off and stared at the blank screen. I wonder what I can do? All of those years on the police force still ought to count for something. He got up, left his apartment and headed for his car.

It took him more than half of an hour in heavy traffic to make it downtown. He parked in front of the police station, and walked up to the counter inside. He spoke to the officer at the counter, and produced the identification he carried that showed he was a retiree of the department. "Mind if I talk to some of the guys in homicide?"

"No, that's okay." The officer pushed a button to activate the door to let him into the back. "You remember where it is?"

"Unless they've moved it."

"They never move anything around here."

Jack moved down the familiar corridors until he found the homicide department.

He looked around for a familiar face. He found James Henderson.

"James. How are you doing? And what are you doing over here in homicide?"

"Jack. I'm doing just fine. I made Sergeant last year and they transferred me over. Haven't seen you in a while. Are you still holding down a stool at the Red Lion?"

"They still have stools that need holding down."

"What brings you downtown?"

"Do you know who's working the Marshall case?"

James reached out and punched some keys on the computer behind him. "I think McNair's on that. Yeah, McNair and Woods."

"I don't know them," Jack said.

"I know McNair. I've never really spoken with Woods much. I hear she's alright. Why? You want to talk to them?"

"I'd like to if I can."

James looked around the room. "They're not in right now, but I'll try to set something up. Like I said, I know McNair. He's a good guy, straight up fellow."

"I'd appreciate it. Let me give you my number."

James grabbed a pen and pad off of the desk. "Shoot." He wrote down the number Jack gave him and threw the pad back onto the desk. James chuckled. "I guess if you're not there I can reach you at the Red Lion, huh?"

"You got it. Everything about the same around here?"

"No, not since we got that jerk for a Chief the Mayor gave us two years ago. I guess he was just coming in as you went out. He's turned out to be a real pain in the you know where, but you didn't hear it from me."

"Since when do you pay attention to a Chief of Police?"

James laughed. "Well this one you got to pay attention to, and he wants to know what's going on with everything. It seems like if the wrong people are getting parking tickets we hear about it over here in homicide." James shook his head. "You were right to get out when you did."

"Sounds like it. Well, give me a call if you can set something up, okay?"

"Will do. Did you know this woman, this Marshall?"

"Yeah. And I know her husband real well. Bradley. He was with me just before he found her."

"Cripes. He's alright, this Bradley?"

"Yeah, he's a good guy. I sure hated to see something like this happen to him."

"Well I'll reach out to McNair. Things have changed around here. But not so much that the word of a stand up guy with as many years on the job as you don't mean nothing."

"I appreciate that, James."

"Don't mention it."

Jack left the station and headed back to his car. On the way, he thought about how it had just gone. I had hoped to talk to the officers in charge of the investigation, but maybe I'll get to yet. I'll just have to be patient. Poor Brad. I'll get something to eat and then head over to the Red Lion. Maybe I'll see him there.

Brad drove from the Skybar to the Red Lion in a daze. He instinctively sought out his friend, Jack, to get his opinion on what Lisa had told him. Entering the Red Lion, he looked around. He's not here. I'll wait a while.

Brad took a seat at the bar and ordered a club soda with lime from Rusty. He sat hunched over and tried to make sense of what Lisa had said.

When Renee said she was at Richard's, had she meant Richard Pierce, the mayor's son? That just can't be. Not to take anything away from Renee. In her work, she met some of Houston's better placed in society, and she was certainly pretty and stylish enough to date in their circle.

What doesn't make any sense is that she would see anything at his place that would frighten her. Or that the son of the mayor would have anything to do with her murder. No, that doesn't make sense at all.

The murder must not be connected. She must have driven to my place after getting upset at Richard's and then been the victim of some random violence. But it wasn't a burglary. Nothing in the house was disturbed that I recall, except for Renee being there. Brad cringed at the memory, and forced himself to think of how Renee was positioned.

There was no sign of sexual assault. She was just brutally shot and left dead or dying on the floor. I had assumed her murder was connected to her phone calls, connected to whatever she saw that frightened her. But it makes no sense for the son of the mayor to be mixed up in this.

Brad felt a hand on his shoulder.

"You haven't gotten too far ahead of me with those fizzy waters have you? I'd hate to have to haul your ass out of here."

Brad looked up at Jack's smiling face. "Hi Jack. I was looking for you."

"And you found me. Or I found you. Whatever, the outcome is the same. Damn, if I'd realized you had the weight of the world on your shoulders, I would have kept my hands off them."

"What? No, that's alright. I'm just a bit perplexed."

"So tell me about it. That's why you were looking for me, right?" Jack turned around and caught the attention of the bartender. "Rusty, I need a beer."

"I just talked to Lisa." Brad said.

"Renee's friend?"

"Yeah." Brad paused, staring at his drink. "She told me that Renee was with Richard Pierce last night. Richard Pierce, son of Stuart Pierce."

"Our mayor?"

"That's the one."

"Hoo boy. Well that explains a lot. I knew that name was familiar." Jack got his beer and took a sip from it.

"It explains what? I thought it just raised more questions."

"What do you know about this Mr. Richard Pierce?"

"Not a thing, really. I know he's considered an eligible bachelor around town."

Jack snorted. "Not by anyone I know. From what I've heard the sonofabitch has a bit of a mean streak."

Brad sat for a minute processing what Jack had just said. "So it doesn't surprise you that Renee would call from his place frightened?"

"Not from what little I've heard about him. Of course, my info isn't first hand. It's just what I hear on the street."

"What else have you heard?"

"Only that he likes to throw his daddy's weight around." Jack took another sip of beer and studied Brad's face. "What you really want to know is did he have anything to do with Renee's murder?"

"I just assumed that he couldn't."

"Well I wouldn't make that assumption. On the other hand I'm not gonna be quick to make accusations against the power and might of City Hall without plenty to back it up." Jack said.

"So you think he could be involved?"

"In a word, yes. And like I said, if you quote me I'll deny it."

Brad took a sip from his glass and sat staring at it. "So what do I do now?"

"You probably should tell the police what you know."

"Shouldn't they find this out on their own?"

"They probably will, but you'll be saving them some steps," Jack said.

"I didn't really come away from my last encounter with them holding any kind of warm and fuzzy feeling about what they were doing."

"What? They were a little rough questioning you?"

"Well, yeah. I guess you could say that. They just seemed a lot more interested in my business than what happened to Renee."

"They had to do that. You are the husband. That makes you the first suspect. They have to eliminate you before they move on."

"I guess you're right. It just didn't make for a relationship where I feel great about talking to them."

"Still, you need to tell the police what you have. Whether Richard was involved or not, he was one of the last to see Renee alive. They need to talk to him, to find out what was going on with her before she was killed," Jack said.

"You're right."

"They'll probably get to him eventually, but they'll get to him quicker if you talk to them. I'll find out some more about Mr. Pierce if I can. I know you're curious. But I warn you, it's not going to be pretty."

"Worse than Renee getting killed, Jack?"

"Touché."

Brad and Jack sat for a few moments sipping their drinks. "So what else is going on with you? Not that you need a lot more to keep you busy," Jack asked.

"Not that much. I have this newspaper reporter dogging me."

Jack looked over at Brad. "Why do you have a smile on your face when you say that?"

"She's pretty."

"Oh! My advice? Don't run from that. You could use the diversion."

"I try to run every time I see her coming, but my feet fail to respond," Brad said.

"Smart feet. Let me buy you another fizzy water. I want to hear more about this pretty newspaper reporter."

CHAPTER 7

Jennifer stopped at the supermarket on her way home Friday afternoon. A little quality time with Kevin was called for, so she decided she would pick up something special to cook for them both.

She headed straight for the meat section without a clue what to buy. A pre-packaged teriyaki pork loin caught her eye. The package said bake at 350 for 30 minutes. That sounded easy enough. She picked up a package of rice pilaf, and headed to the fresh produce section. Steamed carrots sounded nice. She added the makings for a salad. On her way to the wine section she passed by a rack of fresh bread and added that to the cart. After picking out a white wine she knew both she and Kevin liked, she made her way to the checkout.

Standing in the checkout line she went over everything in the basket. This should make a nice meal without too much trouble. I have some candles; I'll put those out too. It seems like it's been a long time since Kevin and I have spent some time alone.

She entered her apartment and called Kevin's name. No answer. I wonder where he could be? Probably rehearsing. Since they got that new drummer they rehearse a lot. I didn't forget a gig did I? No, I remember he mentioned last night this was the first

Friday night he had off in a while.

I'm sure he will be in before long. Except for the new drummer, the band has been together a long while. Over two years. Kevin said the drummer was working out really well. He shouldn't be late.

Jennifer started emptying the shopping bags. She put the wine in the refrigerator, found a pan for the pork loin and put it in the oven. She started the rice and carrots, and put together the salad.

Going into the dining room, she pulled a couple of crystal candleholders out of the sideboard. These had been found at a flea market shortly after she and Kevin had moved into the apartment together. They had purchased them as a sort of house warming gift to themselves. That had been almost a year ago. Hard to believe it's been that long.

They used to have so much fun together. When did they get so busy? Well, tonight they would take time to be together. I hope he gets home soon.

Jennifer got a couple of candles from the sideboard and arranged them in the candleholders on the table. She went back into the kitchen. The rice was ready. So were the carrots. Just a few more minutes on the pork.

When will Kevin get himself home? A few minutes later Jennifer turned the oven off. She left the pork in the oven to keep it warm. I hope it doesn't dry out.

Jennifer looked around the apartment. Food, wine, candles. Something was missing. Music. She turned on the stereo and tuned it to smooth jazz.

Nothing else to do but wait. She sat down on the couch and hoped the wait would not be too long.

It's been an extremely long day, starting with

that call from Bruce about the homicide. Then to the office to research the Marshalls. Then tracking down Brad Marshall.

That was some piece of luck. Of course, my first encounter with him could have gone better, but it looks like things have been smoothed over now. The guy did have me into his office to chat this afternoon. I was not really expecting that. I mean, I had hoped, but I did not really think he would see me. That turned into an interview for Tuesday. Good.

Jennifer leaned back into the couch. I wonder if he finds me attractive? He did call me pretty after all. Ha! Old Bill Caruthers accusing me of falling in love with Brad. That's a laugh. I guess a woman could do worse though. He's pretty good looking, and he has all that money. He's nice too.

Jennifer closed her eyes. She drifted off with a smile on her face.

Jennifer stretched and looked around the room. Except for a lamp in the corner, the room was dark. How long have I been sleeping? Jennifer got up stiffly from the couch. I should not have fallen asleep.

On the dining room table was a used plate. It looked like Kevin had eaten without her. That bastard! She stormed into the bedroom to find Kevin stretched out on the bed.

"Kevin, you sonofabitch. Wake up."

"What? Kevin opened his eyes and smiled at Jennifer. "Oh, hi Jen."

"You ate without me, you bastard."

"You were asleep babe, I didn't want to wake you up."

58

"You should have. I fixed that dinner special for us."

Kevin sat up in the bed. "And it was some kind of good. I almost didn't find the pork, but I smelled it and went looking for it. Found it in the oven," Kevin nodded, still smiling.

Jennifer's eyes started to get wet. "That's not at all what I had planned."

"Oh baby, come here."

"No."

"Please baby. I didn't mean to hurt you. You were up early this morning. You've been working a lot lately and I thought you needed your sleep. Come here."

I guess it was my fault. I shouldn't have fallen asleep. Jennifer got up on the bed and snuggled close to Kevin, her eyes still wet. "I just wanted to spend some special time with you. We seems like we haven't seen each other much lately."

"I know. It's been hectic. You've been working hard. The gigs have been steady, and we've been working in the new drummer."

"He's still working out? Where were you tonight? Practice?"

"Uh, yeah. Practice. Over at Jake's. He's a better drummer than we've ever had."

"Well, you're home now. I've missed you."

"Missed you too, babe."

Kevin and Jennifer shared a brief kiss.

"Mmm, I like that," said Jennifer.

"Besides," said Kevin. "There's still plenty left. If you're hungry I'm up for more. You did a good job. That stuff is great. Forget I've eaten. Let's eat."

Jennifer laughed and wiped the tears from her eyes. "Okay. I'm starved."

Saturday morning, Brad opened his eyes and immediately recognized his hotel room. He stretched and looked at the clock. Just past nine. He'd slept a little late, but then he had needed it. He felt good and refreshed.

He dressed in the same clothes he wore the night before. He had one more change of clothes at the office, but at some point soon, he was going to have to do something about clothes. I need to call the police and tell them what I found out about Richard Pierce being with Renee. I'll ask them when I can get back into my house.

Brad felt hungry and looked forward to breakfast. He opened the door to leave and noticed a newspaper lying just outside. Picking it up, he saw it was a Houston Chronicle. Did I order this? Nice thing to have it anyway. I'll take it with me to breakfast.

He made his way downstairs to the restaurant and to a table. He ordered his eggs and bacon with wheat toast and coffee. Looking at the front page, he found the article about Renee's murder below the fold.

There was Jennifer's byline. According to this, I say I found her murdered in the home we shared. That's not right. We didn't share the home. Well, on paper I guess we did still share it, but we didn't both live there as this makes it out to be. Also, what is this 'according to Bradley Marshall'? I didn't just say that. It's what happened.

Brad continued to scan the article. There wasn't much at all from the police. According to them there are no suspects at this time. That's all? I guess they might not say much even if they had more. They don't usually comment on an investigation.

The rest seems to be just fluff. Calls me a local success story. Calls her a socialite who was an interior designer for Houston's wealthy. That seems pretty shallow. Renee was a lot more than that, and deserved more.

This is incredible. How can an article paint a picture that is both sensationalist and pedestrian at the same time? It's just a run of the mill murder of the rich story. Renee deserves better. It seems wrong to see her in the paper referred to as the deceased. But is it the newspaper's fault? Isn't it the fault of whoever killed her? It still isn't right. Somebody has to pay for this. I need to finish up here and get to the office so I can call the police. I need to tell them what Lisa told me last night.

"Hi there!"

Brad looked up to see the smiling face of Jennifer Hart. He looked at her over his newspaper without saying anything. She took the chair opposite him.

The waiter came to the table with Brad's breakfast. Jennifer told him she would have toast and coffee. Brad continued to look at Jennifer over the paper. She's a little pushy. I don't recall inviting her to sit down.

Something was different about her. She practically glowed. "Hello, Ms. Hart."

"It's Jennifer, remember?"

"I was just reading your article."

"Yeah? What did you think?"

"It wasn't up to your usual caliber of work."

Jennifer's face fell slightly. "You didn't like it?"

Brad folded the paper and put it on the table. "It had some inaccuracies. For instance, you say here that Renee shared the house with me. Renee lived in a townhome on Memorial."

"Yeah, that's a bit of a technicality. Legally you and her still own the house together, do you not? The divorce wasn't yet final. And one of my sources said that your house was the address on her driver's license. Besides, it makes the story better."

"You print lies about people if it makes the story better?"

Jennifer stiffened. "I must not have stated that very well. Of course we don't."

"Another thing. You make it sound as if me coming home to find my wife dead on the floor was just a story I made up. It's not just my story. It's what happened. Why don't you say that?"

"The facts are that you coming home to find Renee murdered is what happened according to you. That is all I can write."

"Then you don't believe me?"

"Of course I believe you, Brad. But I can't write what I believe, only the facts."

The waiter returned with Jennifer's toast and coffee. Brad dug into his breakfast and they ate in silence.

"Thank you for granting me the interview. Ms. Abernathy set it up for Tuesday morning," Jennifer said.

"Good for her. Somehow as of this morning I'm

rethinking my position on that."

"Don't you want to get your side of the story out?"

"I want to get the truth out."

"Okay, so what is the truth?"

Brad sat looking into Jennifer's face. Should I tell her about Lisa and Richard Pierce? No. Not now. I don't want Renee's involvement with Pierce dragged through the mud in the newspaper. Without more to go on, they would just speculate on what was going on between them. And I don't want Richard Pierce to read his name in the paper before the police talk to him.

"I can't tell you."

"Why not?" Jennifer sat up straight in her chair.

"I just can't tell you right now. Maybe soon."

"When?"

"I don't know."

They ate for a few more minutes in silence. Jennifer still had that glow about her that Brad noticed when she first arrived. I could get used to having a pretty woman around at breakfast.

"Brad, I have to ask you this. Did you have anything to do with Renee's death?"

"Of course not! How could you ask that?"

"I'm a reporter, Brad. It's just something I had to ask. You say you have something to tell me but you won't tell me what it is. I had to get that out of the way."

They continued to eat. Brad wondered whether it was wrong to trust a reporter at all. Maybe he shouldn't be talking to her. But I like having her around. She's bright and energetic. Even though she's here because of

Renee's death, she makes me forget about it for a little while.

Jennifer sipped her coffee and then put down the cup. "You know, I was telling my boyfriend last night . . ."

Brad didn't hear the rest of what she said. Her boyfriend. Of course, she had a boyfriend. Why hadn't that occurred to me? His face flushed. Now the reason for her glow is clear.

This woman had him behaving like a schoolboy with a crush. That is dangerous given her occupation. Brad was tense and uncomfortable. He signaled for the check. "Ms. Hart, I think it's not a good idea for us to be talking like this."

"What's wrong, Brad? Was it something I said?"

The waiter came with the check, which Brad signed. He rose from the table. "You have your interview scheduled. I'll see you then."

Jennifer didn't say anything else. Brad left the table in a hurry. He felt relieved to be out of her sight. Why should it matter to me that she has a boyfriend? I've seen the woman only twice before this morning.

Boyfriend or not, I need to keep in mind who and what she is. Having breakfast with the press is probably not a good idea. She's probably just the beginning of the interest the press will have in me. The television people will likely as not start hounding me soon. They have already been calling the office. I need to think about changing hotels and checking into someplace discretely. It would be more convenient to move closer to my health club anyway.

Brad checked out of the Hyatt Regency downtown

before heading to his gym. His plan was to work out and get cleaned up, then go to the office and call the police. Later he'd check into a hotel near the gym.

CHAPTER **8**

Richard Pierce found his robe and pulled it around him. The doorbell rang again. "Hold on, I'm coming." He stumbled to the door and opened it. His father was standing there holding a couple of small bags and had a newspaper tucked under one arm.

"Come on, let me in. I've been out here all morning. You aren't up yet?"

Richard stepped aside to let his father, the Mayor Stuart Pierce, into the apartment. "I'm up now."

The Mayor headed straight for the dining room table where he placed the bags. "I brought coffee and donuts."

Richard closed the door and started toward the dining room. He rubbed his eyes. "Sounds good. To what do I owe the pleasure?"

"What? I can't have coffee and donuts with my own son?"

"Sure dad. Good to see you. It's just you don't come around that often, that's all."

"Are we alone? If we're not alone get rid of the bimbo," the Mayor said.

"We're alone, Dad."

"Good. I hear you missed the money drop Thursday night, Ricky." The Mayor pulled two cups from one of the bags and sat one down across the table where Richard was sitting.

"Yeah, I had some car trouble. Must have gotten some bad gas. It's fine now, the car I mean."

"I also hear a security guard got whacked. Was that part of the same business?"

Richard took the top off of the coffee and took a sip. "That couldn't be helped, Dad. That must have been a new guard. I gave the usual guard a C-note to stay out of the way. He must have called in sick or something."

"So that was your business."

"But it couldn't be helped, like I said. Duane said the security guard thought they were drug dealers or something and was reaching for his radio."

"I don't like to see a bunch of killing in my city, Ricky. It's bad for business." The Mayor sipped his coffee and reached for a donut.

"What bunch of killing, Dad? It's one security guard."

"It's one that you contribute. And that just adds to the killing that's already going on. Have you seen the paper?" The Mayor opened the paper and tapped on it. "Murder right here on the front page. I know the election is a year off and it seems like a long time away. But it's not really that far off from now. All I need is, God forbid, for us to become the murder capitol, or some such shit, and I can kiss this job goodbye. You understand what I'm saying, Son?"

"You worry too much, Dad. Everything is under control."

"Under control, huh? You got the money put out to be distributed?" The Mayor took a bite out of his donut.

"Yeah, I did that yesterday."

"Good. And don't tell me not to worry. That's my job."

Richard and his father discussed some of the coming money transfers and the prospects for the Rockets basketball team this year over the remaining donuts. The Mayor left and Richard looked at the front page of the paper.

Scanning the article about the Marshall murder, Richard was reminded that he still needed to do something about the husband. This is a nagging little loose end that needs to be tied up. It says here his name is Bradley, Bradley Marshall. I can't have that little bastard running around town dropping my name in this shit. I don't know exactly what he knows and I don't even know where to find him.

Hubby's not going to be at home, that place is still a crime scene. So he just came home to find his wife murdered, did he? That gives me an idea.

Richard got his telephone directory from his bedroom and made a call. "Chief Griffin, please. This is Richard Pierce. I know he's not in right now. Page him and have him call me. This is an emergency." Richard left his number with the officer on the other end of the phone and hung up. He sat considering his plan. It was brilliant.

It was only a couple of minutes before his phone rang with Chief Griffin on the other side.

"What is this, Richard?"

"It's Mr. Pierce to you. You haven't forgotten who I am?"

"I haven't forgotten. What do you want?"

"That Marshall murder. The husband did it, that Bradley fellow."

"How do you know that?"

"Never mind how. That's my business. I just want you to get that murdering menace off of the streets."

"What about evidence?"

"You'll figure out something. Or I'll make sure that you get replaced with someone that can get the job done."

"Does your father know about this?"

"Where do you think this comes from? He was just over here discussing our rising crime problem with me and how dissatisfied he was with how you were handling things. I took your side, said we needed to give you more time. Do you want me to call him back and tell him I've changed my mind?"

"Of course not. I'll see what I can do."

"Just do it," Richard said, and hung up. That's sweet. That was a hell of a lot easier than me chasing him down to whack him. Let the police chase him.

After he's arrested for murder he can say whatever he wants. Nobody will believe him then. Best of all, it doesn't add a whit to Daddy's precious murder rate. As a matter of fact, it resolves one. Daddy would be proud.

It was even fun. Hell, it's always fun to throw a little weight around. What's the use of power if you don't get to use it?

Monday I'll call the District Attorney and make sure this case gets his full attention. He's not an appointee like the Chief, but he's elected. That's almost as good since an elected official in this town is always looking for campaign contributions and it just so happens we have a little cash these days.

Brad left the health club to go to his office. Since it was Saturday, Rose would not be there. But he needed to change clothes again and that would be a good place from which to call the police. When Renee made that frantic call to him shortly before she was killed, she was evidently with Richard Pierce. That's something the police need to know if they're ever going to find out who killed her.

It was such a nice day Brad put the top down. Driving the streets of Houston, he couldn't help but think that Renee's killers could be out enjoying the beautiful day. It wasn't right. They have to be caught. They can't be allowed to roam free enjoying days like this.

Approaching his office building, Brad decided to skip the parking garage and park on the street. There was plenty of space today since it wasn't a workday. He pulled in behind a van parked in front of the building.

As he was getting out of his car he noticed the sign painted on the side of the van, Channel Two. I wonder what they're doing out here? He saw a couple of people at the front of the building, one of them with a camera on his shoulder, and froze. Of course. Damn. They saw me. Too late now.

Brad started for the front door.

"Mr. Marshall, do you have anything to say about

your wife's death?"

Brad kept moving toward the door. "No comment."

"Surely you have something to say about her murder?"

"I have nothing at this time." Brad entered the building. The security guard was moving toward the door with his palms held up at the television crew as if to tell them not to come inside.

"I'm sorry, Mr. Marshall. I can keep them out of the building but I can't keep them off of the sidewalk. Free country."

"That's alright, Ben. Thanks." Brad said.

At the elevators Brad took a security badge out of his pocket and inserted it into the slot for after hour access and pushed the button. Damn television cameras. On a Saturday no less. It must be a slow news day. I guess I'm lucky it took them this long to catch up with me.

Up in his office, Brad changed clothes and sat down at his desk. He pulled out the cards for Sergeants McNair and Woods and dialed the number.

"This is Bradley Marshall for Sergeant McNair, please." Brad waited a few moments.

"Sergeant McNair here."

"Sergeant this is Bradley Marshall. I have some news for you about my wife's murder."

"Mr. Marshall. I'm glad you called."

"Well, remember that Renee called me upset and frightened just before she was murdered? I know now she was with Richard Pierce."

"I see. Why don't you come down here and we'll talk about it."

"Come down there? I don't think that's necessary, I can tell you all I know over the phone."

"I just think it would be better if you came down here."

"Look, I talked with Lisa Davis and she said that Renee was with Richard Pierce Thursday night before she was killed. I would think you'd want to talk to Pierce."

"Well of course. Where are you calling from?"

"Where am I calling from? What does that have to do with anything? You act like you're not paying any attention to what I'm telling you."

"Of course we're paying attention. Like I said, I just think it would be better if you came down here so we could talk this over."

"I'm not the one that needs to come down there. Richard Pierce is the one you need to be talking to."

"And if this all checks out, then I'm sure that we will want to talk to him."

"If it checks out? What do think, I'm making this up? You guys are incredible!"

"Calm down Mr. Marshall. There's no reason to get upset."

"There's plenty of reason. You said to call you if I found out anything else. Well I did find out something and you act as if you're not interested in it at all!"

"Of course we're interested. Come on down here and we will take down everything you have to say."

"Come down there and you'll take it down? Why aren't you taking it down now? Why don't you want to talk to Richard Pierce? Is it because he's the son of our Mayor?"

"Now Mr. Marshall, there's no reason to start with any accusations. Why don't you just agree to come down here and . . ."

Bradley slammed down the phone. He raised his clenched fists up to his temples and took a deep breath. It would be easy to scream. He lowered his hands and sat there staring at the phone. That went well.

McNair did not want to listen to me. All he wanted was for me to come down to the station. How is that going to help? The last time I was there all they did was ask me a bunch of useless questions, and from what just went on over the phone there's no reason to think a return trip down there is going to be any different. Besides, if he had sounded interested in what I had to say I'd be down there in a minute.

Are they even going to check on Richard Pierce? It didn't sound like it. How are they going to find Renee's killer if they don't follow up on what was going on with her when she called me?

Maybe they did hear me and they're just not acting like it. I don't know that much about police business. I could be wrong about them, although I don't see how.

I'd like to talk to Jack about it. He spent enough years as a policeman he knows how they work. Lord knows I can't figure it out.

Brad got up from his desk and went to the window. He looked out over the city. Over four million people down there and somewhere among them were Renee's killers. They could be just walking around down there as if nothing happened. Hell, I could walk past them on the sidewalk and not know it.

Back in the Marines things were simpler. You

knew who the enemy was. There were good guys on one side and bad guys on the other and everything was clear. Well, more clear than now anyway. Renee's killers don't wear uniforms or badges. They'll have to be tracked down.

Why can't the police find Renee's killers? It's their job to find them. It doesn't seem as if they are interested in looking in the right places. Is Richard Pierce mixed up in this? Certainly he knows something. He at least knows why Renee was upset when she called me.

There has to be something logical here that I don't understand. The police have their reasons for behaving the way that they do. I'm sure Jack can explain it to me.

Brad looked in the direction where his house would be. Damn. I forgot to ask him when I could get into my house. Brad remembered the sight of Renee's body lying in a pool of blood on his floor and a chill ran down his back. There's no hurry in going back there. It's not going to be that easy. I'll deal with that later.

I need to get some clothes, though. I'll just buy some. I don't want to go back to that house yet anyway. I'll do a little shopping now, and I'll catch up with Jack tonight.

CHAPTER **9**

Jack Wilkerson had just arrived at the Red Lion Saturday afternoon when Rusty placed a phone on the bar in front of him and held out the receiver.

"Phone call for you, Jack."

"Thanks, Rusty," Jack said, taking the phone. "Jack Wilkerson here."

"Jack this is Sergeant Tom McNair. I'm working the Marshall homicide. James said you came by the other day."

"Yeah, that's right. I know Bradley. As a matter of fact, he was with me when Renee was killed."

"Yeah, well. You might be interested in what I have to tell you. Can you come down to the station?"

"Is right away too soon?"

"No, that'd be fine. I can't get away or I'd come there."

"That's fine. I'll be right there." Jack hung up the phone. I didn't expect that. I wonder what he has to say. Whatever it is, I'll find out soon enough.

Jack left the bar and drove downtown to the police station. This time he asked for Sergeant McNair. They made a phone call and told him the Sergeant would be right out.

Waiting for the Sergeant, Jack tried not to be nervous. He didn't have to wait long.

McNair held out his hand. "Jack Wilkerson?"

Jack shook his hand. "Thanks for meeting with me."

"Let's step outside. I hear you use to be with the department?"

"Twelve years. I signed on right after I got loose from the Marine Corps."

"I have eighteen." McNair said as they stepped outside onto the sidewalk. "Look, I probably shouldn't be telling you this, but I'm just so damn frustrated I need to tell somebody. Complain really. James said you came by, was interested in the case. And you being from he department, but retired and all."

"What is it, Sergeant?"

"You know this Bradley fellow pretty well?"

"Yeah, I do. He's a good kid."

"Well, we're being told to make him for the murder."

"What do you mean your being told to? Who's telling you to do that?"

"I'm not sure exactly where it's coming from but it seems like it's as far up as that dip-shit chief we've got now."

"Doesn't the case go where you say it goes?"

"Wilkerson, I've been in homicide for five years. I've had my cases criticized for how I ran them but I've never been told how to run them. They've always been my cases. This is the first time that anything like this has ever happened to me."

"And you're not being given any room on this?"

"None at all. I was told to make Marshall the murderer or hang up my badge. I'm just two years away from retirement, Wilkerson. I'm not going to let one case ruin my career."

"I see."

"You got to like the guy some for it anyway. The time line says that he could have done it. And he's at least five million dollars richer because of it." McNair said.

"Brad didn't do it."

"You're that sure of it, huh?"

"Yes. I'm that sure," Jack said.

"Well I didn't really think he did it, either. We brought him down here the night of the murder and sweated him pretty good. He didn't budge off his story one bit."

"Yeah, he told me. He didn't budge because he was telling you the truth. That's the kind of kid he is."

"Also, we've got no proof he fired a gun that night."

"He didn't kill her, Sergeant."

"Well he's gonna need a lawyer pretty soon. We're trying to locate him and pick him up. We're going to be getting the television media involved. This thing is very high profile. I don't like it but there's nothing I can do."

"I'll try to get word to him that the best thing to do is give himself up. Last I talked with him he told me that Renee had been with Richard Pierce the night she was killed."

"Yeah. He told me that over the phone." McNair said.

"So?"

"So what? Maybe you didn't understand me. I've got a murder case and I've got my murderer. Do I think that Richard Pierce is mixed up in this somehow? I'm not going to say that out loud even to you."

"I think I'm starting to get the picture."

"It would probably be healthy for you if you did get the picture. I shouldn't have to remind you that we have one dead here. I don't want to see that number grow."

"I hear you. Tell me this, do you have other homicides with similar characteristics as the Marshall case?"

"Hell, we had one the same night. A security guard. Shot three times. A .38 with tape on the trigger and handle thrown down beside him. And you're doing exactly what I told you was dangerous, sticking your nose into things that will get you listed as a case number on my desk."

"That's all. No more questions. I really appreciate you calling me down here." Jack said.

"No sweat. I did it to make me feel better, but it didn't work. This still sticks in my craw. But like I said, I'm not going to risk my retirement on one case. If Bradley Marshall didn't do it, then the courts will straighten it out."

"Except we all know courts are not always the true halls of justice, Sergeant."

"Not my problem. I'm gonna try and not loose any sleep over it."

"I hear you. Well, thanks again."

"Sure thing."

Jack turned and walked slowly back toward his car. Crap. Bradley was in a mess. It's Saturday. I don't even know how to get in touch with him. I don't have his cell phone number. I never needed it.

The only thing I know to do is head back over to the Red Lion and hope he shows up there. Likely as not, the police will find him before I do.

What a mess. Richard Pierce has to be behind this. That makes him good for the murder. I thought it might be coincidence, those phone calls. It's hard to think of someone in the position of the son of the mayor getting involved in murder. But he's actively making Brad out to be the murderer. This has to be coming from him. Who else would it be?

Driving to the Red Lion, Jack went over what he might be able to do to help Brad. He couldn't come up with much. Perhaps I can find out a little more about this Mr. Richard Pierce and his business. I'll have to be careful. I really don't want to end up like Renee. I've got to do what I can to help, though. Brad is more than just a friend; he's ex Marine. Semper Fi.

Brad left his office to go shopping for clothes. It was something he didn't like to do. For most of his casual and business casual wear, he relied on Renee to make decisions for him. Buying clothes was an area where he didn't have a lot of experience and he was afraid it might show in his selections.

Stepping outside of his building, he was confronted again with the television crew. There seemed to be at least two crews now. Word must have gotten out that he was here.

"Mr. Marshall, how did you feel when you found your wife murdered?"

"No comment at this time." Brad noticed Jennifer

Hart standing behind the crowd gathered around him. She wore a slight pout on her face. He moved through the crowd to where she stood. "What are you doing here? You have an interview set for next week."

"It was my boss' idea."

"Come with me." Brad led her over to his car. "Get in."

Jennifer shouted back toward the crowd, "Bobby, I'll meet you back at the office."

They both got into the car. Calls came from the crowd on the sidewalk. "No fair!" and "Hey, I can treat you better than she can." In seconds they were roaring away from the crowd.

"BMW Z-3. This is a nice car." Jennifer said.

"I was drunk when I bought it. Normally I wouldn't buy something quite so flashy."

"Not that I care, but where are we going?"

"Shopping."

"Shopping for what?" Jennifer asked.

"I need some clothes, and I could use some help picking them out. You obviously have good taste in clothes."

"Thank you. I'm glad to be off the sidewalk. Thanks for that too."

"You're welcome. You did look a little, well, pathetic back there. I kind of felt sorry for you, and like I said, I need some help picking out clothes."

"Most men need help picking out clothes. But I'm not sure I like being called pathetic."

"Well, at least you were not crowding up against me like the rest of them trying to get a quote."

"Like I said, this was my boss' idea. It was either

this or a bunch of rescued dogs that were being abused in southwest Houston. I don't like to see animals being abused, so I let Jerry take that one."

"It's nice to hear that I rate above abused dogs," Brad said.

"I'll bet you aren't in favor of getting an early start on that interview?"

"You got it. The interview can wait."

"Well, right now I'm so glad to be off that sidewalk, I don't care. Besides, I love to shop."

"Why does that not surprise me?"

Brad steered the car onto the freeway toward the Galleria shopping mall. Jennifer slid down in the seat slightly and closed her eyes. It felt comfortable and right having her in the car with him. This shopping trip isn't going to be as much drudgery as I thought it would be.

Brad parked the car and they made their way into one of the many department stores that helped make up the Galleria complex.

"What kind of clothes are we looking for, Brad?"

"I'd say business casual, mostly. Maybe a couple of dress shirts. Say, you are good at this aren't you?"

"I'm very good at this."

"Great. Because I'm not."

"What, did Mommy always dress you?"

Brad's face reddened. "Well, yeah."

They wandered around the store until they came to the men's clothing department. Jennifer got size information from Brad and set about searching the racks.

Brad felt as if he should help, so he picked out a shirt and held it out for consideration. "What about this?"

"Too boring. Here." Jennifer handed him a shirt. "This would look nice."

"It looks the same as the one I picked out."

"No, it doesn't. Yours had brown squares. These are green with a touch of blue. It'll bring out your eyes."

"They need that?" Standing next to her, Brad was stirred by the smell of her perfume.

"What?"

He searched her face. "My eyes. They need bringing out?"

"Don't be silly."

"I'm just trying to understand."

"You weren't kidding. You really aren't any good at this."

"Oh I don't know. I've enlisted the help of an expert at very favorable rates. It seems I might be pretty good at this business," Brad grinned.

"Come on. We have a lot more to find. I'm sure you didn't come here after just one shirt."

"No. I need a half dozen. And almost as many slacks. And probably a sports jacket."

"Then we'd better keep shopping."

With Jennifer's help and a visit to two other stores, Brad soon had the requisite shirts, slacks and a sports jacket selected and purchased. He also thought to purchase a small travel bag with wheels to carry them in.

"Let's stand here a minute. I think I may have most of what I need," he said.

"Okay."

Brad and Jennifer stood overlooking the ice skating rink. Watching the pairs skate, he couldn't help but wish that he and Jennifer were among them. But that would be entirely out of the bounds of their relationship. She was so much fun to be with. It felt good just to stand here with her.

"Is that it?" Jennifer asked.

"Is that what?"

"Is our shopping done?"

Brad paused. "Well, not exactly."

"What else, then?"

"I didn't really plan on you being along for the rest of it. But it's not something I can put off, actually. You see I need socks, and well, underwear." Brad blushed.

Jennifer laughed. "You're embarrassed. There's no reason to be. Everyone wears underwear. Well, mostly everyone."

"Well, still."

"Would it make you feel any better if I bought a bra and panties while we were here?"

"No! That wouldn't help at all."

"Wait a minute. Didn't I read that you were in the military? Marines wasn't it?"

"Six years." Brad said.

"Were you ever shot at?"

"Yes."

"You survived that but you are afraid to buy underwear with a woman along?"

"Being embarrassed in front of a pretty lady is much worse than being shot at. Trust me."

"Okay then. Let's just get it over with. Boxers or briefs?"

Brad stood there for a minute. This wasn't going to be easy. "Lets buy the socks first and I'll work on my courage."

"I've got another idea. How about you tell me what kind of socks and I'll pick them out while you buy the underwear."

"Even better!"

Minutes later they had completed their shopping and carried the bags along with the small suitcase to the car. They placed all of the packages in the trunk.

"Where should I drop you?" Brad asked.

"Back at my office, at the Chronicle."

"You got it."

Brad and Jennifer climbed into the car and buckled their seatbelts. He paused.

"I really appreciate you helping me, Jennifer."

"Don't mention it. It was fun."

He didn't want it to end. He liked having her with him. "Before I drop you off, how about some lunch?"

"I'm up for that."

"Good. I know just the place." He smiled and started the car. At least it doesn't have to end yet.

CHAPTER **10**

Jennifer waited for the car to come to a stop before she hopped out and ran around to the driver's side. "I enjoyed lunch. Thanks Brad."

"Thank you for helping me with the shopping. Now I'll be dressed smartly. I didn't have a prayer of getting there on my own."

"Glad I could help. I'll see you Tuesday, if we don't run into each other before then."

"Tuesday then." Brad smiled and pulled away.

Jennifer turned and started walking toward the entrance to the building. That was really fun. He kept me laughing through most of lunch. Good thing I was there to help him with his shopping, though. Like most men, he doesn't know the first thing about clothes.

She entered the building and rode the elevator to the fourth floor. Walking past Caruthers' office, she heard her name. "Hart. Where have you been? Your photographer came back without you."

"I just had lunch with the husband of our number one murder victim."

"You mean you just had lunch with the number one suspect in the killing of our number one murder victim, don't you?"

"What are you talking about? Brad isn't a suspect."

"I just got off of the phone with some of my people down at the police department. He's wanted in connection with the murder of Renee Marshall."

"That can't be! He couldn't have killed her!" It seemed as if all the air had left the room.

"And why not? You know more than the police? Why weren't you on top of this? I don't expect my reporters to run around town with their heads up their butt."

"Sorry Bill. This must have just happened. I was on the sidewalk this morning with Channel Two and Channel Eleven and nobody had a clue then."

"If you had called in every once in a while like you are suppose to I would have let you know. We could have called the cops and been there to get the shots of him being arrested. Except we couldn't have gotten the shots because you sent the photographer home. Why was that?"

"He invited me to go shopping with him. His car is a two-seater. There wasn't room for Bobby."

"Shopping?!? You went shopping with him? Oh great. I don't know if this is good news or bad. My reporter is the killer's girlfriend. So we have exclusive access, but she's too busy picking out clothes with him to find out why he killed his wife!"

"I'm not his girlfriend and he didn't kill his wife. Besides, I have an interview set for Tuesday. He wasn't going to talk about the case until then."

"Whether he killed her or not, the police are after him for it and that is news. Whether he bought a brown shirt or a blue one is not news. We print the news, or has your involvement with Mr. Marshall made you forget that?"

"That's not fair, Bill. You know me better than that.

What color shirt he picks out may not be news, but the fact that he's shopping the Galleria oblivious to a manhunt for him is news and you know it."

Caruthers rubbed his chin. "That's not bad. Go write it. Keep in mind that by the time it runs he may be caught."

"You got it." Jennifer said. She turned and started toward her cubicle, deflated by not having to stand up to Caruthers any longer.

This can't be. Brad could no more have murdered Renee than I could have. He's sensitive and funny. On the other hand there is that military side of him that I don't know anything about.

Jennifer sat down at her computer. What a mess. She had just been shopping and had lunch with a murder suspect. They had to be wrong. What if they were not wrong? She bounced back and forth in her mind getting nowhere.

She opened up a fresh document and stared at the blank screen. I am a professional. I've got to put my personal relationship with Brad, whatever it is, out of my mind. If the police are calling him the murderer, then I have to think of him that way, at least when I write about him.

An hour later she had her article written. She read back over it. She remembered the sweet, boyish companion she had just left while she read her description of a cold calculating man wanted for murder. It made her slightly sick in her stomach. This wasn't right. It wasn't right to present a lie to the readers.

Her finger hovered over the delete key. If I write

what I know about him, Caruthers will not even accept it. No, this is what he's looking for. The police have labeled Brad a murderer, so the news is that Brad killed his wife. She moved her hand away from the delete key and submitted it for review.

Jennifer stared at her computer screen and tried not to cry. I shouldn't even care. What is this guy to me anyway? Perhaps the police are right and he did kill his wife, she told herself. She reached over on her desk for the box of tissue.

─────────────────────────

Brad steered the car into traffic after saying goodbye to Jennifer. He couldn't wipe the smile off his face. I can't remember the last time I enjoyed myself so much.

He drove for a few blocks oblivious to where he might be going before it occurred to him that he needed a destination. He needed to find a hotel and check in since he had abandoned the Hyatt Regency.

He steered the car back toward the Galleria area, which was also near his health club. He had thought having a room near his office would be the most convenient, but it hadn't worked out that way. As it was, he was driving from downtown out to his gym and back in the mornings. Being near the gym would eliminate half of that.

The main reason he was changing was to avoid the press. Jennifer had tracked him to the Hyatt Regency. It would only be a matter of time before the television stations followed her lead. He had an idea on how to avoid them at a new hotel. "I hope it works," Brad said to himself.

Brad pulled into a parking lot on Westheimer. He got out of the car and opened the trunk of the car. He transferred all of his new clothes to the suitcase he had just purchased and closed the trunk.

Brad continued down Westheimer until he reached Post Oak where he made a right. He pulled into the entrance to the DoubleTree Hotel. He put the top up on the car before getting out. Retrieving his luggage and laptop computer from the trunk, he was approached by a valet. He handed the valet his keys, received a ticket and continued into the hotel.

A young man smiled at him from behind the front desk. "Can I help you?"

"I hope so. I have a rather peculiar request." Brad took out his driver's license, business card, and American Express and laid them on the counter. "I am a computer security specialist. I am conducting an audit for one of the major oil companies here in Houston. They think that I was called away to Los Angeles, so my presence here is supposed to be somewhat of a secret. It might alert members of the company that I am still investigating them when I want them to think that I am out of town. I wonder if I might register under an assumed name?"

"This is your correct name, Mr. Marshall?" The young man studied the driver's license and business card.

"Yes. I have no problem with you knowing my name, it's just if someone should call for me, I want them to be told that I am not here."

"I don't see a problem with that. What name would

you like to be registered under?"

"Jack Wilkerson." Brad hoped Jack wouldn't mind if he borrowed his name for this. It was what popped into his mind.

"And how long will you be staying with us Mr. Wilkerson?"

"About a week. If I finish up early I'll let you know. Also, I'll need Internet access from my room."

"There's a small surcharge for that."

"I understand. That's quite alright."

Minutes later Brad was stepping into his room. He spent a few minutes putting the clothes away. If this turned out to be home for a few days he wanted it to be as comfortable as possible.

He set up his computer and logged onto his servers downtown. With that crap about his call to the police going on, he hadn't checked the status of his servers. He did that now, and finding that everything was running correctly, he sat back in his chair.

What a day. From utter frustration over the police, to having a great time with Jennifer. That girl makes your troubles melt.

I still can't get over the police and their attitude. Are the police even going to talk to Richard Pierce? Surely they will. I can't believe that being the son of the mayor would keep you from being asked a few questions about a woman you were with just before she was murdered. Not in this town or any town.

And what if they do question him? What if he doesn't know anything? Renee could have been the victim of some random shooting, a burglary gone bad.

No, that doesn't square with the facts. There was

nothing taken in the house. It wasn't a burglary. And a random shooting wouldn't explain the phone calls. She was frightened when she called me. Minutes later she was dead. That has to be connected, and that means that Richard Pierce is connected to her murder in some way.

There's got to be a way to get the police to see all of this. Jack was a policeman for a lot of years, I forget how many, after he left the Marine Corps. If anyone can help me with them, he can.

Brad looked at his watch. It's a little early to be looking for Jack at the Red Lion. Maybe I'll take a nap. He logged off of the computer and stretched out on the bed.

Lying there on the bed, all Brad could think about was Jennifer. The way her hair fell around her face, the way she walked, the way she laughed. He tossed and turned and finally decided that a nap was out of the question.

Maybe it would be better if he lost himself in his novel for a while. He went back to his computer, logged onto his server, and downloaded the latest copy of his novel. For the next couple of hours he was lost in a futuristic world of his own making.

Brad got up from his computer and looked around the room. I should probably change before I go to the Red Lion to look for Jack.

After changing clothes, he examined himself in the mirror. He was right to carry Jennifer along to help pick out his clothes. She was good at it. He was very satisfied with how he looked.

He went down in the elevator and crossed the lobby to the front entrance. It was nice to know that no camera crews would be waiting for him here. Assuming a name at registration was a stroke of brilliance.

He gave the valet his ticket and waited for his car. His next meeting with Jennifer would be the interview. Kind of formal. That sucks. I'll have to think of something else to go with it. Maybe I can think of some excuse to get her to dinner.

Brad smiled. So what if she has a boyfriend. That's not the same as married. It's alright for me to try.

When Brad's car arrived, he tipped the valet and sped off toward the Red Lion. It was a little early yet, but being Saturday, Jack may very well be there. If not, I'll just wait. I'm starting to get hungry and their hamburgers are plenty good.

Brad enjoyed the drive to the Red Lion. Weaving through the traffic on the short drive, he imagined different ways to lure Jennifer into seeing him again away from the formal setting of the interview planned. The interview would give him plenty of time to try different means to get her out on more of a date. It might not work but it was worth a try. I'm pretty sure she had a good time today as well. Maybe a return trip to the Galleria, this time for some ice skating. Or maybe just a quiet dinner somewhere.

Brad parked his car and walked into the Red Lion. Jack was at his familiar place at the bar.

"I came here looking for you, Jack. Heh, I used your name to check in at the DoubleTree. I hope you don't mind."

"No, I don't mind. If you hadn't, you probably wouldn't be here now. The whole town is looking for you, pardner."

Brad took a stool next to Jack. "What do you mean?"

"I just saw your happy face on TV." Jack slid a napkin over to Brad on the bar. "Write down the number of your criminal defense attorney. I know you have one. I met that smarmy Italian at one of your cookouts. Might as well write down your cell phone number, too. I don't have it, so I couldn't get a hold of you."

Brad took out his phone and wrote names and numbers on the napkin. "What is this all about?"

"The short answer is, you're in a middle of a mess. I met with one of the detectives on your case today."

"I called them this morning. I tried to tell them what Lisa had told me about Renee being with Richard Pierce. They weren't interested in hearing it."

"Yeah, well. They're being told not to be interested."

Brad's stomach developed a cold, sick feeling. "I was afraid of that. I kept telling myself that it couldn't be true, that in this town or any town, being the son of the mayor wouldn't matter that much."

"It does matter. It matters plenty."

"Jack, if they don't talk to Richard Pierce, how will they ever find out who killed Renee?"

"As far as they are concerned, they know who killed Renee. And from the looks of things that just walked in the front door, they're about to apprehend the murderer." Jack picked up his beer and slowly took a sip.

From behind him Brad heard a loud voice. "Bradley Marshall, step away from the bar. Keep your hands where we can see them." He glanced behind him to see two uniformed police officers with their guns drawn and pointing at him.

"I would suggest that you do as they say and avoid any sudden moves, pardner. This was what I was going to tell you about," Jack said, putting his beer down.

"You have the number of my lawyer," Brad said to Jack.

"Now!" the voice from the officers came again.

Brad moved off the stool and held his hands out from his body.

"Absolutely. You know I'll take care of it." Jack picked up the napkin Brad had written on and put it in his pocket. "Might be a couple or three days before you get a bail hearing, what with it being Saturday and all. Sit tight. And as they say on TV, don't say anything to anybody. Did you drive here?"

"Yeah."

"I'll make sure that Rusty knows to leave your car alone. This is not the time to reach into your pocket to give me the keys," Jack said.

One of the officers put his weapon away and pulled Brad's hands behind his back. Brad winced when the handcuffs pinched his wrists. He was turned toward the door and gently pushed forward.

From over his shoulder he heard a high pitched whiny voice, "When do I get the reward? I was the one that called you. When do I get the reward?"

CHAPTER **11**

Brad sat in the small cell of the jail. He tried to shake off the daze that enveloped his mind, but he seemed to be drowning in it.

He had come to the cell by way of an interrogation room. Sergeants McNair and Wood had entered the room and asked if he would answer some questions. He had told them he wouldn't answer any questions without his attorney present, and they left. What he wanted to do was ask them questions. Why were they doing this to him? Why weren't they questioning Richard Pierce about his involvement in Renee's murder? Before he could think to ask them anything they left.

Now he sat on a steel bunk, alone in a steel room. On the bunk were sheets and a thin blanket. His only other possessions were the orange jumpsuit he wore with some plastic slippers, and a bar of soap that he had placed on the steel sink, next to the steel toilet. There was a small desk and chair in the cell. The chair was more of a stool that was affixed to the floor. The cell looked barren.

Brad stared at the bars in front of him. His jaw and fists grew tight. How dare they? How dare they cage me like an animal, judged unfit to participate in free society out there. I've done nothing wrong. Yet here I am in a cage.

Brad had been in jail twice before. Both times were for public intoxication. Both times he was thrown into the drunk tank with a lot of others. And both times he slept through most of the experience. He was, after all, drunk. This was different. This was obviously a part of the jail reserved for felons and more dangerous criminals. Here and now he couldn't sleep it off and forget about it. He wasn't drunk. He wasn't guilty.

Brad wanted to scream and yell and beat his hands against the bars. He couldn't. Behaving like that would validate what they were doing to him; that he had to be caged because he didn't know how to behave in a free society. His jaw drew tighter until it hurt.

He stood up and walked to the bars. Outside the bars was a common area surrounded by two stories of cells like this one. In the middle of the common area were five steel picnic tables.

Upon a far wall was a television. The television was on and seemed to be showing an episode of the program 'Cops'. The cops were arresting a couple of hoodlums.

"Hey, Armand. Isn't that your brother they got there?" Brad heard someone shout from one of the other cells.

"Naw, man, that's my cousin," came the reply. There was a lot of laughter in the cells.

Up high and behind a thick glass was a control room where a guard watched over the section. The guard didn't seem to be paying any attention to what was going on below him.

Over in the general area of the television was a

telephone. It looked like an ordinary pay telephone. Brad instinctively knew it could only make collect calls, since money was not going to be allowed in here. He wanted desperately to talk to someone. But even if he could get to the phone, he didn't know who to call. He didn't know who he could call and say 'look, I'm in jail and I just need someone to talk to.' There was no one like that.

Brad went back to the bunk and sat down. In the midst of this loneliness, he started reaching out in his mind for something else to hang on to. His lawyer. Sooner or later Jack will get in touch with John Cantrinni and they will start the process of getting him out of here.

What was it Jack said? It might be Tuesday before I get a bail hearing. This is only Saturday. I might go out of my mind well before then. Surely Cantrinni will come see me soon. I just need to hang on until he gets here. He'll be able to tell me more about what will happen and when.

Brad tore at the back of his neck, trying to ease the stiffness he felt. I can't believe this could all be the doings of Richard Pierce. This isn't how it's supposed to work. Those cops know I didn't kill Renee, don't they? How could they ignore the evidence and have me arrested?

They're going to look pretty foolish when we get to trial and they don't have any evidence that I killed Renee. Brad felt a sickening feeling in his stomach. Innocent people get convicted all of the time. This could get a lot worse before it gets better.

I hope Cantrinni comes to see me soon. He'll have

something to say on the matter. Plus, it'll be great to see and talk to somebody. Anybody. Sitting here with nothing to do will drive me out of my mind.

Brad tried to count the bars across the front of his cell. Before he got halfway across, his mind wandered back to the injustice being done to him. I'm a respectable businessman, not some criminal. I don't belong here. This is a huge mistake. As soon as this is cleared up I will be out of here.

Brad felt sick. This is not a mistake. This is a plot against me. Richard Pierce arranged this little vacation for me. There is no other explanation for it. What was that Jack said? They're being told to not be interested in Richard Pierce. Pierce's behind this. He has to be.

So all of City Hall will be trying to make me guilty of Renee's murder. What if they succeed? What if I have to spend the rest of my life in a cage like this? Plenty of innocent men get convicted. There are innocent men in prison now. I could wind up another one of them, just so that Richard Pierce doesn't have his name come up in connection with Renee's murder.

I'm not going to let that happen. Cantrinni will get me out of here. Then I'll find out what I can about Richard Pierce. I can't just sit around and let them put me in prison for the rest of my life. I've got to do something to prevent it.

But I can't do anything right now. I can't do anything but sit here and wait. Wait for Cantrinni. Wait for a bail hearing. Wait for something to eat. Damn, I'm hungry. I must have missed dinner around here. Bastards probably had me taken to that interview room when they could have brought me here to be fed.

Brad sat on his bunk like a coiled spring, wanting to jump up at the bars and scream his innocence. He chose instead to sit and fume over the injustice of his imprisonment.

Brad heard his name on the television. He got up and went to the bars and looked out. The evening news was playing and they were announcing that Bradley Marshall had been apprehended and was being charged with the murder of Renee Marshall. Charges have not yet been filed, but will be soon. There was an old photograph of him on the screen.

So now it was official. As if my being here didn't make it official enough. Now all of Houston thinks of me as a murderer. My God, what must my parents think? They know I'm innocent, of course, but what will this put them through?

Bradley went back to the bunk and sat down. He put his face in his hands and closed his eyes. Did I do anything to deserve this? No, of course not. There for a while I was no model husband, but I never lifted a hand to harm Renee. This has to be straightened out and soon.

Brad went back to trying to count the bars of his cell. He didn't do very well this time either.

Brad suddenly felt very tired. He lay down on the cot and pulled the blanket over his head. His mind was swimming from one thought to another, making sleep impossible. So he lay there, without moving. He thought of his novel, and for a while wished he were somebody else, in another place, in a future time.

Brad heard the clanking of metal doors and shortly after that, two men in orange jumpsuits wheeled carts into the common area outside of the cells. This must be breakfast. He looked up at the clock and saw it was a little after six, Sunday morning.

The door in front of him opened and all around him he saw men step out into the common area from the cells that surrounded his. He moved through the doors of his cell. The man who came from the cell to his right went up to a large bucket on wheels and grabbed a carton of milk and then went to one of the carts where another man handed him a tray. Brad fell in behind him, grabbing first the milk and then a tray and following him to a place at one of the large picnic tables.

Brad looked down at the tray. It seemed to be scrambled eggs with toast and sausage. Brad took the plastic fork on the tray and tried the eggs. Bland, but plenty good when you're starving. The sausage was the same. It didn't take Brad long at all to clean his tray and empty the milk.

Brad looked around the tables. There seemed to be about twenty-five others. Brad didn't know what to do with his tray, so he waited for someone else to finish.

The scrawny man across from him smiled with a grin that was missing one of his front teeth. "You came in last night. I saw you."

"Yeah." Brad said.

"I'm Derek. Derek Pagell." Toothless said.

Brad paused. His instincts told him not to trust anyone in here. "Jack. Jack Wilkerson." Well, Jack said he didn't mind me using his name at the hotel. I hope he doesn't mind one more time.

Toothless grinned at him and nodded his head. "What are you in here for?"

Brad looked at Toothless. This is the felony wing. If I'm going to continue a charade it has to be a felony. "Drugs. How about you?"

"MRP."

"MRP?"

"Motion to Revoke Probation."

Brad nodded as if he understood. What he understood was that the answer told him nothing about the underlying charge, the charge that had Toothless on probation. Brad felt satisfied that he had made up a story for this man. If he had known about it earlier he would have been suffering from MRP himself.

What the hell. I'll give it a shot. "What were you on probation for?"

"Oh, a bunch of stuff."

Just as I thought. No answer at all. Brad noticed a number of others that had finished. They were returning their trays to the carts, and throwing their empty milk cartons in trashcans that were now provided. Brad got up with his tray and did the same.

Brad wandered around the common area to stretch his legs. It felt good to have a little room to walk. Some of the others gathered in groups of four or five to talk. A couple of the others wandered aimlessly like Brad. The wanderers stayed away from each other, involved in their own thoughts.

After about ten minutes a buzzer sounded and the others started returning to their cells. Brad did the same. Soon the buzzer sounded again and the doors to his cell closed. Brad was closed off from the world again and alone in his mind.

The breakfast wasn't a lot but he felt much better. Some hot coffee would have been nice, but hot coffee in a room full of felons would probably be out of the question. One slight disagreement could lead to a face full of burns.

Here I am objecting to them treating me like an animal that has to be caged, and I'm thinking of these other men as not being much better. I'm thinking of them in the same terms that I object to being applied to me. Does that mean I'm no better than those that put me here?

There's a difference. I'm innocent. Innocent until proven guilty, and I haven't been proven guilty. Hell, I haven't even been charged with a crime yet. I've just been pulled off of the street and jailed.

Still, I don't know that there aren't others in here under similar circumstances to my own. I don't know that all these men are guilty of crimes. I'm here, and I'm not. I just assume that because they're here, they can't behave themselves with hot coffee.

Is that fair to them? No. Should I think of them differently? Probably. Do I care right now? No. I've got too much to worry about without trying to solve the injustices of our criminal justice system except where it applies to me. I've got to get out of here. That's all I can think about right now.

A guard appeared in front of his cell. "Open five." The cell doors opened. "Marshall, you have a visitor."

Bradley stepped through the cell doors and turned to his right to the exit door of the cellblock. He walked out into the hallway and followed the guard's instructions from hallway to hallway until he came to a doorway.

"In there," the guard said.

Brad went into a small room to find John Cantrinni sitting at a table.

"Brad!" John said with a smile.

"John. Good to see you."

"Good to see you. Although I'd rather it be under different circumstances, of course."

"Well, we work with what we've got."

"So, you decided to give up that penny ante stuff and start giving me some serious attorney's fees."

"I've always been concerned about your financial well being, John."

"I know you have, Brad. I got a call from a Jack Wilkerson. He said we'd met but I didn't remember him."

"He's a friend. You met him at one of my cookouts."

"Oh well. I saw you on the news, anyway. I would have come looking for you. Are you alright? Do you need anything?"

"I need to get out of here."

"Well, yeah. Right. Your bail hearing will most likely be Tuesday. I can press for tomorrow but what with the weekend, I doubt we'll have much luck."

"I understand. Just do what you can, John."

"They will most likely oppose bail. I doubt they will be successful. They might be successful in getting it set quite high. I assume that's not going to be a problem?"

"My assets are plenty liquid. They were about to be divided because of the divorce. Bail shouldn't be a problem. Contact Rose Abernathy at my office. She has signature authority over my accounts, for business purposes. She also knows whom at the bank to talk to. Like I said, it shouldn't be a problem."

"Normally I advise my clients not to tell me whether or not they did it. It makes my job easier. Since I know you and I know you didn't do it, that's not an issue."

"Of course I didn't do it. We were getting divorced, but there was a part of me that still loved her."

"Why don't you tell me what happened?"

Brad told John about the phone calls, his trip to the Red Lion and coming home to find Renee's body. He told him about his meeting with Lisa, and what Jack had told him just before he was arrested.

"Damn. Sounds like you're gonna make me earn my money." John said.

"I didn't kill her. Doesn't that count for anything?"

"It counts for a lot. I just meant that in addition to any circumstantial evidence that makes you appear guilty, it looks like we might be fighting City Hall on this one. That's all."

"Are you up for the fight?"

"Brad! I'm surprised at you for even asking. You know me better than that."

"Oh course. I'm sorry John, I didn't sleep particularly well last night."

"It's alright. Actually I should be thanking you. With all of the media attention, this could be the biggest case of my career."

"Oh. I'm so glad to be able to help out an old friend. I'll think of how this is helping you out while I'm sitting in that cell back there. It'll make the hours fly by."

"Sorry. I know it's tough. Hang in there. We'll get you out of this."

"I know you will. I'm just a little cranky," Brad said.

"With good reason. Like I said, you'll probably get a bail hearing Tuesday morning. We'll arrange everything and then you should be out Tuesday afternoon. I know it's not much but the wheels of justice and all that. Just be patient."

"Thanks John. I'll be alright. I don't have any choice. Somewhere out there are the people responsible for Renee's death. They need to be in here, not me. I'll do whatever it takes to make that happen."

CHAPTER **12**

Richard Pierce rolled out of bed and started pulling on his clothes. He glanced back at the bed. What was her name? Lisa. Now that the morning fuck is out of the way I wish she would leave.

"Don't you have someplace else you need to be?" Richard asked.

"Not really. Are you trying to get rid of me?"

What does it sound like you dumb cunt? No, I better not piss her off too much. I might want to sample some more of that some time. "It's just that I have some business I need to take care of."

"Oh."

She's still not moving. What is it with her?

Lisa sat up in the bed. "Richard? Can I ask you something?"

"What is it?"

"The night that Renee was killed. She left the Skybar with you."

Richard glared at Lisa. "Renee was fine when she left here that night. But if you ask me, she probably just stuck her nose somewhere it didn't belong and started blabbing about it. That can get a person in trouble. Do you understand me?"

"Yeah. Sure Richard. I didn't mean to make you mad."

"As far as you're concerned, I never knew Renee. Is that clear?"

"Sure, Richard. Whatever you say."

Richard stared at Lisa. That bitch is scared to death. Good. That ought to keep her mouth shut. She doesn't know anything anyway. So what if I was with Renee that night. The last I saw Renee she was alive, just like I said.

"Good. I'm glad we understand each other. Now get dressed. Like I said, I need to take care of some business."

Richard went into the living room. He turned on the TV, wanting to get some local news. This isn't the time of day for that. He turned the television off and turned on the stereo. Looking out the windows, he watched the traffic on the downtown streets below and wondered what to do next.

Sometime today I probably should go by the office and look over the books. I need to make sure the distribution of the money has been entered correctly. Man, I hate to work on Sunday. It shouldn't take long though. I'll reward myself later with a trip to a tittie bar.

I need to find out what's going on with that Marshall business. They should have him in jail by now. Would the newspaper say anything? Only one way to find out. What's taking that bitch so long?

Lisa appeared from the bedroom. "I'm ready."

"Ready for what?"

"I need a ride back to the bar. I left my car there, remember?"

Oh shit. Why did I give that bitch a ride? I must

have had too much to drink. "Oh, yeah. Come on."

Richard and Lisa left the apartment and went down to the parking garage. The got into the black Lincoln Town Car and left the garage headed south.

At an intersection Richard spotted a man selling newspapers. He signaled to the man and held out two dollars, which the man exchanged for a Sunday newspaper. Richard placed the huge newspaper on the seat between himself and Lisa.

"Darlin', look at the front page and tell me if you see anything about Renee's murder in there."

"Okay." Lisa picked out the first section of the paper and began to scan the page. "Oh my God."

"What is it?"

"It says here that they arrested Brad for Renee's murder."

Richard smiled. He looked over at Lisa, who looked back at him with an expression of shock and horror. "What's the matter?"

"You look like you're happy they arrested Brad."

"I'm glad they arrested someone for killing that sweet girl. Of course I am."

"But Brad couldn't have killed her." Lisa shook her head.

"Well the police seem to think that he could have. They arrested him didn't they?"

"There has to be some mistake."

"Maybe you're just mistaken about this Brad fellow. People can fool you."

"Not Brad. He came to the Skybar asking me about Renee. He was trying to find out who might have killed her. I told him about..." Lisa put her hand up to her mouth.

"About what? About me?"

Lisa stared back at Richard. She looked too frightened to move.

Richard tried to control his rage. "You remember what we talked about back at my place? Keep your nose out of my business. And keep your goddamn mouth shut."

Oh fuck. So this Marshall fellow knows that I was with Renee that night. Maybe that's not too big of a mess. He's in jail. He's a murderer. Nobody is going to listen to him now. Still.

"You remember what I'm telling you. You didn't see me with Renee that night. Am I clear? Tell me, am I making myself clear?" Richard demanded.

"Yes, Richard. Yes. You were never with Renee that night. I know when to keep my mouth shut. You can count on me."

"Alright then."

Richard drove the rest of the way to the bar in silence. This wasn't so bad. They did have the little prick in jail. That's good news. That's very good news. And it really didn't matter what little he knew because his credibility was zero right about now.

Richard pulled up to the curb. "You take care."

"See you soon?"

"Sure, babe. I'll see you soon. Remember what we talked about."

"Okay, Richard."

Richard pulled away and started back for his apartment. With her finally gone and the news of Bradley Marshall's arrest, he could smile as big as he wanted. He reached over and cranked up the stereo.

Things are looking pretty good right now. That Lisa isn't too bad to have around. I mean, I wouldn't want her around much in the daytime. She's pretty enough for the daytime, but too dumb. She and those big firm tits are lot of fun at night, though.

Man, she squeals like a little pig in bed. Not like those throaty moans her friend Renee bellowed. God, I hope I live long enough to hear all the sounds I can fuck out of women. Richard's head bobbed to the music.

I think I'll take the newspaper back home and read over this article a couple of times. This is something to be relished. Tomorrow I'll call the DA's office and remind him Marshall is a menace to society who needs to be kept off the streets.

Brad walked through the large double steel doors of the jail Tuesday afternoon and onto the sidewalk. He stood looking at the sky. He took a deep breath of the downtown city air. It smelled good to him. It smelled like freedom.

The first thing he wanted was a shower. He'd had a shower earlier this morning in the jail. That shower stall was covered with mold. He wanted to take a shower in a shower stall that was clean, and then put on fresh clothes. Clothes that didn't smell like they had been stored in a jailhouse bin for days.

He looked around and noticed a small group of people moving toward him. They carried cameras and microphones. Oh crap. Here come the reporters.

"Brad."

Brad turned around toward the familiar voice to see John Cantrinni hurrying up the sidewalk toward him. "Hello John."

"Let me do the talking."

"You got it."

Brad stood there with John while the crowd converged upon them. The questions started before the crowd of reporters got in place.

"Mr. Marshall, how does it feel to be out of jail?"

"Mr. Marshall is glad to be free and is looking forward to proving his innocence." John said.

"And who are you?"

"I'm sorry. I'm John Cantrinni, Brad's attorney. That's C-a-n-t-r-i-n-n-i."

"Did you kill your wife, Mr. Marshall?"

"Of course not. Bradley Marshall had nothing to do with the death of his wife and we look forward to proving that in court," John replied.

"If you didn't do it, then why are you being charged with her murder?"

"We are not prepared to answer that question at this time, except to say that his arrest has political implications."

"Political implications? Can you be more specific?"

"Not at this time. I'm sorry."

John continued to handle their questions expertly. Brad noticed Jennifer Hart standing in the back, making notes. She wasn't asking any questions.

He continued to watch Jennifer. After some time their eyes met. She looked as if she was in pain. She broke eye contact and looked back down at her notebook.

"That's all we have at this time. Thank you," John said. "I have my car back here, Brad. I'll give you a ride where ever you need to go."

"Give me just a moment. I'll be right with you." Brad walked through the dispersing crowd and up to Jennifer. She was still standing there writing on her notepad.

"Jennifer."

"Hi Brad. I guess you're glad to be out of there."

"You can't imagine."

"You missed your interview this morning." Jennifer said into her notepad.

"My what? Oh, yeah. I was called away."

"I understand. Those things happen."

She certainly is reserved. She doesn't even look me in the eye. "They don't happen to me very often. How about we set another date for the interview?" he said.

"Sounds good." Jennifer looked at the ground between them.

"Get in touch with Rose. Tell her I said it was okay."

"I'll do that."

"We'll see you Jennifer."

"See you."

Brad turned and walked back toward John. That was strange. She wasn't her usual bubbly self. I guess she doesn't like talking to jailbirds.

Well, none of this is my fault. I didn't ask to be arrested for a crime I didn't commit. Brad's stride got a little bolder. Why do I even care what she thinks anyway?

"Ready to go?" John asked.

"I'm ready."

"Who was that you were talking to?"

"Her name is Jennifer Hart. She's a reporter for the Chronicle."

"Brad, we haven't talked about it, but I really have to advise you against talking to the press. That's my job. You can get yourself into real trouble without realizing it by saying the wrong things."

"Actually I wasn't talking to her as a member of the press. Well, we had an interview set up for this morning, but of course I was indisposed."

"Good thing. No interviews."

"I didn't want to talk to her as a reporter. I really wanted to date her."

"Oh, well in that case. That's a really fucking bad idea."

"It seems as if it doesn't matter now anyway."

"No. It matters. It matters that you understand that it's suicide and all of the reasons why it is suicide. Brad, I can help you prove your innocence, but I can't stop you from convicting yourself if you're hell bent on it. Repeat after me, I Bradley Marshall.

"I Bradley Marshall." Brad said.

"Do not date anyone."

"Do not date anyone."

"Especially reporters."

"Especially reporters."

"Got it?"

"Got it?"

"Now cut that out. This is serious, Brad. Plenty of attorneys will fire their clients for talking to the press, much less sleeping with them. For both of our sakes, put that woman out of your mind and forget about her."

They arrived at John's car. "You're right, John. Like I said, from the treatment I just got it looks like she's not the least bit interested any more, so the whole discussion is mute."

"Glad to hear it. Now, where do you need for me to drop you?"

"I left my car at the Red Lion Bar & Grill, over on Alabama Street."

As they pulled away from the curb, Brad stared at the buildings around them. He noticed the people on the sidewalk, walking freely wherever they wanted to go. He was back among the free.

He looked up at the sky again. He could actually see the sunshine pouring between the buildings and filtering to the sidewalks. A traffic signal reminded him that there were rules that a person is supposed to abide by to remain out of jail. He had obeyed the rules, and still they had arrested him.

Somewhere deep inside of Brad a little breath of rage lingered over the indignation of his arrest. For the moment it was being overwhelmed by his heart bursting with the emotions of his freedom.

He thought of all of the things he wanted to do, right this minute. Go to the beach, eat at a restaurant, take a nap, listen to music, work on his novel, see Rose Abernathy, the unflappable Rose Abernathy, just to make sure his life was at least temporarily where he had left it. All of the things he couldn't do as of this morning, now he could.

Maybe not right this minute, but he was free to do them. Right now it was overwhelming that he could do all of these things if he chose to. Right now it was wonderful to be overwhelmed.

CHAPTER **13**

Jack Wilkerson looked at his watch Tuesday afternoon and saw that it was four o'clock. Good, the first of the news programs would be coming on. He put down the western that he had been reading and turned on the television.

Jack saw Brad's face on his screen, along with Brad's lawyer answering questions outside of the jail downtown. Thank God, he's out. Jack listened as John Cantrinni answered questions from the press. He's letting his high priced mouthpiece answer the questions. That's smart. Make him earn his money.

Problem is, he's going to be working even harder for his money when this stuff comes to trial. Jack's stomach churned. Brad's going to have City Hall pressing hard against him.

The telephone rang.

"Jack?"

"Is that you, Pete?"

"Yeah. I heard you want to see me?"

"Yeah. Can you be at the Red Lion in half an hour?"

"Sure thing."

Pete was an informant, a snitch. He used to be Jack's snitch, back when Jack was with the Police Department. Pete supplied Jack with information and in return Jack looked the other way at Pete's petty crimes, mostly bookmaking.

Jack checked his wallet. He took out a one hundred dollar bill and put it in his shirt pocket. Pete would expect to be compensated for his time, especially since Jack was retired.

Jack still knew people that could make trouble for Pete, and Jack normally wouldn't pass Pete quite so much green. But Jack wanted to impress upon Pete the seriousness of the matter.

Jack turned the television off. He walked out the front door and strolled toward the Red Lion. It would take him about fifteen minutes to walk there.

Walking to the Red Lion instead of driving was a habit of Jack's for a couple of reasons. First, he didn't want to drink and then drive home. Second, he joked to himself, if he didn't walk to get his beer he wouldn't get any exercise at all. He made that same joke to himself every time he started the walk to the Red Lion, even though this trip held more importance than just beer.

Walking along, Jack couldn't take his mind off of his friend Brad. He had to do whatever he could to help his friend. He didn't have a lot of people he considered close friends, and Brad was one of them. Kind of strange, considering the difference in their ages. Brad could be his son. I certainly talk to Brad more often than Julie, my daughter in Dallas.

They had the bond of the Marine Corps. But it was more than that. We hit it off immediately. He parries my verbal jabs and punches right back. I enjoy talking with him. Over the last couple of years we've become close friends and that is that. I've got to help him because that's what friends do.

Absorbed in his thoughts, Jack reached the Red Lion before he knew it. Inside, he mounted his usual stool.

Rusty placed a draft beer in front of Jack. "How's it going?"

"I've seen worse. Much worse." Jack looked around the bar. Pete wasn't here yet. He looked at his watch. It shouldn't be too long. Pete was rarely very late. Business man that he was, appointments meant money for him. He was punctual out of habit.

As if on cue, Pete walked in the front door and headed straight for Jack. "Draft." Pete said to Rusty. Jack and Pete waited for the beer to be delivered before they spoke to each other.

"So what's got you calling me out, Jack? I thought you retired."

"I did. I'm just doing a favor for a friend." Jack lifted his beer to take a sip from it.

"I always thought of us as friends, Jack."

"Did I ever say different? I need you to find out all you can about someone."

"If they like a little action on a game now and then, or have a friend that does, I might already know their business. You know that, Jack. So who is it?" Pete lifted his beer to his lips.

"Richard Pierce."

Pete sat frozen for a moment with the beer mug at his mouth. He slowly placed it back on the bar. He sat there staring straight ahead. He opened his mouth as if to speak, and then shut it. Finally, he opened his mouth again. "The Richard Pierce, the Mayor's son?"

"The one and only."

"You're trying to get me killed. I don't know nothing about no Richard Pierce." Pete shook his head and fidgeted on his stool.

"Calm down, Pete." Jack took the money from his front pocket and slid it on the bar over in the direction of Pete. "I'll make it worth your while. And let me remind you; while I'm not with the department any more, I still have plenty of friends that are. I can make a lot of trouble for you if I decide we're not friends any more."

Pete reached out and took the money from the bar and put it in his own shirt pocket. He sat there for a moment. "He's bad news, Jack. One mean reckless fuck. And he runs the part of his daddy's business that Daddy wants to keep secret."

"Go on."

"Word is if you wanna do business downtown, you gotta do business through him. And there's a lot of business being done, what with the reconstruction of downtown and all. There's not a lot more I know."

"So there is some serious money involved."

"Big money. But off of the books. He's got a couple of goons that do some work for him, Duane Clark and Reggie Johnson. Duane likes to bet on the local boys, Astros, Texans, Rockets. That's how I know 'em. He doesn't usually come to me first, but some of his action gets pretty large. Then I cover some of it."

"Find out what else you can about them. Like I said, I'll make it worth your while. I want to know the details about Pierce's business, who he's doing business with, what it's about. That sort of thing."

"I don't have any choice do I?"

"Just like old times, friend."

"Just one thing." Pete said.

"What's that?"

"When, not if, but when they find my corpse in a dumpster, make sure I get a decent funeral with flowers. And I want women there crying over me even if you gotta pay 'em."

Brad left the DoubleTree Hotel feeling like a new man. The hotel room where he had not yet stayed the night had still welcomed him with a homey feeling, and he had enjoyed the shower and fresh clothes with near childlike giddiness. After grabbing a quick dinner at the hotel restaurant, he was ready to head out to the Red Lion and try to find his friend, Jack.

Jack was right where he expected to find him, on his familiar stool. Brad bounced onto the stool beside him. "Don't you ever move from this spot?"

"I try not to. You got out and about and see what it got you?"

"My trouble came looking for me. It found me here, remember?"

Jack chuckled. "Oh yeah, now I remember. This place was quiet and respectable until recently. Maybe I should start a petition or something to ban murderers from this joint."

"Real funny." Brad accepted a club soda that Rusty put in front of him and nodded. "Thanks, Rusty."

"Hey, I saw you on TV today. You didn't look too bad for a jailbird." Jack said.

"Yeah, keep it up with the name calling." Brad said.

"What? I thought I just gave you a compliment."

"I notice nobody pays you to think."

"There's still some life left in him. Yes, there is still some fight left."

"Hell yes. I haven't given up yet. When I was being hauled out of here Saturday, you were saying some things. You didn't get to finish. I want to hear the rest of it."

"What was it about, exactly? Refresh my memory."

"You made a statement about how the police were being told not to look any further than me for Renee's murderer." Brad said.

"Oh yeah. Well, that's basically it. I met with one of the detectives on your murder case. He wasn't convinced you did it, but he was being told to make it you."

"Is that sort of thing common? Or am I special?"

"You're special. This had never happened to him before. Usually the homicide guys run the cases wherever the leads take them. The bosses stay out of the way. Oh, they might bitch and moan about how long it's taking or stuff like that, but they don't interfere with the case."

"And in this case they're getting involved."

"Jumping in the middle of it and telling the detectives who the murderer is. Not asking them anything about the case and not giving them a choice. They were told to make sure you did it."

"Crap."

"That about sums it up, yeah."

Brad sipped at his drink. "And this is coming from?"

"Well it's coming from the top. But we both know

where the original source of this plan is located, don't we?"

Brad nodded. "I keep telling myself that they can't convict me of something I didn't do, but deep down I'm still a little worried."

"Smart man. You should be worried. Plenty of guys are in the pokey for things they didn't do."

"I keep thinking of that."

"Of course, most of them didn't have decent lawyers. At least you can afford to buy a little justice for your side. But you've got City Hall against you."

"Not all of City Hall. Just a branch of it, for all we know."

"Okay. I never said things were hopeless." Jack said.

Brad took a sip from his club soda. He screwed up his face and paused. "Renee must have been killed because of something she found out. When she first called, when she was so frightened, she said that she saw something she shouldn't have."

"So you want to know what it was she saw?"

"It must have been something to do with the business of Mr. Richard Pierce." Brad said.

"Agreed."

"If I can find out what that was, then I might be able to turn it against him."

"I'm ahead of you on that. I've got some feelers out. And I've found out a little. Some general stuff."

"Such as?" Brad asked.

Jack turned toward Brad. "You've got to be careful here, my friend. Remember that poking a nose into these matters has already cost one life."

"I haven't forgotten."

"Richard Pierce is the front man for a lot of his Daddy's business, evidently the under-the-table business that Daddy doesn't want noticed."

"Corruption in the Mayor's office? Isn't that novel."

Jack nodded his head. "You know all of that construction that's going on downtown? Evidently there are some payoffs involved. Sonny boy handles those."

"There's a lot of construction. It wouldn't take much to add up to a lot of money."

Jack nodded again. "I'm trying to find out some more details."

"You think that Renee stumbled on to this business?"

"She may have happened upon a piece of it, or some dirty business related to it. Who knows? Pierce, the son, has some fellows working for him that aren't very nice guys. There's no telling what she saw."

"We may never know."

"That's right. But I think you're still on the right track. If we can find out what Richard Pierce is up to, we might be able to get him out of the way, and this made up case against you will dry up and go away."

"God, I hope so."

"We just have to be careful, like I said..."

"I know, I know. One casualty already."

"It's only one that we know of. The main thing is we don't want any more." Jack said.

"So we'll be careful. I'll have to give this some thought. Obviously marching up to the guy and asking him what he's up to is completely out of the question."

"Wouldn't do you any good at all. Like I said, I've got some feelers out." Jack said.

"Well I'm not just going to sit back in the background on this. I'll come up with some way to get some info on him. I just have to sleep on it." Brad said.

"Didn't they give you a nice bunk downtown?"

"No, it wasn't nice at all. Oh, I almost forgot. I borrowed your name while I was in there. Not that I didn't trust the other guys in my cell block, but you know, they have criminals and shady characters in there, Jack."

Jack laughed. "Not a problem, Brad. I'm actually quite flattered."

"Well it backfired. Since I pretended to be you the only book they had to read in my cell block was a western."

Jack howled. "Some real literature and plenty of time to enjoy it, and it sounds like you're complaining. You think if you had used your own name then the one book might have been science fiction? That's just too rich."

"I'm not sure it worked, anyway. I was on the news while I was a guest of the county. Somebody may have recognized me. I got some funny smiles and waves."

Jack howled even louder. "Are you sure they weren't just making a pass? I'll bet you're not experienced in jail house dating etiquette."

"Well, I managed to get out of there without acquiring a girlfriend." Brad grew somber and frowned. The events on the sidewalk earlier came up in his mind. Yeah, it seems that I have no girl and no prospects of one in my life at all.

CHAPTER **14**

Jennifer turned off the television Tuesday night in disgust. There's nothing worth watching. She didn't feel like sitting around the apartment alone with nothing to do. Kevin was playing a rare Tuesday night gig with his band. I know, I'll pop over and see him. It's been a long while since I've gone to watch him play.

She drove to the bar where he was playing and gave her name at the front door. She was on a guest list for the band, saving her the cover charge. Once inside, the loud volume of the music became familiar, and she saw her boyfriend up on the stage with his guitar. She smiled. Looking around at the fairly small crowd, she had no problem finding an empty table at the back.

I guess it's to be expected that the crowd would be fairly small on a Tuesday. Jennifer listened to the band for a while. They were quite good, and the new drummer was an improvement, as Kevin had said.

A waitress appeared to take Jennifer's drink order and she ordered a margarita. Jennifer looked around at the crowd. It was not only small, but quiet as well. Oh well, Tuesday isn't much of a party.

Jennifer thought back over her day. It sucked. These days her whole job sucked. It didn't used to be that way. I used to like my job.

This Bradley Marshall stuff is depressing. He didn't

kill his wife. My instincts are never that wrong about anybody. Yet I have to watch him being treated like a criminal, not just by the police, but also by my own newspaper. I have to treat him that way myself. This afternoon I couldn't even look him in the eye.

I really like this guy. I know he wouldn't hurt anyone. So why is this happening to him? Why do I have to be the one to write about it? Usually I'd give anything to be assigned to such a high profile story, and now that I have this one all I can think of is how I don't want it.

Maybe I should ask Bill to reassign me. No. I can't do that. If I start opting out on stories then my career is dead.

Still, I don't know if I'm doing the story justice. Sure, I call myself a professional, but am I really acting professionally here? Maybe I should be using my connection to Brad to get more of the story. Can I do that? That almost seems like lying to him. So what if it is? Isn't that what I'm paid to do?

This is a mess, and I don't like it. Whatever happens to Bradley Marshall, I have a job to do. Like it or not, I'm going to have to find a way to do it. I'll have to put whatever feelings I have about his innocence out of my mind. His problems aren't mine, and I have enough problems of my own trying to get the story.

Tomorrow I'm going to be the dedicated journalist I used to be. Tomorrow I'll be on fire. I'll call and get an appointment for an interview with Brad and that will be that.

The waitress returned with Jennifer's drink. Jennifer took a sip of the drink, pronounced it acceptable, and focused her attention back on Kevin. If only his band would become a big hit so he'd be rich like Brad. Ha! Fat chance of that. They were good, but not superstar good. Would Kevin take me with him if he achieved that kind of success? I don't really know. We've only known each other a couple of years.

Good, it looks like the band is taking a break. Oh, great. Kevin has to stop to be admired by the local groupies. Has he even seen me? Yes, he looked up this way, he sees me. Damn, he's taking forever.

Kevin wove his way through the tables to where Jennifer was sitting. "Hi. I didn't expect to see you here tonight."

"I got bored at home. You have a fan club?"

"What's that?"

"I noticed your admirers."

"Oh that. They were just complimenting the band. You like our new drummer? This is the first you've heard him."

"Yeah. I like him. He's the improvement you said he was."

"Yeah. We're satisfied with him. You going to stay long?"

"No. I can't be up that late. Like I said, I was just bored. I wish I could carry you out of here now and take you home with me."

"That'd be nice, but we have a couple more sets to play."

"I know. I probably won't stay much longer."

"Okay. I better go. I want to talk to the boys about making some changes in the next set." Kevin leaned over and kissed Jennifer. "See you at home."

"Wake me up when you get home."

"I will."

Jennifer watched him walk away. Sometimes it seemed they barely had a relationship at all. The biggest problem was they kept different hours. Then there was the difference in their careers. I'm not even sure you can call what he does a career. He certainly can't afford to pay for even half of the apartment. I don't know what he'd do if I didn't subsidize his existence.

Whatever our relationship, he's mine and that makes me happy. He'll be successful one day. Jennifer looked around and noticed Kevin talking to another member of the band. See, he's working on that now.

Brad entered his office Wednesday morning. It was good to see Rose sitting at her desk.

"Hello Rose."

"Mr. Marshall! It's good to have you back. You look good."

"Thanks, Rose. Any messages?"

"I've put some on your desk. Nothing urgent, Mr. Marshall."

Brad went into his office and closed the door. He smiled. It was good to be back in his familiar space. He put the newspaper he was carrying on the desk and looked out the window at the city below.

Things were a little out of whack right now. No, things were a lot out of whack. I'm being charged with Renee's murder and her killers are walking around out there without a care in the world. That will change.

That has to change.

Brad heard his intercom buzzer. "Mr. Marshall, there's a Mr. Sheridan for you on line one."

George and Leslie Sheridan were Renee's parents. Brad pushed a button on the phone. "Okay, Rose. I'll get it." Brad sat down in his chair and picked up the receiver. "Brad. This is George Sheridan."

"Hello George."

"Brad, I want you to know, me and Leslie, we don't believe a word of what we've been reading in the papers. We know you couldn't have had anything to do with Renee's death."

"I appreciate that, George. I really do."

"Well, there's just no way, I mean. Even with the troubles that y'all had, you were always very good to Renee. The police are being stupid not to see that."

"I'm afraid I'm not the one to talk to about police competency right now. My attorney wants me to keep quiet."

"Yes. I can understand. The main reason I'm calling, Brad. Would it be alright with you if Leslie and I took care of the arrangements for Renee?"

Brad paused. Of course, the arrangements. He had been jerked around so much lately he hadn't thought about them. "Of course, George. That would be fine. Given the publicity I seem to be generating, it might be best for Renee if I'm not involved more than necessary."

"That really didn't enter our mind, Brad. We just want to be involved. We knew you had your hands full right now, what with these outrageous charges."

"I don't even know the status, I mean, have they

released her body? The authorities and I have been on an adversarial track lately."

"Yes. I talked to the coroner. They will release Renee to us, given the circumstances." George said.

"I would like to attend the service, of course. If you don't mind."

"We don't mind at all, Brad. Leslie and I talked about that. We want you to be there. Renee would want you to be there. Like I said, we don't believe any of that stuff we read in the papers."

"Thanks. That means a lot, George, it really does. Let me know about the funeral. Leave a message with Rose if I'm not in."

"Will do, Brad. You hang in there. It will all work out."

Brad hung up the phone and sat staring at it. Given that he and Renee were almost divorced it was more appropriate for her parents to make the arrangements anyway. It was nice of George to call, though. I suppose it will be a media event when I attend the service. Too bad. I'm not missing her funeral because of what they're saying about me in the press.

Brad looked down at the newspaper in front of him. Speaking of the press, what are they saying about me?

Brad looked through the paper until he found the article about himself being released from jail. The article was on page six. At least he wasn't page one news right now.

He scanned the article and began to frown. It still made him out to be a murderer. Alright, so it didn't call him that in so many words but it never missed the chance to repeat the fact that he was charged with the crime of murdering his wife. It mentioned that he benefited financially from her dying instead of divorcing him.

All in all, it wasn't a pretty picture of Mr. Bradley Marshall. It made it sound like letting him get out of jail was a huge mistake being made by our system of justice.

Brad put down the newspaper. He thought of his conversation with Jack the night before. I need more information on Richard Pierce. I'll start with what everyone else knows about him.

Brad logged onto his computer and brought up web pages for the Houston Chronicle. He clicked on the link to access their archives of articles and searched for the name 'Richard Pierce'.

A screen full of articles appeared and he started by selecting the one at the top. It described a charity event. Among the attendees was one Richard Pierce. Article two, another social event that he had attended. After several of these, Brad learned only that Richard Pierce keeps a fairly active social calendar.

I would expect that. He is after all, the son of the Mayor. Nowhere in the articles was any mention of an address, or place of business. The only reference to Richard Pierce is that of being the son of the Mayor.

There's got to be a better way to research Richard Pierce. The newspaper would know all sorts of things about Mr. Pierce that they didn't print.

Brad smiled. John said I couldn't talk to the press. He didn't say I couldn't ask them questions. He searched the Chronicle web pages for a phone number and dialed.

"Ms. Jennifer Hart, please. This is Brad Marshall."
He sat waiting to be connected.

"Jennifer? This is Brad."

"Hi Brad. I wasn't expecting to hear from you."

"I know. I need to talk to you. I wondered if you
were free this evening?"

"I suppose so. I can't really say no, can I?"

Brad chuckled. "How about around six? We could
grab something to eat. You like Tex-Mex, right?"

"Sure. You want to pick me up here, in front of the
Chronicle building?"

"That would be great. I'll see you then."

Brad couldn't wipe the grin off his face. I'll have to
be careful what I say, not to talk about the case. Will
she guess what I'm up to by the questions about
Richard? Does it matter? It wouldn't hurt for Richard
to get a little press coverage himself. Still, I don't want
to tip my hand.

I'll just feel out Jennifer on the subject and see how
it goes. If nothing else, I'll get to see her again. I could
use a pretty face to look at across the dinner table.
After the last few days I deserve that at least.

Brad's thoughts took him back to the night of the
murder. The smile left his face. He saw Renee lying in
a pool of her own blood. He remembered looking
through her phone for the Richards. Pulling his own
phone from his pocket he brought up the entry for
Richard Pierce. There was no address, just a
telephone number and an email address.

An email address! The smile returned to Brad's
face. This might be something I can work with. This
might very well be something indeed.

CHAPTER **15**

"Hi, Dad," Richard strolled into his father's office Wednesday afternoon and plopped down in a chair.

"Hi Son. Glad you came by. How's business?"

"Like clockwork, Dad. I'm making a pickup tonight. It's just a small one, from the Bartoulli Brothers."

"No trouble from anyone?"

"No. No trouble. Watson is still bitching from time to time, but he pays."

"His payments are in line with everyone else, right?"

"Yeah Dad. He pays the same percentage as everyone else and his contract is set so that he makes plenty of money after our cut. He just likes to bitch. Everything is under control. If I were going to complain it would be on the other end."

"The other end? What's the problem?"

"A couple of the laundries want to take several days to get the cash onto their books and cut us a check. I've talked to them. They're just nervous. They take a little leaning on. It's no big deal."

"I expect you can handle it. All of that money I spent on your business degree better be good for something."

"Come over to my office, Dad. I'll be glad to show

you the books."

"Naw, I wouldn't know what I was looking at. Debits, credits, I never could keep that shit straight. That's why I sent you to the University of Texas. Are you sure those books are safe in your office?"

"Yeah Dad. You have to know the password to get into them."

"Okay. I guess now I'm being the nervous one. Say, don't forget about the symphony Friday night."

"Oh, Dad."

"Don't oh Dad me. You know it's important that you show up at these things from time to time." The Mayor searched for a piece of paper on his desk, and finding it held it out for Richard. "Here Ricky, I want you to take this girl with you."

Richard feigned surprise. "Dad!" His father's girlfriend, Clara Burke was in the habit of setting him up with society girls for society events.

"I don't want you showing up with no stripper. You need to be seen with some class women around town. Don't forget you're the son of the Mayor."

Richard looked at the piece of paper. "I don't know this girl."

"Doesn't matter. It's been arranged. She's expecting your call. Clara set it up. Clara said she's a nice girl."

"I don't get a vote in this do I?"

"No Son, you don't. Make your old man happy and go along with this. I don't ask you to go to many of these things."

"Alright Dad. I'll give her a call." Actually, some of these tight ass bitches Clara Burke sets me up with turn out to be a lot of fun when nobody is looking. Not all of them, but enough to go along with these matchmaking efforts of hers. Besides, it keeps Dad happy and off of my back.

The Mayor started searching through his desk drawers. "Where are my antacids? Here they are." Finding a packet of tablets, he took two and put them in his mouth.

"Something upsetting you, Dad? Like I was saying earlier, business is good."

"It's not that, Son. It's just all the rest of the shit in this town. The City Council is breaking my balls over the budget changes. I read in the paper yesterday our city's most famous murderer is running loose in the city, out on bail. His lawyer made some threat about how his indictment has political implications. How about that? Political implications. I've never heard of that man before in my life."

Richard was careful not to raise his voice in any way. "This murderer you're talking about. Is it that Marshall fellow?"

"The one and only. My only relief right now is it's off the front page. But if he or his lawyer keep making these noises, who knows how long that will last? Do you know anybody with a political axe to grind against him?"

Richard kept himself calm. "Can't say as I do, Dad. I'll keep my ears open and let you know what I find out."

"You do that Son. I'd sure like to know what that sonofabitch meant by political implications."

Richard stood up to leave. "I'll check it out, Dad.

Hey, I've got to go. We'll see you later, okay Dad? Friday night at the latest."

"Okay son. Give that girl a call."

"Will do, Dad." Richard turned and left his father's office. This will not do. This is one fucked up mess. I expected Marshall to rot in jail. Now he's not only out of jail but making noises that upset my father. This has got to be fixed.

When I get back to the office I'll have to make some phone calls and find out what's going on here. There's got to be a way to get Marshall back off the street. The District Attorney needs to find that way, and find it now. It's time to light a fire under somebody's ass.

Brad left his office parking garage Wednesday, just before six, and steered his car toward the Chronicle building. He should be feeling a little foolish, in that what he was about to do was a foolish thing. His lawyer had warned him not to see anyone socially, especially not a member of the press.

He didn't feel foolish. He felt a little naughty, doing something he wasn't suppose to do. Anyway, this wasn't really a date per se. He had a legitimate reason for seeing Jennifer. She might have information that would be beneficial to him. It would be easier to approach the subject over dinner.

So everything was above board and all of that. He still felt naughty. Perhaps it was because he expected to have a good time. He smiled.

Brad pulled up to the curb in front of the Chronicle building and almost immediately Jennifer got into the car beside him.

"Hi there." Jennifer smiled at him.

"Hello yourself. So, what's tomorrow's headline?" Brad pulled the car out into traffic.

"Peace in the Middle East, terrorism has been abolished, and time travel will become commonplace within the year."

"Oh. Slow news day, huh?"

"You could say that."

"Well at least I'm off the front page."

"Don't think I'm not grateful for that."

Brad looked over at Jennifer. She was sincere. "You don't like writing about me?"

"About you being arrested and in jail, charged with murdering your wife? Give me a break. Brad, I know you didn't kill your wife. It bothers me to have to write some of the stuff I do."

"If I didn't do it, why can't you just write that?"

"Brad, you know better. You're a smart guy. Your saying you didn't do it is not news. My saying you didn't do it is certainly not newsworthy."

"I do see your point."

"I knew you would. Like I said, you're a smart guy," Jennifer said.

"Through all of this, I always recognized you had a job to do. I never took anything written in the paper personally. It's been a little hard at times. Some of the slant seems to run against me. But I never blamed you."

"Thanks, Brad." Jennifer smiled. "This must be very hard on your parents. Have you spoken to them?"

"I talked to them a little today. They're worried, but

137

there's not a lot I can do about that, except work to prove my innocence. They wanted to know if they should come into town, but there's nothing for them to do here. I don't even have a place for them to stay. Hell, I still don't have a place for me to stay."

"The police haven't released your house to you yet?"

"To tell the truth, I haven't asked them. I'm not sure I want to go back there yet."

"I can imagine. You still at the Hyatt Regency then?"

Brad paused. "I don't think I should answer that, Jennifer."

Jennifer laughed. "Hiding from me, are you?"

"Actually, I'm hiding from the press. As much as I enjoyed our little breakfast chats I don't think my attorney would approve. I'm sure he wouldn't approve of this."

"I won't tell him. About our dinner together, I mean."

"Good. You're still up for Tex-Mex, right?

"Sure."

Brad entered the ramp to put them on the Southwest Freeway headed south.

"Jennifer, you said you believe I'm innocent, right?"

"Sure, Brad. Why?"

"I need some information. I'm pretty sure you can help me find it."

"What is it?"

"I want the address of Richard Pierce."

Jennifer looked at Brad and didn't say anything for a moment. "Your lawyer mentioned something political involving your case. You think Richard Pierce is involved in Renee's murder?"

"I can't answer that, Jennifer. This is the favor part. I don't want you to write about the fact that I'm asking, or that I suspect him of anything."

"I see." Jennifer paused, her brow furrowed. She cocked her head to one side. "I can do that. Business or personal?"

"What's that?"

"Do you want his business address or personal residence?"

"Oh, I see. Both I guess."

"I'm sure we have them in our files at the paper. I'll dig them out. Tomorrow, alright?"

"Sure, that would be fine. Just call the office. If I'm not there leave the information with Rose."

"Is that all?"

"Well, no. The other is more personal. Just a question. I'm a little embarrassed to ask."

"Go ahead, Brad. We know each other pretty well by now."

"I got the impression before, and I don't know where, well, how do I say this? That you are involved with someone?"

Jennifer smiled. "First of all, I'm flattered that you would ask, Brad. Yes. I'm involved with someone."

Brad felt a hole in his stomach. "I see." He tried not to show his disappointment to Jennifer.

"But I do enjoy our time together, and we can still have a nice dinner tonight. Okay?"

"Okay." This was probably not a really bad thing. Her being involved keeps her off limits, where I should be keeping her anyway.

I promised John I wouldn't get tangled up with a reporter. This just makes it easier. "I enjoy spending time with you too, Jennifer. As long as you're a reporter and I'm a murder suspect, I'm not supposed to even talk to you. But to tell the truth, I really did want to see you again. I intend to enjoy dinner with you, especially since your boyfriend isn't here."

"Good. Then that's settled." Jennifer smiled. "Where are we going?"

Brad steered the car onto the exit ramp. "Right here. Lopez."

"Oh super! I've never been here."

"I discovered it years ago. Since then it's become a favorite of mine." Brad pulled into the parking lot.

"I trust your good judgment."

"Is that a fact? You know, you're a smart lady."

"Thanks. But of course I am." Jennifer laughed.

Pulling into a parking space, Brad stopped the car. He turned toward Jennifer and smiled. Jennifer was smiling back at him.

CHAPTER **16**

Jack loaded his truck with his fishing gear in the pre-dawn hours of Thursday morning. The weather report said it was going to be a beautiful, clear day, not too hot and certainly not cold. This will be perfect. I need to get out of the house.

Within a few minutes, Jack was driving south on I-45 towards Galveston, listening to the radio. Like the old joke, Jack liked two kinds of music, country and western.

Jack was looking forward to getting out on the bay. When he thought of his friend, Brad, he frowned. It's tough to see such a good kid in the middle of such a mess.

I should be hearing something back from Pete soon. That little weasel has always come through before. I don't know what good it will do, but information is power, or that's what they say. The more we know about the business of Richard Pierce the better position we'll be in to deal with him.

Dealing with Richard Pierce is not going to be easy, regardless of what we know about him. We already know enough to be sure of that.

There's got to be more I can do. After all, I've been trained to investigate crimes. What would I do if I were working this as a case of my own?

At this point I'd probably go back over all of the evidence. If not now, at some point I'd back up and look at everything again just to make sure I wasn't missing anything. That's not a bad strategy now. I can do that. While I'm waiting on Pete to get back to me I can review everything that put Brad in this pickle.

Brad came in the bar and told me about Renee's phone calls. That's when we first knew something was wrong with Renee. Brad said that she'd mentioned she was at Richard's and he found out she was with Richard Pierce by talking to someone. What was that girls name?

Lisa. I can't remember her last name. This Lisa said Renee was with Richard Pierce that night. It might be worthwhile to talk to this Lisa. I might jog something in her mind Brad forgot to ask about.

After the phone call where Renee said she was at Richard's, Brad went home to find Renee dead. The police should be through with the house by now. I'll ask Brad if I can have a look at it. It doesn't hurt to have eyes on his side look at things. I might not see anything else, but it's worth the time to check it out.

Next time I see Brad I'll ask him about Lisa, and seeing the house. I'll retrace the steps that got him into this jam. You never know what might turn up. Besides, it's the least I can do for Brad. He deserves better than what he's getting.

Of course, regardless of what turns up, at some point Mr. Richard Pierce is going to have to be dealt with. There's got to be a way to get to him. He has to have a weakness. I'll have to ask Pete about this.

As it is, I don't know. I have no idea how to go

about getting to Pierce. That's going to require a lot more thought. Well, I'm about to be knee deep in water with the sun coming up over Galveston Bay. There's no better place for thinking.

―――――――――――――――

"Let me get this straight. You're going to send Pierce a virus in his email?" Jack asked. He and Brad were sitting with a table between them at the Red Lion late Thursday afternoon.

"Well, yes." Brad replied.

"But this virus won't damage his computer, or spread itself like other viruses."

"Of course not."

"It'll just send you his files."

"Exactly. Well, that's what I hope it will do." Brad took a sip of his club soda.

"Leaving aside the question of whether or not you can do that, I assume that you can. Isn't that illegal?"

Brad screwed up his face. "Technically, yeah. It is."

"Then there are two questions to ask, Brad. The first question is, will he know you're doing it?"

"Not at all likely. This is playing in my ballpark, Jack. I shouldn't have to remind you I'm a computer security specialist. I know where the holes are in computer security. Most people don't spend the money and time to plug those holes. I'll be counting on that with Pierce."

"What if he has some security measure in place?"

"I know what the popular ones are. I'll be disabling those if I detect them. He might be able to stop me from getting at his files, but it would be almost impossible for him to catch me."

"They catch computer hackers all of the time." Jack shook his head and sipped his beer. "I don't want to see you get into more trouble."

"More trouble than I'm in now? They catch guys who do it a lot, Jack. It's like robbing banks. If you keep robbing banks you'll be caught eventually. If you set out to rob just one bank there's a good chance you'll get away with it."

"I don't know. I'm still uncomfortable with it. But it's funny you bring up robbing banks. It leads well into my second question. This is illegal, breaking into another guy's computer. Are you okay with that?"

Brad frowned. "To tell you the truth, I haven't really come to terms with it. I've been trying to look past it." Brad played with his straw in his glass, avoiding Jack's eyes.

"I mean, you spent several years of your life with computers helping people keep the bad guys out, Brad. With this, you're becoming one of the bad guys you helped guard against."

"I know. And that doesn't feel too good."

"I wouldn't think it would."

Brad settled back in his chair and sat for a moment, listening to the old Bob Segar tune, "Come to Poppa", playing in the background. Finally he spoke. "My back is against a wall here, Jack. I don't intend to sit around while these guys railroad me into a life sentence. Or worse."

"I hear you. In the end, you have to do what you think is best here. When I was a policeman, not
144

everything I did to catch the bad guys was strictly legal. It's a judgment call, how much you're willing to compromise to justify the end."

"The age old question of ends justifying the means?"

"Well, yes. As I said, it's your call. It sounds like you've made up your mind to do it, in spite of your reservations."

Brad paused. "I've already started working on it."

"Be careful. Take your time. Don't get caught. It may not seem like much now, but you don't want to be charged with computer crimes when you're guilty. It's easier to defend yourself against something if you're innocent. I don't know if that's true but it sounds good."

Brad chuckled. "Yeah, it sounds like it ought to be true."

"What are you going to do with the information, assuming you find something out from his computer?"

Brad lifted his eyebrows and sighed. "I haven't thought that far ahead. I guess it depends on what I find. I'm sure he's doing something that when Renee found out about it, got her killed. If I know what that is, I'll be in a better position than I'm in now."

"Yeah, knowledge is power, or so they say. That's something I've been mulling over myself."

"Right. Knowledge is power. Right now I don't have much of either." Brad said.

"Whatever you find out, run it by me before you act on it. Like I've mentioned, I have an iron or two in the fire myself. I'm trying to find out more about Mr. Richard Pierce through more old fashion methods. I still have a source or two left from my days with the

Department. Let's gather all we can before we decide what to do next."

"I'll do that. There's no hurry. I don't even have a hearing scheduled for weeks. Cantrinni is trying to put this off as much as possible, letting the publicity die down."

"That's probably a good idea. Hey, I went fishing today."

Brad raised his eyebrows again. "So? Good for you. Catch anything?"

"First off, yeah, I caught four trout. Nice ones, but that's not the point. Haven't I taught you anything? Fishing is good for thinking."

"Oh, okay. What did you think about?"

"I thought if I were working this case as a policeman, what I'd do at some point would be to retrace my steps. I'd go back over all of the evidence to make sure I wasn't overlooking something."

"I see. That makes some sense."

"Some of this stuff I haven't even looked at for the first time. I thought if you don't mind, I'd start at the beginning and go through everything that got you into this mess and make sure we're not overlooking something."

"No, I don't mind. I appreciate the help, Jack. It's more than I would ask you to do."

"I'll need a key to your house. I assume the police have released it from being a crime scene?"

"To tell you the truth, I haven't asked them. I've been staying in a hotel because I didn't want to go back there anyway. And the police and I have been too adversarial for casual conversation about the state of

146

my property."

"I understand. Being retired from the force, I can probably talk my way in either way."

Brad took a key off of his key ring and pushed it across the table to Jack. "I found her just inside the front door. You know, I just thought, there's a chance that they've let my maid, Tina, in. It could be cleaned up by now. Like I said, I just haven't had it in me to check."

"I understand. I'll let you know what shape it's in. I probably should have volunteered to do this anyway. Another thing. This girl that told you Renee was with Richard Pierce the night she was killed? Who is she again?"

"Lisa. Lisa Davis."

"Right. I want to talk to her."

"Sure thing. I'll give you her number." Brad took out his phone and transferred Lisa's name and number to a napkin, which he slid toward Jack.

Jack took the napkin and glanced at it before putting it in his shirt pocket. "I'll let you know what she says as well. There's just one last thing."

"What's that, Jack?"

"Are you busy tonight?"

"No. You need some help with something? You're helping me enough, you just name it."

"Yeah. Like I said earlier, I have some fresh gulf trout at my house and I need help eating it. I don't know that we can eat all of it, but with your help I can make twice the dent on it I can alone."

Brad laughed. "I'll be glad to help. Honored, actually. Lead me to it."

CHAPTER **17**

Jennifer got off the elevator and slinked toward her desk Friday morning. It seemed hard to get excited about her work these days, hard to get excited about anything. She decided it was just a phase. If she kept her head down and kept working through it, time would take care of it.

She thought she made it past Caruthers' office without being noticed when she heard her name called.

"Hart. Get in here. I see you're in here early as usual. Does this mean you have a lot of interesting news for our readers today?"

"Good Morning, Bill. No big news. I was going to check my email, then check with you for any assignments."

"What about this Marshall thing? Nothing new on that?"

"No. Not right now. I'm still monitoring it."

"Have you talked to him lately?"

Jennifer considered her options. Lying in the newspaper business was dangerous. Your credibility was everything. There was the outside chance she was seen with Brad at dinner Wednesday night. More likely she was seen getting into his car in front of the building. "I had dinner with him night before last."

"Oh Ho! I don't suppose he told you why he did it?"

"He didn't kill her, Bill. I've told you that before."

"And I've told you, killers saying they didn't do it is not news."

"I can't make him admit to something he didn't do, and he didn't do it."

"His lawyer said something about there being some political slant to all of this. Have you found out what he meant?"

"Not yet. I asked Brad about that and he wouldn't tell me. He said he could tell me later, but not yet."

"You need to find out what he was talking about."

Jennifer sighed. "Right now Bradley Marshall trusts me. In the long run that's worth more to me as a reporter than pushing him too hard and pushing him away."

"I guess you're right. Are you sleeping with him?"

"Bill!"

"What? I was being sensitive here. If you had been a guy I would have used the 'f' word."

"The point is it's none of your business."

"I'm not so sure about that. If you're sleeping with him then I feel pretty good about the level of information we're going to get out of him."

"Well I'm not sleeping with him. Do I still have a job?"

"Sure. For now. But this could be a world-class story, Hart. Maybe even a Pulitzer. You should think about these things before you go keeping your legs together."

Jennifer shook her head. If Bill Caruthers were not such a caricature she would be offended. "I'm going to my cubicle."

"Yeah, get to work. And think about what I said."

Jennifer grabbed her bag and continued on her way to her desk. She plopped down in her chair and sat thinking over what Caruthers had said.

No way she would ever sleep with someone just to get a story. Not that the idea of sleeping with Brad Marshall is that bad. If I weren't involved with Kevin, I might just consider it.

That's out of the question, though. As long as I'm living with Kevin, then Kevin it is. Going to bed with someone else isn't something on my radar screen. It's just wrong. I don't want Kevin acting that way, so I don't.

Jennifer heard her phone ring.

"Jen, it's Kevin."

"Hi Kevin. I was just thinking about you."

"Where are my blue jeans?"

"Your blue jeans? You mean the ones you wore yesterday? They were dirty. I put them in the hamper."

"They weren't dirty. I'd only worn them once."

"Well excuse me. If you want to wear dirty clothes then I'll stay out of your way about it."

"Thanks."

He hung up! He didn't even say goodbye, just hung up. Sometimes I'm not at all sure what I see in him. He's never considerate toward my feelings or me. He only thinks about himself. For two cents I'd drop Mr. Kevin Barker.

I'm sure I could do better. Someone like Brad for instance, that keeps me laughing and makes compliments instead of ranting about day old blue jeans and hanging up on me.

What am I saying? It must be this phase I'm going through. I'm sure Kevin isn't awake yet. I'll call him back later. He'll be awake and will have found his jeans. I'm sure everything will be alright then. I hope so.

Brad stepped into his office Friday morning and was greeted by the smiling face of Rose Abernathy. "Good Morning, Rose."

"Good Morning, Mr. Marshall. How are you doing this morning?"

"I'm fine, thanks."

"Mr. Marshall, I just want to say that you've held up really well through all of this. I don't know what the police must be thinking, but I'm sure everything will turn out alright."

"Thanks, Rose. I appreciate that. Any messages?"

Rose held out a small stack of paper slips. "Just these. Nothing important. A Mr. Grimley from Channel Two is calling regularly now. He's become quite the flirt. I'm not sure that I mind his calls. Sometimes I even look forward to them," Rose chuckled.

Brad looked through the messages. Rose was right. There was nothing there. "Be careful, Rose. These press people have a way of ingratiating themselves into your lives."

"Oh, I wouldn't worry about me, Mr. Marshall. It's only a little harmless fun."

"I know, Rose. I'll be working on something this morning that requires my concentration. Hold my calls unless it's important."

"Will do."

Brad walked into his office and closed the door. He put the message slips on his desk and stood looking out the window. Watching the traffic below he went over his schedule in his mind. Today he would attack Richard Pierce through his email account.

Tomorrow was Renee's funeral. He would lay to rest a woman he had at one time pledged to be with for the rest of his life. Or hers. As it turns out, 'till death do us part' was exactly the result, in spite of the impending divorce.

He wondered if Renee's spirit was looking down on them. He knew that if she were, she would be incensed that her murderers had not been caught.

Brad crossed over to the closet and took out his suit. It was still in good shape, it would do fine for tomorrow. Two white shirts were fresh from the cleaners. He was set for the funeral.

Tonight he was to have dinner with his parents. They're coming into town today for the funeral tomorrow. Actually I think they're coming into town more to see me.

It will be good to see them. They need to see me, to see that I'm doing alright. I know this is worrying them to death. They're probably more worried than me. At least I can work to do something about it. All they can do is read the newspapers and think the worst.

Brad looked over at his desk and computer. It was time to get to work. He sat down and logged in. He had already started work yesterday setting up for his attack.

He had downloaded a file transfer program written in Java, a language he knew Pierce's computer would understand. Normally the program listened for commands to tell it which files to transfer over the network. Brad modified the program, first to connect to his server at his office, then to transfer all the files, one by one, located on Pierce's computer. This formed the basis for his program or virus attack.

This was actually the easy part. Brad then set about making the program into a virus. The first thing the program would do would be to copy itself to a remote part of the computer and then register itself so that it would start if the computer were restarted. That way if the transfer was interrupted it would restart.

Then he searched through a list of known virus detection programs and disabled them if they were found. Since his program wasn't a known virus it wouldn't be detected as such until he had a chance to disable all of the virus protection. He then disabled network protections.

Next he put in a feature to email himself a text message to his cell phone that the virus was installed. Brad smiled. It's good to be king. He added another email to tell him when it was finished, and told the program to erase itself when everything was done.

Brad sat back in his chair and surveyed his work. Not bad. He looked at his watch. It was after noon. Not bad for a morning's work.

Creating something always gives me a sense of fulfillment. This one is a little bothersome, though. Viruses are evil things, and this one is no different. This is breaking and entering, and theft of information.

153

Pure and simple, and it's wrong.

Brad frowned. A part of him wanted to reach out to the delete key and erase what he had done. No way he would allow himself to do that. Good or bad, he was going through with this. I'll do everything I can to find out what was behind Renee's death and bring down those responsible for it.

Only two things remained. The first was to hide the virus in an email. This was going to be tricky. To activate the virus Pierce would need to look at the email. He wouldn't have to do anything else, but he must read it. The subject line was all-important.

Brad sat deep in thought. Of course anything referencing Renee's death would be sure to get his attention. It might however get too much attention. He wanted Richard to read the email, but not become alarmed.

Of course! Pierce was the mayor's son. Brad attached the file to an email titled "From the Mayor's Office". Pierce would have to look at that. It was also vague enough to be used by common spammers, or senders of unwanted email. In the body of the email he wrote, "For hot young girls visit..." and made up a web address.

He changed the from address to be from "The Mayor". A quick check on the city's web site and he had the Mayor's official email address to attach as well. Now to send it.

He logged onto his server. He didn't want to send the email directly from his server. If anything should go wrong he didn't want it traced back to him.

He needed another server to send the email from.

154

One of his former clients came to mind. They still owed him money. Well, now they would pay him, if he could get in. He gave the password to unlock a file he kept with accounts and their passwords. He connected to the client's computers and tried to log in. He was in! They haven't changed their administration password. They would pay for that too.

He transferred the email to their computer and entered the command to send it toward Pierce's computer. He sat with his hand on the key, making sure he had done everything right.

Brad's stomach was in a knot. This felt wrong. He had spent much of his life combating against this sort of thing. He had written and installed tools to protect computers against unauthorized access and use. He studied how criminals or hackers gained access and devised ways to detect them, track them, and thwart them. He had felt good about what he was doing. He had been wearing the white hat.

Now, here he was, committing the crimes of breaking and entering and theft. Even if it was for a good cause, it was at its core an evil thing to do. How badly do I need to find out what was behind Renee's death?

Brad pushed his finger down on the key to send the email. It was done.

CHAPTER **18**

Richard held the car door open for Ms. Katherine Bellows. The car was parked on the circle drive in front of her parents' estate in River Oaks. He walked around the car in his tuxedo to the drivers side and plopped himself in the car.

"And so we're off." Richard started the car and put it in gear.

"Not a minute too soon. I'm glad to be out of that place."

"You're father seemed nice enough, Katherine."

"Call me Kathy. He's a bore, but he is my father. He means well, as does my dysfunctional mother."

"You live here with them?"

"Actually I stay in Europe as much as I can. They insisted I come back this fall for a visit so here I am. How about you? Do you ever go to Europe?"

"Not as often as I would like. My father is pretty well tied to this town, or course. I stick around to help him with things."

"Help him with things. That's mysterious enough. Your mother?"

"She died when I was five."

"Oh, I'm sorry," Kathy said.

"It's alright. You like the symphony?"

"No, I don't. I like rock and roll. But enough

of my parents' friends will be there that I suppose we had better make an appearance or else I'll catch hell about it."

Richard chuckled. "Same here. My father will be there. Along with his lady friend, Clara."

"If I start to snore, wake me up."

Richard laughed. "Only if you do the same for me."

"Deal. Do you have plans afterwards? Or are you busy with your Dad's city stuff?"

"No, I didn't make plans. You said you like rock and roll? There are a couple of bands playing around town tonight. We could catch something after this social gig if you want."

"That sounds great. I'm not in town enough to know what's going on around here. I have a couple of friends here. But one's in New York right now, and the other one said her damn dog just died, of all things."

Richard raised his eyebrows. "Her dog died?"

"Yeah, I don't know what's up with her. I certainly don't want to go over there and help her cry over her friggin' dog."

Richard grinned. This girl is alright. The evening might turn out worthwhile after all. She's not much for tits, but I sure wouldn't mind checking out that pert little backside that swims around in that dress. "We'll skip the doggie funeral then and go cry over some Texas blues."

"Sounds good. That's one thing I do miss in Europe. Although we hear more of that sound over there than you'd think."

Richard continued the chatter with Kathy all the way to Jones Hall. They took their seats beside the

Mayor and Clara. After brief introductions, Richard was left to sit in silence and think.

The books are all up to date. I saw to that this morning. There's no reason to think Dad will not get another term as mayor, but if the unthinkable happens and he's defeated a year from now we'll still walk away from this town plenty rich. Plenty rich indeed, if there is such a thing.

Good, the music is starting. The sooner it starts the sooner it'll be over. Then I can get Kathy out of here. A few drinks and some dancing, and then later to my place. I can almost feel her bare ass in my hands now.

That Bradley Marshall thing is still a pain in the ass. From what that jackass District Attorney said to me today, they just need a little more time to come down harder on that prick. Well, I'll give them a little more time, but not much. Marshall is not going to become a problem for Dad and me. No way, no how.

Brad picked up the phone in his room and dialed the number to his parent's room. His father answered.

"Dad, you and Mom about ready?" Brad asked.

"We're all ready, Son."

"I'll be right there, then."

Brad hung up the phone and got his sport jacket out of the closet. He ran a brush through his hair one last time and then stepped out into the hallway.

His parents had driven in from Livingston earlier that afternoon for Renee's funeral tomorrow. At his suggestion they stayed at the DoubleTree, where he was staying. They were one floor beneath him. Brad decided to not wait on the elevator and took the stairs.

He rapped on the door. His father, Leonard Marshall, opened it.

"Hi Dad."

Leonard held out his hand. "Brad. Good to see you."

Brad took his father's hand in his for a warm handshake. "Good to see you, Dad."

Brad's mother, Joyce, was rising from a chair further back in the room. She approached Brad and gave him a hug. "How are you, Brad?"

"I'm fine, Mom, really."

"Let me get my purse then, and we'll go." Joyce picked up her purse from the bed and they left the room, walking together down the hallway toward the elevator.

"How was your drive down?" Brad asked.

"It was okay, I had to drive." Joyce said. "It's gotten to where driving in the city makes your father too nervous."

"I can drive alright if I want to." Leonard said. "If your mother wants to, then I let her."

Brad pushed the button for the elevator and they were left standing to wait.

"This is a nice hotel," Leonard said. "Nicer than we probably would have picked on our own."

Brad winced. "I can take care of the bill, Dad."

"Oh no. We got it, no problem. You're mother deserves a nice night or two away from home now and again."

"Yeah, it's real nice here. I was staying downtown, but the press got to be a bother. They let me check in here under another name."

"Oh, that explains it. We asked about you at the front desk. They said they hadn't heard of you. We started to call you to see if we were in the right place." Leonard said.

"I told your father right or wrong, I didn't want to drive around looking for a place to put my feet up any longer. I made him check in here anyway." Joyce said.

"Then they said they had the reservation you made for us, so we knew we had the right place." Leonard said.

The elevator arrived and they moved inside, choosing the lobby floor.

"I should have warned you about that. I just didn't think. I'm sorry."

"No bother. We're here now. Why don't you drive? You know more where we are going." Leonard said. "Here are the keys."

"Okay. We'll have to take your car anyway. Mine only has two seats."

They continued to the car. Brad's father got in the front seat with Brad.

"Is seafood okay?" Brad asked.

"You know it's fine with us." Leonard said.

"I thought we would drive down to Kemah. It's built up a lot since you've been down there."

"I'll bet they still cook shrimp down there in Kemah." Leonard said.

"Yeah, Dad. They still do."

"That sounds real fine. Good thing you're driving. It's been so long since we've been to Kemah we'd have to drive around looking for it." Leonard said.

Kemah was down on the bay, and just far enough out of the city to feel like it was just out of the city. Brad wanted a change of venue for the evening.

They had barely gotten onto the freeway when Leonard finally breached the subject of the murder charges.

"Have you talked to your lawyer lately, Son?"

"Not since the arrest. I have a meeting coming up with him soon. I'm sure he's going over the documentation now, preparing preliminary motions, that sort of thing."

"What does he think about all of this?"

Brad thought of Cantrinni's remark that Brad was finally generating some decent legal fees for him and smiled. "Well, like I said, we haven't talked about it much. He knows I didn't do it."

"He did say that much, then?"

"Yeah, he made a comment about it. He said he usually tells his clients that he doesn't want them to tell him whether or not they are guilty, that it makes it easier for him legally. He said that in my case he knew I didn't kill Renee." It feels strange to say her name now. It didn't used to feel strange.

"Well, that's something. He might work harder for you knowing for sure that you're innocent." Leonard said.

"He's a good lawyer, one of the best." Brad said.

"That's probably even more important." Joyce said from the back.

"It sure doesn't hurt." Leonard said. "Do they have any idea who actually killed her, Brad?"

Brad couldn't tell them about the involvement of

Richard Pierce. If they knew that the Mayor's office was somehow involved in painting him guilty, it would worry them to death. "No Dad. There's no idea. The police aren't looking for anyone else since blaming me clears the case for them. It could have been just some random killer."

"Yeah, it could have been random. Do you know why she was at your house?" Leonard asked.

"I have no idea. She had a key. I guess she let herself in, or her killer used her key to get in."

"It's just such a big mystery." Leonard said.

"You don't let it worry you to death, now Brad." Joyce said. "It will turn out okay. We keep you in our prayers."

"I know, Mom. I don't want you and Dad to worry either. Like I said, I have a good attorney. He knows I'm innocent. The police don't have a case. I wasn't even there when she was killed. I'll be fine."

"I know you will, Son. I know you will." Leonard said.

Brad looked at his father. His father looked worried. Nothing I can do about that. He's going to worry, as is Mom, and there's nothing I can do to fix that right now.

CHAPTER **19**

Jack pulled up to the traffic light and stopped. He looked at the ten story building on the corner and judged it to be the one. He made a right turn and pulled into a supermarket parking lot across the street from the building. Pulling a piece of paper from his pocket, he checked the address again. Yes, this is it.

Inside he looked around at what appeared to be a kind of lobby. A large man sat behind a podium in the corner.

"Skybar?" Jack asked.

The man pointed to the elevators with barely a movement. "Top floor."

Of course. Some place calling itself the Skybar would be on the top floor. Jack pushed the button for the elevator and waited. And waited. Finally he was able to get into the elevator and away from the gaze of the big man in the corner.

Top floor. Jack pushed the button and rode the groaning old contraption to the top. He got out to find a doorway with another man behind another podium.

"Ten dollars."

Jack pulled out his wallet. I don't know what they have in here that they're so proud of as to charge ten dollars. It certainly isn't that racket they play for music. It's not country and it's not western.

Jack paid the man and stepped inside the club. The music blared louder once he was inside. She said she would be at the bar in a blue dress. That must be her there. Pretty girl. Too much makeup though, and showing a little too much skin.

Jack approached her and took an empty stool beside her. "Are you Lisa?"

The girl looked at him. "You're Brad's friend? The one that called?"

"Yeah. That's me."

Lisa looked around the bar. "Buy me a drink?"

"Sure." Jack caught the eye of the bartender. "Another drink for the lady, and I'll have a beer." Jack turned to Lisa. "You come here often?"

Lisa eyed Jack. "You trying to pick me up?"

"Would it work if I was?"

"No."

"Then it's just a question."

Lisa played with the straw in her empty ice and then looked around the room again. "Brad's in a lot of trouble."

"I know. I'm trying to help him."

"He's a nice guy. I hate to see him get hurt."

The bartender returned with the drinks and Jack paid for them. He settled back down on the stool. Lisa gulped at her drink and looked around the room once again before returning her attention to the straw in her drink.

"I understand you saw Renee here the night she was killed," Jack said.

"Nope. I didn't see anything."

Jack's eyebrows went up. So this was how it was

164

going to be now. "But Brad told me..."

"Brad must have misunderstood me. I didn't see nothing that night." Lisa was nervous. She looked at her drink, gulped and played with the straw.

"I see. Brad's in a lot of trouble, Lisa. I was hoping you would be willing to help. You said you hated to see him get hurt."

"Look. I'd like to help Brad, but there's nothing I can do. The only reason I agreed to see you was so you could tell him he needs to be careful. He could get hurt real bad and I wouldn't want to see that happen. You know what happened to Renee."

"Yes. I know what happened to Renee."

"Like I said, Brad's a nice guy. He doesn't deserve it. But I really shouldn't even be talking to you." Lisa scanned the room yet again.

This girl is scared silly. I don't blame her. "Well, I really appreciate you seeing me, anyway. Take care of yourself, Lisa."

"You too. Thanks for the drink. I'm sorry I can't help Brad, but there's nothing I can do."

"I understand." Jack climbed off of the stool and headed for the door. As disappointing as it was, the girl was making a lot of sense. Renee had evidently gotten herself killed and Lisa knew it. You can't blame Lisa for not wanting to follow in Renee's footsteps.

Unfortunately, this leaves Brad in a bad spot. Lisa was the only witness he knew that put Renee with Richard Pierce the night of her murder.

Jack looked around the room. I wonder who else might have seen them? If I have to I'll come back here with a picture of both of them and find someone with enough guts to say they saw them together. Whatever it takes, we have to get Brad cleared.

The telephone in Brad's room rang at nine o'clock Saturday morning. Brad suspected it was his father. He was right.

"Bradley, did you want to ride with us?"

"No Dad, you and Mom go ahead. I think I'd rather make this trip alone. You know where it is?"

"Oh yeah. Lawndale, right? You're mother had a cousin buried there just last year. Down 45. We know where it is."

"I'll see you there then."

"Okay, Son."

Brad hung up the phone and stood staring at it. Saying goodbye to Renee was not something he wanted to do with company along.

He took his jacket from the hanger and put it on. He stood in front of the mirror one last time to check his tie and his hair. Everything looked fine. It was time.

He left the room and took the stairs down to the parking garage. Walking to the car he felt as if a thousand eyes were watching him. Looking around he saw no one.

It's probably just a premonition. Too many eyes are going to be on me at the funeral. That's not the way it should be, but there's nothing I can do about it. Nothing is going to keep me away.

Brad felt a gnawing in his stomach. I probably should have had more than toast this morning. The toast was hard enough to eat. Too late now anyway.

Brad got in the car and started it. Music filled the interior. Brad reached out and turned the music off.

Driving the more than half hour to Lawndale Funeral Home and Cemetery, Brad was filled with a mixture of dread and determination. He pulled into the parking lot, got out of his car, and forced his legs to move him down the walk to the entrance.

Just outside the door, he paused. There was no way around the fact that this was going to be awkward. He was accused of killing the deceased. But he didn't kill her, and despite their differences, he had still loved her when the monsters responsible took her life.

By law he was still her husband. Till death do us part. Regardless of how we had planned to part, death had parted us. He had every right to be there. Still, there will be stares. There's no way around that. I can't change it. Let them stare.

Brad went through the doors and looked for the chapel, finding it to his left. He stood just inside the entrance to the chapel. A few faces turned to look at him.

I hadn't thought of this. Where does the accused murderer of the deceased sit? Brad saw Renee's parents on the front row to the right.

He walked down the aisle, feeling the eyes on him until he reached the pew just behind them. After he sat down, Leslie Sheridan reached behind her and Brad took her hand. She squeezed Brad's hand and smiled slightly.

Brad took a deep breath and looked at the coffin. It was closed. Inside was Renee. Inside was the body of a woman he had loved and with whom he had shared six years of his life. She had given him a daughter, a beautiful daughter that God had taken back from them. A lump came up in his throat.

Brad noticed his parents taking seats beside him. Like Leslie, his mother reached out and squeezed his hand. The lump in his throat got worse. His eyes began to feel damp. Damn. He wiped his eyes with the back of his hand.

Brad sat there, trying to put the stares that he felt on his skin out of his mind. This is supposed to be about Renee, not the spectacle of me being here.

Finally, a man approached the podium and began to talk about Renee. Brad heard the words but didn't try to make sense of them. The words he spoke talked about Renee, as a friend would describe her. He knew Renee as a wife.

Memories of Renee came flooding over Brad, good memories of her laughing, her teasing him with fire in her eyes. Brad wiped his eyes again. All of the sudden he could hold it in no longer, and he burst into tears with his hands covering his face. Sobbing into his hands, he struggled to regain control. He felt his mother's hand on his back.

As quickly as the tears came, they subsided. Brad wiped his eyes once more and looked up. From deep inside he felt the familiar burning vestiges of rage against whoever caused the death of Renee. He made fists and held them in check, wanting instead to wave them in the air in front of him. His breathing came deeper and he grew stronger on the anger within him.

The speaker lead a prayer, and then two attendants

moved the flowers from Renee's casket to enable it to be opened. One of the attendants then came to the pew of the Sheridans, motioning to them that they could get up to pass by the casket. Brad and his parents then filed in behind Renee's parents.

Brad stood a little back and away from the casket while the Sheridans took one last look at their daughter. Brad thought of the time, not so long ago, when he had to bury his own daughter, his and Renee's. But God had taken their daughter. This was the work of man.

Finally they moved on and Brad took their place in front of the casket. Brad's parents moved in beside him. Renee looked so peaceful, so beautiful. His knees felt a little wobbly. His mother took hold of his arm. Brad weaved and stiffened his legs.

Goodbye love, he whispered. I will find out who did this to you. They will not get away with it.

He made his legs move to take him away from the casket. Fighting back tears he followed the instructions of an attendant through a door and into a waiting limousine. His mother and father got in beside him.

They sat for a moment before anyone spoke. Finally his father broke the silence. "That was a real nice service."

"The music was nice," his mother said.

"I didn't hear it."

"Of course you didn't, son. But it was nice, just the same."

They sat in silence. Brad's thoughts gave up trying to compete with his emotions and left him in a vacuous heap in the seat.

At some point they started to move for a brief ride.

The car doors opened and they were ushered to chairs placed at the graveside, beside the coffin.

The same man who spoke before opened a small book and read from it. Brad recognized it was probably the Bible. Brad no more heard these words than the words or music that preceded them.

The man closed the book and approached the Sheridans. He shook their hands, and then everyone stood up. Brad looked at the coffin. There was a pain in his chest that seemed like it would take forever to go away.

Brad looked around. For the first time he was curious who might be attending. He saw Dianne Parks, with her husband Larry. There was Lisa. He noticed a few other friends of Renee's. There were Sergeants McNair and Woods. Strange that they would be here. I guess they just wanted to see who else would show up.

There's John Cantrinni near the back. Oh, that's Jack with him. Nice of them to come. They noticed Brad looking at them and Brad nodded. They nodded back.

Brad took one last look at the coffin. He clenched his fists and his jaw drew tight. What a waste. What a waste of a beautiful woman. What a waste of a beautiful life.

CHAPTER **20**

Early Saturday afternoon Jennifer put the finishing touches on an article about a traffic accident on I-10. Young as she was, she had still been at this long enough these types of articles were written without much thought.

Today this was a good thing, because Jennifer was suffering from a headache. She submitted the story and sat in her chair considering her options.

The Marshall case needed to have the daily routine check to make sure nothing new had popped up. The District Attorney's office should be closed today. Still, it doesn't hurt to check. If Caruthers asks, I need to be able to tell him I'm on top of it.

She picked up the phone and dialed Charley Dunhill, her contact with the District Attorney.

"District Attorney's Office, Dunhill speaking."

"Charley, this is Jennifer. I'm surprised you're there today."

"Yeah well. I don't like it much, but we're here."

"Anything new on Marshall?"

"Well, I... I can't say right now, Jennifer."

Jennifer sat up in her chair. "What do you mean you can't say? You mean you have something and you can't tell me?"

"Well it isn't official yet. We don't know for sure. I

should know more in a couple of hours."

Jennifer paused. "If it's something that's just not ready yet, you can trust me to sit on it for a little while, you know that."

"I can't this time, Jennifer. Like I said, I just don't know for sure. I'll know in a couple of hours. I'll try to give you a call then, okay?"

"Charley? Come on, this is Jennifer you're talking to."

"Sorry Jennifer. I just can't. It's not firm enough yet."

"Okay Charley. If I'm not here call me on my cell. You have my number, right?"

"Yeah. I gotta go, Jennifer. I'll be in touch."

He hung up before she could ask him any more questions. That jerk. Jennifer put the phone down and screwed up her face. *Here I am with a splitting headache and Charley Dunhill says he might call in a couple of hours. What's his problem?*

I could sit here for days and Charley might never call. Oh, my head. If it gets any worse I think I'm going to be sick to my stomach.

Jennifer looked around her cubicle. She heard rustling in the space beside her.

"Jerry, you there?"

"Unfortunately"

"Jerry I'm going to head home. I have a headache."

"Take some aspirin."

"I did already. It's not working. Anyway Charley Dunhill said he might call me in a couple of hours. If you notice a call coming in on my phone, pick up for me and try to get a message." Jennifer paused. "And contact me on my cell as soon as possible to make sure I know that the call came in, okay?"

"One answering machine, at your service."

"Thanks Jerry. I think he's just yanking my chain. He'll probably never call, but you never know."

Jennifer transferred Charley's number to a piece of paper to call him back later in case she didn't hear from him. She'd have to make sure this didn't amount to anything.

She picked up her purse and headed for the door. Driving home, she tried to not move her head much and puzzled over what Charley had said. It couldn't be anything. The case seemed to be at a standstill. There were the uneventful motion hearings coming up, but the trial wouldn't be for months.

Still, what had them working on a Saturday? Maybe she shouldn't have left the office. Too late now.

Jennifer opened the front door or her apartment and was greeted with odd sounds. She followed the sounds to the bedroom. Kneeling on the side of the bed was a young woman, entirely naked. Kevin stood beside the bed and was grunting with effort, his pelvis colliding with her backside while she squealed her appreciation.

"Kevin!"

Kevin froze, his face filled with terror.

"You sonofabitch! How dare you?"

Kevin turned to face her, his arms held out, his manhood obscenely flopping before him. "Jennifer. What are you doing here? I can explain."

Jennifer rushed toward him, her hands clasped together into one big fist. She brought her hands down on his chest as hard as she could, sending him reeling backwards. He stumbled over the side of the bed.

Jennifer turned and stormed out of the room. She stood for a moment panting, the images she had just seen playing over again in her mind. She wobbled, and then plopped down on the couch. Drawing a deep breath, she held her hands up to the sides of her throbbing head. "No!"

Kevin came into the room wearing only a pair of jeans. He approached Jennifer with his arms held out and sat down on the couch beside her. "Jennifer, let me explain."

"Get away from me and get out! Get your things and get out of here!"

"I know you're upset, but . . "

"Your damn right I'm upset. I don't need this. I don't need you. I've given you everything and this is the way you repay me?"

"Just calm down."

"I will not calm down! Get your things and get out. I don't want you here. Can't you understand that? Collect your clothes, most of which I bought for you by the way, collect your bimbo, and get the hell out. Now!"

Kevin got up from the couch and went back into the bedroom. Jennifer heard them murmuring as she put her face in her hands and started to cry.

Brad was seated with his parents Sunday morning at the restaurant in the DoubleTree hotel. They would be checking out of the hotel and going back home to

Livingston, Texas later this morning.

"You're looking better this morning, Brad," his mother said.

"I feel better. I needed some rest after yesterday."

"I understand. You just rested then, last night?"

"I tried to work on my novel. It didn't go very well."

"I wouldn't think so, after yesterday. Once everything settles down, then you can get back to writing on it. I don't know that I ever told you, but we're real proud of you for trying to write a book. No one in the family has ever done that before."

"No, you haven't said. Thanks, Mom."

"Some of them writers make a lot of money."

Brad smiled and shook his head a little. "I don't need a lot of money, Mom. The fact is I have plenty."

"I know, but just the same."

"I imagine you'll have considerable less than you do now when that lawyer gets through with you," Leonard said.

"Now Leonard," Joyce said.

"Well it's not fair, Brad having to spend his own money having to defend himself. Then when he's found innocent the District Attorney collects his paycheck and Brad here collects a bill to pay out of his own pocket. It's not right. That's all I meant."

"I apologize for not having dinner with y'all last night, but I didn't feel much like eating," Brad said.

"I see that's changed. You made short work of your breakfast," Leonard said.

Brad chuckled. "I was hungry."

"That was a real nice ceremony. I have a cousin

buried there in that cemetery, you know," Joyce said.

"Dad reminded me yesterday."

"Cousin Maurice. Maurice Taylor. Do you remember him?"

"I don't think so."

"I'm not surprised. You were pretty young the last time you saw him, as I recall."

"I remember going to that family reunion of your family when I was about five. Would I have seen him there?"

"I expect so. That's probably the last time you saw him, when you were about five." Joyce nodded and reached for her coffee.

Brad folded his napkin and put it on his plate.

"I called your brother in Dallas last night, let him know you were alright," Joyce said.

"How's Michael?"

"Michael and Kimberly are getting along fine. So are the kids. He's concerned about you, you know."

"He shouldn't be. There's nothing he can do about it."

"He worries just the same. He said to tell you that you're in his prayers and he's sure everything will work out fine."

"I do appreciate that."

"I think he'd like to come down for a visit, but he said they've got some big project starting up at work," Joyce said. Brad's brother was a manager for a food distribution company.

"I appreciate the thought more than the visit. As much as I like to see my brother, as I said, there's nothing he can do here right now."

176

"I know. Give him a call though. He'd appreciate hearing from you that you're alright."

"I'll do that, Mom."

The waiter approached with the bill, which Brad snagged and signed.

"Thanks for breakfast, Son. Well, I guess I'm all done. You ready to go, Mother?" Leonard asked.

"I'm ready."

Brad walked with his parents to the lobby. He told them he needed to check on something at the front desk, so they said their goodbyes and parted.

Brad went up to the front desk.

"Can I help you?"

"You have a Leonard and Joyce Marshall in room four twelve. I'd like to take care of their bill." Brad put his credit card on the desk.

"Of course." The man pressed keys on a computer, which started a printer making noise. He was presented with a sheet of paper that he glanced at and nodded. A moment later the transaction had been completed.

His father would never let him take care of the bill unless he went behind his father's back and paid for it before he could object.

Leaving the front desk, he passed through the lobby to the gift shop. He found the stacks of newspapers and selected a Houston Chronicle from the top. He tucked the massive Sunday paper under his arm without looking at it and paid for it before going up to his room.

Inside his room, he walked over to the table near the windows and lay the paper down. He glanced at the headlines and froze. No. It couldn't be. There must be some mistake. They're not talking about me.

The headlines read "MARSHALL CONFESSED". He choked on his own saliva, his hand coming up to his mouth. He scanned the lines beneath the headline. *While in jail immediately following his arrest and awaiting bail, Bradley Marshall confessed to the brutal murder of his wife, Renee Marshall, to a cell mate, sources within the District Attorney's office report. According to them he bragged about the killing to at least one other person, and stated that he was sure to get away with it.*

CHAPTER **21**

Brad stumbled onto the hotel room bed, and sat staring ahead. The room vibrated around him. Still choking he fought to breath. This can't be happening. This just cannot be.

Brad struggled to his feet and approached the table where the newspaper still lay like a thick flat snake. He reached out and pulled it toward him so that he could read the article more carefully.

According to the article he had bragged about killing Renee to a Derek Pagell. Who was Derek Pagell? Brad searched his memory of his time behind bars. Suddenly a toothless face swam to the front of his mind. Was that Pagell?

Brad reached out and clawed the air in front of him, trying to erase the toothless grin from his mind. His arms clasped around himself and he shivered. This is bad. This is real bad.

He went to the window and looked out at the parking lot below. Not finding the answers he was looking for, he looked around the room. The space between the window and the door became a place to walk. Brad paced back and forth several times, his arms still clasped around him, interrupted only when he paused to shiver.

Cantrinni! John Cantrinni needs to know about this.

Brad phoned Cantrinni's office.

"Law Office."

"I know this is Sunday, but I need to speak to John Cantrinni."

"This is his answering service. Would you like to leave a message?"

"Yes. This is Brad Marshall. Have him call me at the DoubleTree, room six fourteen as soon as possible."

"Is that all?"

"Yes, thanks."

Brad sat down on the bed. He shook his head and rubbed his hands on his knees.

They had no evidence. I hadn't touched the gun; I hadn't fired the gun; I wasn't even there when she was killed. But with this Pagell there in court testifying that I said I did it, who knows what will happen. I could spend the rest of my life behind bars.

He went to the bathroom and splashed water on his face. Looking at himself in the mirror, he decided he looked scared. He dried his face and looked again. Yep, white face, wide eyes, scared alright. He brushed his hair and took a deep breath. I'll get through this, he told himself. One step at a time.

Hearing the phone ring, he tried to keep from running to answer it.

"Brad, this is John. I guess you read the morning paper."

"How could this happen John? That sonofabitch says that I said I did it!"

"I should have warned you about the possibility of something like this. The first thing is to calm down. This sort of thing happens all the time. Well, not all the time. But it happens."

"Why would he make something like this up?" Holding the phone to his ear, Brad's hand trembled.

"He's trying to get time cut off of his sentence. He's trying to give the District Attorney something he wants and expects something in return. Like I said, it's not all that uncommon."

"And he can do that?"

"Well, yes. Did you talk to this Pagell fellow at all?"

"I talked to him for about two minutes. That is if it's who I think it is. I didn't use my real name, and I told him I was in jail on a drug charge. I guess I was right to be suspicious of him."

"Looks like it. I guess he watches the evening news. He must have recognized you from the television coverage."

"I thought someone might recognize me, but I never thought of something like this."

"Well try not to let it bother you. I know that's hard, but we'll deal with it. Come see me tomorrow at the office. Can you do that?"

"Tomorrow? Sure, I can do that. So this isn't that big of a deal?"

"Well it's not good, don't misunderstand me. But we can handle it. Just come to see me tomorrow, and don't think this is the end of the world. It isn't."

"Okay John. You know best. Thanks."

Brad put down the phone and went back to the desk. The newspaper, while still ominous, looked less frightening now. He noticed the byline, his old friend Jennifer Hart.

He rereads the article, this time trying to view it objectively. Try as he may to put his emotions aside, line after line makes him cringe.

The third time through it he fares a little better. Trying to withhold any personal reaction the tone still seems particularly venomous toward him. Here, she describes Renee's murder as her being 'slaughtered in her own home, allegedly by the man she loved and trusted the most . . .' Strange. She knows Renee and I were being divorced, and that Renee lived on Memorial, not at the house. She's usually at least a little more clinical than that, even when she's harsh. I guess she decided venom sells today, truth be damned

Brad put the paper down. He went to the window and gazed out on a sunny day. Whatever happens with John and this jailhouse snitch the plan to get more info on Richard has to move forward, and quickly. I can't put all of my hopes in a fair trial. Not now.

Brad went over to the nightstand to pick up his cell phone. Why doesn't it ring with the message he's waiting for from his server? He checked the charge. The battery was fine. He put the cell phone back down on the nightstand. Come on Richard. You've got mail.

Walking the three blocks from his office to John Cantrinni's Monday morning, Brad carried with him the same apprehension that had haunted him all morning. While he was anxious to hear something encouraging from his lawyer, he couldn't imagine what that good news would be.

"Have a seat, Brad." John motioned toward the two

chairs facing his desk. Brad chose one and sat down.

"This isn't good news, is it?"

"No it's not, Brad. There isn't much of a good way to spin this. Like I said yesterday on the phone, I probably should have warned you that this type of thing was possible."

"I don't see how he could just lie like that and get away with it"

"Is it that there are liars in jail that you find hard to fathom, or that the District Attorney would use that to his advantage?"

"I guess I was just being naive."

"You said you barely talked to this fellow, this Pagell. Did you talk to anyone else?"

"No. I didn't talk to anyone."

"How did you spend your time in jail?"

"Mostly reading, or sitting in my cell. I wasn't in a very social mood."

"Well that's something. They probably wont be able to call other witnesses saying you and Pagell were chatting often. It would look a lot worse if they were able to do that."

"It's worse enough as it is."

"Another thing you need to prepare for is that the District Attorney may move to have your bail revoked. It's just a standard practice and it shouldn't amount to much."

"Revoke my bail? Shouldn't amount to much? Boy, you're a lot of fun this morning."

"I said he may try. There's little chance he would be successful. The underlying reasons for your bail, your community ties and character haven't changed.

You haven't been caught attempting to flee jurisdiction. Just because a man of very questionable credentials makes some allegations is no reason to revoke bail. The DA will argue it's new evidence. We'll argue it's questionable at best."

"So your pretty sure I'll stay out of jail, for now."

"I don't think you'll ever go back, Brad. I still think we're going to win this case."

"To tell you the truth, I'm a lot more worried about it than when I woke up yesterday morning."

"I understand. Frankly, if I was in your shoes I'd feel the same way."

"Oh good. My feelings of impending doom are understandable. I feel better already. All cheery smiles now."

"Hang on to that sense of humor. We've got a long way to go yet, and it may be rough. The DA seems to want this one really bad. Maybe it's because of the publicity, I don't know. He seems to be a little more intense about this one than I've seen him on past cases."

"Like he's singling me out?" Brad thought of the influence of the mayor's office in this town and against him in this case. "There goes my cheery smiles about the future."

"We'll get through it. Just have a little faith, and be patient. I'm doing what I can to slow things down. I don't think the opposition will be as interested in this case if it isn't on the front page of the newspaper."

"I think the involvement of Richard Pierce in all of this has more of an effect than the publicity," Brad said.

"It might. But don't forget that the District Attorney

is an elected official. He answers first and foremost to the people that put him in office."

"Why doesn't that make me feel better?"

"Hang in there. We'll win this thing, yet."

"Is that it?" Brad asked.

"No, there are a couple of other things." John looked down at his desk and flipped through some papers. "Look at this. I was looking at the autopsy report, specifically the list of personal effects of Renee's." John handed Brad a piece of paper.

Brad looked at the paper. "Is there something I'm suppose to be looking for?"

"Actually, what I want to know is, is there something that should be there that isn't?"

Brad looked at a short list of items on the page; Dress, shoes, phone, wallet... "There's no jewelry."

"I noticed that too. I was wondering, didn't Renee wear jewelry?"

"Yes. She almost always wore earrings. She usually wore a necklace of some sort, and when I saw her a week before she died she was still wearing her wedding ring."

"She still wore her wedding ring?"

"Yes. I asked her about it. She said 'well, we're still married,' and I left it at that. Hell, I still wore mine until just after the funeral."

"I don't know that it means anything. I just wanted to check with you about it."

"Sure. Sure thing." Brad stared at the windows behind John. She most certainly had jewelry on when she went out to the Skybar and was seen with Richard. And she didn't have it on when she was found dead in my house. Her jewelry must be somewhere in between.

"You didn't take her jewelry?" John asked.

"No. I didn't."

"This might help us later. To tell you the truth I'm not sure exactly how right now. Let me work on it and I'll get back to you on it."

"You said there were a couple of things. What's the other?"

John looked down at his desk. "The other thing is a little more sensitive. The autopsy report mentioned semen found on the body."

Brad stiffened. "I guess I should have thought of that possibility, but to tell you the truth, I didn't think of it."

"I'm assuming it's not yours."

"No, it's not."

"I'm expecting the DA to ask for a blood test to include or exclude you as the donor. Assuming you're not the donor they will probably just argue jealousy as an added motive."

"I couldn't be jealous about something I didn't know about."

"Exactly. And besides, it helps us in that it proves that Renee was with someone else besides you near the time of her death. Of course, we'll argue that it was her killer's semen."

"I see." Brad wrinkled his nose and squirmed in his chair. "Is there anything else?"

Brad concluded his meeting with John and left the office. So Renee lost her jewelry and picked up semen and I'm still stuck in a mess. Meeting with John didn't make me feel better about a thing.

CHAPTER **22**

Richard Pierce sat in his office Monday and with a click of the mouse his computer connected to the bank and updated his accounts. He stared at the screen.

What he saw didn't please him. Hung Lee's cleaners over on Harwin still had not transferred the money it should have into his account. That business was the only holdout. The others had made their transfers.

He picked up the phone. "Duane. Meet me downstairs in twenty minutes. And bring Reggie."

He stared at the screen. The blood vessels in his neck grew larger. There's always one in the crowd. Why don't they ever learn?

He closed the accounting package called Quickbooks, and opened his email. Here's a mortgage offer. No thanks. What's this? Something from my father's office? No, just an advertisement for hot pictures masquerading as email from the mayor. That's clever. If I was selling porn I'd probably call myself the governor. Ha! Richard deleted the email.

He got his jacket from the closet and went downstairs to meet Duane and Reggie. Soon they were in the car headed west, with Duane in the front and Reggie in the back.

"I just want to impress upon this little punk the

seriousness of the situation. Don't hurt anybody." Richard squirmed in his seat. "Reggie you stay by the front door. Duane, you stay next to me. Got it?"

"We got it."

The click of a round being chambered in an automatic weapon came from the back seat.

"I said no rough stuff, Reggie. Keep that thing in your pocket."

"I will. I was just being prepared."

"Yeah, he was just being prepared. Like the boy scouts." Duane chuckled.

"Your a real comedian. I don't want this going bad. It's just a courtesy call. Don't start waving guns around." Richard said.

"We understand. We'll be cool." Duane patted his hands on his knees. "Hey, maybe we need some music to calm Reggie down, soothe the savage beast like."

"Maybe not. Just shut the fuck up and think about what you're here for." Richard said.

They rode in silence the rest of the way to A1 cleaners on Harwin. The car skidded into a spot in front of the cleaners and all three men got out. They entered the shop with Richard in the lead.

The shop smelled strongly of dry cleaning chemicals. A beautiful young Asian chick looked up from behind the counter and recognized the men. She raised her hands above her head. "No hurt! No hurt!"

"Shut up. Where's Hung Lee?" Richard strode past the counter and into the racks of clothes with Duane on his tail. Reggie moved his large frame to a position beside the front door. "Hung Lee. I know you're back here. I need to talk to you."

Richard peered between rack after rack of clothes, moving through the shop. "Come on, Hung old friend. We're just going to have a little chat, that's all."

In the back Richard came upon a small man cowering next to a large machine. Richard stopped and smiled. "Where's your office? It's over here, right?" Richard pointed over to his right.

Richard snapped his fingers and Duane moved to grab the small man by the back of his collar. Duane followed Richard with the man in tow to an office in the back corner of the building.

"Shut the door."

Duane kicked the door shut. He still held the man so that his feet barely touched the floor. Richard went behind a small desk and sat down as if the desk were his own. He toyed with the papers on the desk.

"You've been a little slow making your payment. Now you did get the cash delivered from central distribution, didn't you?"

Hung Lee nodded. "Yes. Got money."

"Then why haven't you made the payment to me?" Richard looked up at Hung Lee.

"Is too much money. Can't put on books all at once. Would look bad."

"Now see here. We have an arrangement with dozens of cleaners just like yours. They're making good on the arrangement. Shall I explain it to you again?"

Hung Lee was wide-eyed and silent.

"The cash comes in to you from central distribution with a load of clothes. You put in on the books like it was regular business. How you do that is your business, I don't care as long as it looks good. Then you pay it out to me for my part in the business. " Richard smiled.

"That way everything winds up being tidy. You do like for everything to be tidy don't you." Richard slammed his hand down on the desk. "After all, you're a fucking cleaners!"

"I'm going to give you two days. Two days to get that payment wired into my account. Get the money on the books and wire the money just like regular business. If you can't do that then you'll stop having a regular business to clean any clothes. Is that clear, you little prick?"

Hung Lee nodded. "Is clear. I wire money tomorrow."

Richard smiled. "Nice doing business with you, Mr. Lee. I knew you could be reasonable. Next time make sure to take care of business promptly so I don't have to make these little house calls. They upset my delicate constitution."

Hung Lee looked puzzled. Richard nodded to Duane, and Hung Lee was dropped from his grip. Falling to the ground he struggled to maintain his balance.

Richard got up and left the office with Duane. Moving toward the front of the shop, Richard strutted like a matador after the kill. At the front of the shop, Reggie stood watching the front door and the woman behind the counter. "We're all done here" Without breaking his brisk stride, Richard motioned with his arm toward the door.

"You bad man," said the young Asian woman. Her

arms were folded across her chest; her eyes were narrowed into a glare.

"What's that?" Richard stopped and looked at her.

"You bad man."

Richard chuckled. "Not so, honey. I good man. I make sweet young things like you feel real good." He walked up to the woman and grabbed her by the back of the neck with one hand, his other hand grabbing her breast. "You want me to make you feel good?" He pushed her away from him. "You need to grow some tits before I waste my time on you."

The woman staggered back, her eye's wide and her hand at her mouth.

Richard smiled and nodded. "Save up your money and buy yourself some tits, and I'll show you what a good man I am. Got that darlin'?"

Richard waved his hand above his head in a motion for the others to follow him out the door. The woman broke into a run toward the back of the shop. The three men pushed through the door to the outside. They were laughing as they got into the car.

Richard started the car and turned to address the other two. "Good work, boys. I think it's time for a little lunch. And a little celebration. What say we head over to a tittie bar that serves lunch?"

Brad left his lawyer's office. He was exiting the building when his cell phone started playing the tune that alerted Brad to a text message having come in. Brad almost dropped the phone trying to get to the display to see the origination of the message.

Yes! Mr. Richard Pierce now has an infected computer. His files, if everything is going correctly, are being copied to my server. Brad put his phone away and bolted toward his office.

Brad waited at an intersection for the light to change. Why wouldn't it change? There are people with things to do here. He looked over at a construction crew working on the street nearby, and noticed "Bartoulli Brothers, Inc." painted on the side of their dump truck.

Finally, the light changed. Brad crossed the street and got caught up in a pedestrian traffic snarl of sorts with a baby carriage. Of all days.

He managed to find a clear avenue of sidewalk and stretched his legs out short of running. Another traffic light. Another wait. Brad's hands turned into fists. He looked around at the buildings and people surrounding him and saw neither. When the light changed he almost leaped off of the curb to cross the street.

What if something went wrong? The program is not very robust. It will restart if the connection is broken or the computer is turned off, but that's about the only contingencies that it's programmed to handle.

Worse yet is that the program hasn't even been tested. One typographical error and the program will not run at all. I should have figured out a way to test the thing before I sent it.

It has to be running though. It sent my email to my cell phone. So that's something. That's really the biggest test. If it runs at all it will probably run correctly.

I've got to calm down. The program has to run. It

is running. Once I get to my office I can make sure.

Brad flew into the lobby of his building. He tried hard not to run. He didn't want someone asking him why he was in such a hurry.

He noticed the security guard. Did it show on his face that he was committing a crime; that he was breaking into another man's computer and stealing his secret files? Brad looked down at the floor and slowed his pace. The security guard didn't seem to notice him.

The elevators were at their slowest, or at least so it seemed. Within the hour the doors opened up and carried him up to his office.

"Hi Rose."

"Mr. Marshall. A couple of messages for you." Mr. Abernathy held out some telephone message slips.

"I'll look at them later." Brad raced past her desk and into his office. He closed the door and sat down to his computer. With a few keystrokes a list of connections to the server spilled down the screen. Scanning them he came across one from the same Internet domain where he had sent Richard's email.

Good. The connection is made. His hands trembling, he listed the folder on his server where Richard's files were to be copied. He almost leaped out of his chair. Files were coming in.

He looked at the list of files. They were system files; the programs that make a computer run and were the same on most computers. Nothing special about them. Next would come the program files, and finally the data files. The most important files were the data files, the last that would be transferred.

If Brad had known exactly what he was looking for

he would have had the data come first. But a lack of knowledge about Richard's setup and being in a hurry he had gone for the quickest and easiest approach. That's alright. It was working.

Brad listed the folder again. More files and folders had been added from Richard's computer. This would take several hours. I can check the speed, but I have no way of knowing exactly how much data Richard has on his computer.

Brad did some quick estimations on the transfer time by guessing at the size of the information. It would probably take several hours, but not days. By sometime tomorrow it should be finished, if not sooner.

Brad sat staring at the screen. Nothing to do but wait. He got up and went to the windows. Looking out at the streets below he thought of the murder charge against him. He wondered if the information he got from Richard's computer would be of any help.

What could be on his computer that would help me? Suppose I did find out something? How would I be able to use it? I still haven't figured that part out yet.

There are no guarantees; I knew that when I started this. I have to try, anyway. I have to try everything I can. No way am I going to spend the rest of my life in prison while Renee's killers walk around free.

Brad's jaw drew tight. Soon. I've got to be patient. He looked back at the computer screen. I'll know soon. Maybe by tomorrow

Taking a stool, Jack looked around the Red Lion Bar & Grill Monday afternoon. It wasn't very crowded. Almost empty. That was good. He was here to meet Pete Tanner. Tanner had called him and told him he had more information about Richard Pierce and that business.

"I'll have a beer, Rusty."

The bartender pulled a draft beer into a cold mug and sat it in front of Jack. He then made some marks on a pad of receipts and tearing the top sheet off, put it on the counter behind the bar. This was Jack's tab. Rusty automatically ran a tab on Jack unless Jack instructed him to do otherwise.

A tall slender man walked up to the bar next to Jack. "I guess I'll have another beer, Rusty." The man held out an empty mug, which Rusty took to replace with one frosted and full. "Hello, Jack."

"Leo. How's things?"

"Fine. Just fine. Always is when the boss turns me loose for a few to get out of the house."

Jack nodded and took a sip of his beer. You might appreciate her while she's here with you, he thought.

"Been fishing lately?" Leo asked.

"I went last Thursday."

"Galveston Bay?"

"You got it."

"Catch the sun come up?"

Jack sipped his beer. "Of course."

"Thursday was clear."

"Absolutely."

"Sounds perfect."

"Close to it."

"Catch anything?"

"Four trout."

"That's sweet. Doesn't get much better."

"Not much better." Jack noticed Pete coming in the front door. Pete stood still at the sight of Jack talking with someone else. "You're going to have to excuse me for a few, Leo. I have some business to discuss with this gentleman."

"Sure thing, Jack. Nice talking to ya."

"I'll just be a minute." Jack took his beer and got off his stool. He moved toward a booth and motioned to Pete, still standing by the front door, to follow him.

"Jack, how are you doing?"

"Fine Pete. Like you care. What've you got?"

"I'm hurt, Jack. I thought we were friends."

Jack sat back in the booth. "Alright Pete. I'm fine. How are you?"

Pete grinned. "I'm alright. I've been asking around. Trying to find out some more about our friend, Mr. Pierce, the junior."

Jack turned his palms up on the table. "So what did you find out?"

"It's mostly like I told you. The people with contracts for the construction downtown are paying Pierce. A lot."

"You got names?"

"A couple. Watson Construction is one. They have a contract worth fifty mil a year. Word is they're kicking just into seven figures back to Pierce."

"And they're paying the son? How are they doing it? Through some sort of consulting arrangement?"

Pete shook his head. "Nothing that fancy. He just gets paid, under the table."

"Cash?"

Pete nodded. "He don't take no American Express. He takes payments once a month or so. About a hundred large."

Jack let go with a low whistle. "A hundred grand in cash a month just from Watson? Who else?"

Pete looked around the bar before answering. "The Bartoulli Brothers are paying him. Not as much. Their contract is only worth ten mil. There's two or three others in Bartoulli's range."

"We're getting into some serious money."

"And he expects the unions to ante up as well. How much they pay I don't know," Pete shrugged.

"I knew that the Mayor was a friend of the unions."

"They're not friends, Jack. The unions see him as a business partner. He gets a cut of their business, all paid through his son."

"And he treats them right." Jack shook his head.

Pete nodded. "In exchange, he makes sure the contracts go to contractors that use union workers. That's what he tells them anyway. My guess is he'd sell out to anyone that was willing to pay."

"Well, we knew it was rigged. We just didn't know

the details. I appreciate you finding this out for me, Pete."

Pete scanned the bar again. "I'm sticking my neck out, asking questions you know. These people leave dead bodies lying around."

"What do you know from dead bodies?"

"A couple three weeks ago a security guard was in the wrong place at the wrong time. One of Pierce's guys whacked him. Some chick found out about it and they did her too, that same night. I'm telling you, I don't like nosing around in these people's business."

"The woman they clipped, do you know who she was?"

"No. I didn't ask. Didn't want to know. Hell, I don't wanna know what I do."

"Pete, I can't thank you enough." Jack took a one hundred dollar bill folded out of his shirt pocket and slid it over the table top to Pete.

"Thanks. I rather not help you any more with this one," Pete said.

"I understand. You've already been a big help."

Pete rose and took a look around the bar before heading for the door. Jack took his beer and returned to his stool at the bar. He shook his head. I was afraid of this. The bigger the business that Mr. Richard Pierce is hiding, the more he'll be willing to do to hide it. And as Pete said, these people leave dead bodies in their wake. Brad needs to be very careful.

"Rusty, I need another beer." Jack pushed his empty mug toward the bartender to get it refilled. Leo reappeared at Jack's elbow.

"Wasn't that Pete Tanner you were talking to?" Leo asked.

"Who? Oh yeah. That was Pete. I owed him for a Texans game I should have stayed out of."

"Same old Pete. He's collected plenty of my money over the years."

"Yeah. Same old Pete." Jack sipped his beer and thought about the news that Pete had delivered. Pete was right to be nervous.

Was that murdered woman he mentioned Renee? Probably. It made sense. The timing lined up right, as well as the circumstances. Jack resisted the temptation to look over his shoulder.

Brad sat at his computer Monday afternoon immersed in the Science Fiction world of his novel. Lunch had been difficult, his mind returning every other minute to the ongoing transfer of information from the computer of Richard Pierce to his own. Now, after lunch, he had found a way to keep his thoughts occupied.

That is, he was lost in thought until his buzzer interrupted him and he heard the voice of Rose Abernathy.

"Mr. Marshall, there's a Ms. Hart here to see you."

Jennifer? What's she doing here? "Rose, did she have an appointment?"

"No. I would have reminded you, Mr. Marshall."

"That's alright. Send her in."

Brad saved the work he was doing on his novel and sat back in his chair. He resisted the temptation to make a quick check on the progress of the file transfers.

The door opened and Jennifer Hart eased into the room. "Brad. I hope I'm not interrupting anything important?"

"No. But I am a little surprised to see you." Brad stood up.

"I'm surprised you agreed to see me. You promised me an interview a while back and I never collected. I took a chance that you might see me, but I wasn't really hopeful."

"Ah yes. Against the advice of council, I'm always available for a meeting with you."

Jennifer raised her eyebrows. "Well. That's encouraging. I guess I should be flattered."

"On the other hand, as far as an interview, there's not very much I can say right now. Again, at the advice of council."

Jennifer pouted slightly. "There goes my exclusive."

Brad motioned to the chairs in front of his desk. "Please, sit down."

Jennifer plopped herself into a chair and dropped her bag next to the chair. "Thank you, I will."

"It seems that you're finding plenty to write about me, even with the strain of a lack of interview material."

Jennifer looked up at Brad. "I hope you don't blame me for doing my job."

"You know I don't."

"You're right. I know you don't. You've been very good about it. Your reaction to some of the things printed about you, I mean. Your treatment toward me has been much better than I have a right to expect."

Brad folded his hands on his desk. "I try to keep in mind that you're just trying to sell papers. Still, your tone has seemed more, caustic, lately?"

"You mean yesterday's piece? Yeah, well. I was having a bad day Saturday when I wrote that."

Brad leaned back in his chair. "By all means, feel free to rip me a new one for the benefit of a million readers the next time you break a nail."

"It was a lot more than that."

"Yeah? What was it then?"

Jennifer frowned. She looked down and pulled at the fabric of her slacks. "I'd rather not say." She seemed on the verge of tears.

"I'm sorry. I didn't mean to upset you. The article was a shock, but there's no way you could have written it to where I would have enjoyed getting that kind of news."

Jennifer looked up. Where Brad expected to see moist eyes he saw fierce determination. "I'm glad you're so understanding. I couldn't help but be shocked, personally, at your confession."

"I didn't confess to a murder I didn't commit and you know it. Didn't you find the whole thing lacking in credibility?"

"Perhaps. Mind if I ask you a question?"

Brad chuckled. "Probably. Go ahead."

"Outside the jail, when you had just been released, your attorney said that behind your arrest were political implications. What did he mean by that?"

"I can't answer that."

Jennifer smiled and cocked her head to one side.

"Sure you can, Brad. Just open your mouth and form the words."

"I really can't. I'd like to, but I can't. All in good time."

"Off the record then."

Brad paused for a moment. "You know I didn't kill Renee, don't you?"

"Oh course, Brad." Jennifer smiled.

"The person or people who did kill her will not hesitate to kill again if they think they are being exposed. I can't risk that right now. Not until I know more."

"I told you I wouldn't put it in the paper until you told me it was alright."

"I couldn't risk you telling anyone, not even your boyfriend."

"I don't have a boyfriend."

Brad's eyebrows went up. "But I thought you told me . . ."

"I had a boyfriend. He's done with."

Brad leaned back in his chair. So that was the reason for the bad day Saturday. He tried not to smile. "I see."

Jennifer's nostrils flared. "No, I saw. That was the problem. I saw plenty. I saw what a two timing, low life, piece of shit scumbag I had gotten involved with." Jennifer's face grew red.

"I'm sorry."

"Why? It's not your problem. And it's not my problem any more. He's gone and that's that."

"I just meant . . ."

"It sounds like you have a pretty good idea who

killed Renee. Are you going to tell me or what?"

"I'm afraid it's or what. I can't tell you right now. Maybe soon."

"Alright then. Keep your secret. You men seem to like to keep secrets. At least that's my experience."

"What are you talking about?" Brad squinted.

"I thought you were different, but you're all the same. Thanks for your time." Jennifer picked up her bag and stood up. She held out her hand.

Stunned at her abruptness, Brad jumped up to shake her hand. "Come back anytime."

Jennifer turned and stormed out of the room. Brad slid back down into his chair and sat staring at the door. What was that all about? I guess things went badly with the boyfriend. I guess I should feel bad for her. I guess I don't. Brad smiled.

CHAPTER **24**

Jennifer waited for the elevator doors to close and then stamped her feet, her fists clenched tight and waving around her. Why did she loose control like that?

I screwed that up. With some coaxing I might have gotten him to open up some more. He obviously likes me. I could have used that. Instead I berated him for who knows why. Argghh. She stamped her feet again.

The elevator doors opened and Jennifer strode out of the building onto the street. Picking her way through the pedestrians on her way back to the Chronicle building, she tried to come up with ways to put a positive spin on her meeting with Brad.

He did deny that he made any sort of confession in jail. That was not surprising since he denied committing the murder. But still it was a point to mark down in her notes.

He hinted that he knew who killed his wife. Did he say that he knew? No. But he suggested it. He said that he might be able to tell me soon.

Jennifer stood waiting on a light. She adjusted the bag on her shoulder and considered Brad's comments about the murder. He was very hesitant about who killed Renee Marshall.

How am I going to write this? I really don't know

what to do. I want to be able to print that he knows who killed his wife. But if I do that, it's sure to spook him. He might never tell me what he knows. He might not ever agree to see me again.

Jennifer grinned. I still can't believe I got in to see him today. Jennifer lost her smile. Then I blew it. Damn. I really screwed that up.

Jennifer entered the Chronicle building and rode the elevator up. She was almost to her cubicle when she ran into Bill Caruthers.

"Jennifer. Nice of you to drop by."

"I just came from Bradley Marshall's office."

"Don't tell me our number one killer agreed to talk to you?"

"He did."

"Woo Hoo! What is it with this guy? Is he a masochist or something? You tear the stuffing out of him over the weekend and he just comes back for more!" Caruthers smiled and shook his head. "So what'd you get?"

"Not much that I can use, unfortunately. He denied making any sort of confession of course. He thinks he knows who killed his wife, but he's not quite ready to tell me."

Caruthers' scowled. "What do you mean 'Who killed his wife'? He killed his wife. He confessed."

Jennifer's shoulders dropped and she shook her head. "He didn't kill his wife and he didn't confess to something he didn't do. That confession is a jailhouse snitch looking for a better deal on his sentence. You and I both know that."

"Well, we can't print that he didn't confess if we just

ran a story that he did."

"Actually we can say that he denies it, which he does. It may not be front page stuff, but it's something. I've got a feeling that when he does tell me who he thinks did it, it's going to be somebody big, front page stuff."

"Why don't you just write that he knows who killed her?"

"I'm afraid that would spook him. I'm afraid he'd quit seeing me, and I'd never find out who it is he thinks did it."

"So you're holding out for that? Playing Marshall along to try to get the rest of his story?"

"Exactly. He's still agreeing to see me, Bill, even after all of the things I've written. I don't want to loose the access I've got and the story along with it. Not this late in the game."

Caruthers nodded. "I don't like it, but I have to let my reporters report. When I was in your shoes I hated it when some bald old has-been tried to tell me how to do my job. Go to it then, and if you wind up with both hands full of air on this one I'm going to be all over your cute little ass." Caruthers stomped off.

Jennifer dropped her bag on her desk and plopped down in her chair. That was strange. That wasn't exactly encouragement from Caruthers but it was the closest thing to it I've ever heard come out of that old man's mouth. Getting back into Brad's office must have really impressed him. I got lucky there.

Brad has a soft spot for me. Good. I can use that to my advantage. It's about time that I'm the one doing the using instead of the other way around.

That reminds me, I need to get home early. Kevin's getting the last of his things out of the apartment. I want to make sure none of my things disappear with that no good butthole.

Jennifer logged on to her computer and sat for a moment considering how to begin the article and what it would say. The point of the article would be that Bradley Marshall denied making a confession while in jail or at any other time while in custody of the police. She filled in with more background material and had the article written within an hour.

This isn't front page news, but it should make the front section. Brad could see it and it might improve her relationship with him. It wouldn't hurt for him to see an article on his side for once. Perhaps he would come to trust her enough to tell her whom he suspected of killing his wife.

She picked up the phone and dialed the number to her apartment. "Kevin? Good, you're there. Don't leave until I get there. I don't want you hauling any of my stuff out of there." She hung up the phone.

She logged off of her computer and gathered her things. She was about to grab her bag and go when Jerry appeared at her cubicle with a coffee cup in his hand.

"Jennifer. I couldn't help but overhear. Boyfriend problems?"

"Not anymore. He managed to get himself kicked to the curb. After today he's out of my life forever."

"Ouch. I can't say I'm disappointed, though. This might not be the best time, but I don't want to wait too late. How about dinner?"

"Gee, ahh. I'm really flattered and all that, Jerry. But I'm afraid not, and I'm kind of in a hurry."

"Sure. Maybe another time. Think about it and let me know?"

"I'll do that. Thanks." Jennifer picked up her bag and rushed past Jerry and down the hallway.

This is just too strange. First Brad agrees to see me. Then Caruthers is almost nice. Well, nice for him. Now Jerry asks me out. I thought I put on my mega—bitch face this morning just to deal with men and all they can do is be nice. It's starting to make me sick.

Hold on until I get there, Kevin. I may just take back some of those clothes I've bought you. I need to give somebody hell, and if anyone has got it coming it's you.

Brad entered the Red Lion Bar & Grill and looked around. It was almost empty this Monday evening. Brad noticed his friend Jack sitting alone at the bar.

"Jack, I almost didn't see you for the crowd."

"Don't you hate having to fight your way up to the bar? Been this way ever since the newspaper gave their chicken wings two stars." Jack shook his head.

"Maybe we ought to think about relocating our offices." Brad accepted a club soda with lime from Rusty.

"And give up those two star chicken wings? Never. We just need to figure out a way to get this joint mentioned on one of those television news roach reports. That would clear out the riff-raff and we'd still get our chicken wings."

Brad chuckled. "I have some good news. The computer files of Mr. Richard Pierce are being uploaded to my server."

"Right now?"

"As we speak."

Jack took a sip of his beer. "How long will it take?"

"It should be through by tomorrow."

Jack nodded. "What are you going to do with his files?"

Brad scowled. "It depends on what I find out. But I really haven't decided yet. They should tell me something, maybe give me a clue why Renee was killed."

"I may have found something out there."

Brad's eyebrows went up. "You know why she was killed?"

"I'm not sure. I just heard some pieces of information that when I put it with other pieces of information, sounds like it might have to do with her murder. Maybe I better start at the beginning."

"Please do." Brad took a drink from his club soda.

"Pierce is getting kickbacks from most, if not all, of the construction companies downtown. People like Watson Construction and the Bartoulli Brothers. He gets paid in cash."

"I'm guessing a lot of cash."

"You guess right. A security guard evidently stumbled on to them and was killed by Pierce's men. A woman found out about that murder and they killed her too."

"And you think the woman was Renee?"

"I'm pretty sure it was. I asked McNair, one of the

investigators on Renee's case a while back, if there were any other similar murders to Renee's. He said a security guard was killed in the same manner on the same night."

Brad stared at his drink. "How did you find this out, this news about Pierce?"

"Let's just say it's reliable."

"Alright. So now we know why she was killed, and that Pierce or his men did it as we suspected. Now what?"

"I don't know now what."

"I don't know either." Brad paused. "Maybe his files will tell us more."

"And maybe we'll think of something. I just got this news today. I've barely had time to digest it myself."

Brad nodded. "We have some time. I met with my lawyer today."

"That slick Italian? What did he have to say?"

"He mostly tried to calm me down from that crap going on with that bastard saying I confessed."

"I read about that. Of course I knew it wasn't true. I figured it for somebody looking for a deal to cut his sentence."

"That's what it seems to be. Still, it doesn't look good for me."

"Isn't that pretty common though? Didn't John say that it could be dealt with?"

"Oh yeah. He even said he wished he had warned me that something like this could happen. John did say something I've been wondering about though."

"What's that?"

"Renee was found without any jewelry."

"I take it she usually wore jewelry?"

"Sure. She usually wore earrings, and sometimes a necklace. She still wore her wedding ring. We talked about it when we met for lunch just the week before she was killed."

Jack frowned and took a sip of his beer. "I don't know how to say this delicately. I would think that married women usually take off their wedding rings before they hop in bed with somebody other than their husband."

Brad nodded slowly. "You seem to have hit on it. Renee was also found with semen on her. Is there a chance Richard Pierce still has my wife's jewelry, or that he sold it?"

"Not likely he sold it. From what I hear he's not hurting for money."

"That would mean he still has the wedding ring I gave my wife laying around like some sort of trophy." Brad shook his head. "God, that pisses me off."

"It's alright to be pissed off, but don't let it cloud your thinking. These people eliminate their obstacles with bullets."

"Do you think Pierce knows that Renee called me that night?"

Jack frowned. "Likely. Which brings up the question of why he's letting you walk around upright."

"I can't do much to hurt him right now. The police won't listen to me."

Jack nodded. "He probably thinks that as long as you're labeled a murderer you can't hurt him. He had something to do with your arrest. We can guess that from my conversation with McNair." Jack turned to face Brad. "But if he gets wind that you're poking around in his business, or getting his computer files, your life insurance better be paid up."

"At some point he's going to have to know."

"Let's put that off until we know all we can. Until we have all of the evidence we can gather." Jack took a sip from his beer.

"Agreed. You borrowed my key a while back. Did you go by my house?"

"I went by there last Friday. I didn't find out anything. It looks like it's been cleaned up." Jack took a key out of his pocket and slid it over to Brad.

Brad nodded. "That would be Tina, my housekeeper. She comes on Mondays and Thursdays. I had forgotten about her."

"You thinking about moving back home?"

"Not yet. The memory of that night is still a little raw. So what's next?"

"How about some chicken wings? They come very rated by the local rag."

Brad grinned. "Very rated?"

"That's all I can say about them. That and they're chicken."

"Why not. I like to live a little dangerously, in case you haven't noticed."

"Of course you do, as we all do. And I can tell by the look in your eye that life has been too bland to suit you lately." Jack slapped his hands down on the bar. "Rusty, we need some of those spectacular and unappreciated chicken wings to liven up our lives."

CHAPTER **25**

Richard strode into Dave & Buster's Monday night, nodding to the man at the front checking ID's. He climbed the steps to the bar and began to scout the women around him for what might be available.

He had thought about going to one of the hotter spots on Richmond Avenue but had come here instead. The idea of a girl barely out of her teens wasn't really appealing tonight. He was looking for a woman who knew what she was doing.

Not having found what he was looking for, he went up to the bar. "Bacardi and Coke," he told the bartender. A couple minutes later, drink in hand, he circled the large rectangular bar.

He saw a familiar face sitting alone at the bar. Would she do? Why not? She had nice tits, knew how to fuck like a demon, and squealed like an animal. "Lisa? How are you doing?"

Lisa looked up at him with surprise. "Richard. I didn't expect to see you here."

"I'm the one that's surprised. This doesn't seem like your kind of place."

"I like it quiet every once in a while. I come here sometimes to think."

Richard nodded. "Myself. That and I like to play the arcade games in the back. Don't tell anybody but

I'm a big kid." He chuckled. "Can I buy you a drink?"

"Sure."

Richard got the bartender's attention. "Another round over here, please."

"I want you to know that I've been doing like you said. I haven't said anything to anybody."

He looked at her with a blank face. "That's good. About what?"

"You know." Lisa lowered her voice. "About Renee."

Richard looked around. "Lisa. This isn't the place."

"I know. But I wanted to tell you that I haven't been talking to anybody about it. Not even that guy that called me to talk about her."

Richard stared at Lisa, his eyes wide. "What guy? Somebody came to you asking questions?"

"Yeah. But I didn't tell him nothing."

The drinks came and Richard paid for them. He waited for the bartender to leave. "Who was it, Lisa? What was the man's name?"

"I'm not sure I remember. Jack something, I think." Lisa took her drink and toyed with the straw. "Oh I remember. Jack Wilkerson. I remember because I went to school with a Julie Wilkerson. I wonder if they are related?"

"Are you sure his name was Jack Wilkerson?"

"Pretty sure. But I didn't tell him nothing, like I said."

"I have to go to the can. I'll be right back. Don't go anywhere." Richard got up from his stool and headed off in the direction of the men's room. Once out of hearing range he pulled out his cell phone. "Luis Gonzales, please. Luis?"

"Speaking."

"This is Richard Pierce. I need you to find someone for me."

"Living or dead?"

"Very alive. He's been sticking his nose in my affairs."

"I got it. Living and stupid. You got a name?"

"Jack Wilkerson. That and the fact that he's made me a hobby is all I know. Find out what you can about him and get back to me quick."

"You got it."

Richard put his phone away. Luis was the best private dick in town. Richard used him not only in matters of researching people he might do business with, but also to handle other matters of security. It was Luis, for instance, that made sure Richard's apartment and office was kept bug free and no one was tapping his phones. Whoever this Jack Wilkerson was, Luis would find out.

Richard stepped back up to the bar. "Honey, did I tell you yet how hot you look tonight?"

Lisa giggled. "No sir, I don't believe you did."

Richard sat down on the stool and smiled. "I came here determined to talk to the prettiest woman in the bar. Looks like I succeeded." And if you buy that I've found the dumbest cunt in the bar.

Lisa blushed. "I'm not the prettiest."

"No argument allowed. If I say you're the prettiest then it's true. Bartender, we need another round over here."

"Are you trying to take advantage of me?" Lisa's eyes sparkled.

"Will it work?"

"Maybe." Lisa chewed on her straw.

"Then after we finish our drinks..." Richard leaned over to whisper in Lisa's ear. ". . . maybe you and me can go find some place to do nasty things to each other."

Lisa squirmed on her stool. "Oh Richard! Do we have to wait for the drinks?"

Richard looked over at her tits straining to get out of her low cut dress. "No darlin', we don't."

Brad gave the waiter his standard order of bacon and eggs Tuesday morning. He looked over at the Houston Chronicle lying on the table in front of him. It took an extra effort to raise up his hands and take the newspaper off the table and open it.

There was nothing on the front page about him. Brad smiled. Sometimes the simplest things make for a good day. He started flipping through the pages looking for some reference to himself or the murder case against him. Nothing in the first section.

He picked up the 'City and State' section and froze. "Marshall Denies Confession" was the headline. That's not too bad. It's accurate enough.

He glanced through the article and saw that it said nothing new other than his denial of the confession he was suppose to have made while in jail. The article was even soft in it's treatment of him, compared to previous articles. He looked at the byline. It was written by Jennifer. In spite of her blow-up in my office, she must be softening toward me.

Brad put the paper down and smiled. Yes, sometimes the little things make for a good day. John would be mad at him for talking to the press. John can get over it. I didn't say anything other than I didn't confess and I don't mind if the whole world knows I didn't confess to a murder I didn't commit.

Brad took out his cell phone and looked at it. He should be getting a message any time now that the file transfers had finished. He worried about something interrupting the transfers. No point in worrying about that. They were still coming in a few minutes ago when I logged in from my laptop. Data files were coming in, the last of the transfers. The signal they are finished would come any time now. Brad put his cell phone away.

His breakfast came and he tried to be leisurely about eating. He knew that rushing breakfast would not make the file transfers finish any faster, but still it was hard to slow down. He finished his breakfast and ordered more coffee.

Brad looked around the restaurant. He was comfortable here. At some point he needed to decide what to do with his house, either sell it or move back in. At the thought of moving back in, the muscles in Brad's neck grew tight. I might just go for a high-rise condo instead of the house. In any case, that decision can come later, maybe next week. I can afford the hotel. There's no hurry.

He walked down the corridor leading to the parking garage. With a spring in his step he was looking forward to his morning workout at the health club.

Getting into his car, his cell phone rang. Looking at it he saw that it was the message the file transfers had completed. Forget the workout, I'll go straight to the office and see what we have!

Traffic was a mess. Usually Brad avoided the worst of the rush hour traffic with his workout. By skipping it, he was headed for the office while everyone else was doing the same. It took him forty-five minutes to get downtown and park.

Brad stepped into his office with a smile. "Good morning, Rose."

"Good morning, Mr. Marshall. You look chipper today."

"Things could be worse, Rose. How are you today?"

"Oh I'm fine. Never better."

"I'll be busy this morning. Hold my calls."

"Sure thing."

Brad went into his office and closed the door. He was almost trembling as he logged onto his computer and accessed the folder on the server where Pierce's files were housed.

Where to start? Brad looked in the Documents folder and noticed several dozen documents. He pulled one up on the screen and looked at it. It seemed to be an agreement for services, nothing exciting there. It would take hours to look through all of those documents. I'll come back to that later.

He looked at the folder where copies of Richard's Internet surfing were kept, the cache files. He looked at a few of those. So, Pierce likes to look at porn. The newspapers might like to get a hold of that, but it doesn't help me.

He noticed a folder for an accounting program. Now this could be something. He brought up the same accounting program on his computer and tried to access the file. It was password protected, it needed a user name and password to access the file.

Brad guessed that the user name was the same as on Pierce's email address, 'rpierce'. He accessed a folder on his server that he kept for analyzing computer cracker tools, or tools the bad guys he used to protect against might use. He started the program running to crack the password on the accounting file given the user name 'rpierce'.

Brad got up from the desk and looked out the window. This could take a few seconds or a few minutes. There was no guarantee this would work. He might have to try another user name. Brad suddenly wished he had not skipped the gym. Breaking into someone's accounting records, the shower was what he was missing.

Brad turned around and looked at the screen. It was finished already. He sat back down and looked at the password printed on the screen: pussymaster. Brad shook his head and typed in the password. Pierce's accounts came up on the screen.

Brad stared at the information, which at first made little sense to him. Little by little, he began to understand the finances of Richard Pierce. Moneys came into cash accounts from names that Jack had mentioned: Watson Construction, Bartoulli Brothers, and others. From there the money was given to All—Right Cleaners. All—Right then seem to distribute the money to a couple of dozen other cleaners and three strip joints. The cleaners and strip joints then made deposits to Pierce's bank account in the amounts that they received from All—Right.

Brad sat back in his chair. He looked at his watch. Two hours had passed since he started looking at Pierce's books and his eyes were tired. He shook his head at what he had in front of him: the records of hundreds of thousands of dollars coming in to Pierce and being laundered through, of all things, laundries.

It was spectacular in its disguise. Since the imposition of environmental restrictions a few years back, very few laundries or dry cleaners processed their own dry cleaning. They all sent it to a central location. The central location held all of the necessary permits and equipment, processed the dry cleaning and returned the clothes to the individual shops each day. Each day, vans carried clothes and, it seems, sometimes cash back and forth between the shops. The strip joints must have just been thrown in as an easy way to launder large amounts, as the cash that went through them was more than the laundries.

Brad looked again at the screen and shuddered. The information in front of him made the act of looking at it, and everything around him, seem surreal. He sat with his eyes loosing focus; his head shaking back and forth, his mouth slightly open. How wonderful it would be if the delete key would make all of this go away as easily as it cleared the screen. No wonder people were dying around Mr. Richard Pierce. He would surely do most anything, and kill most anyone, to protect such a lucrative enterprise.

He got up and paced around his desk. Jack had told him Pierce was involved in dealings like this, but seeing it in black and white shook him. Brad wasn't just being persecuted by City Hall. It was City Hall armed with a mountain of ill-gotten cash.

Brad sat down and laid his head down on his desk. The weight of the knowledge he learned made him sleepy. Soon he drifted off. He dreamed of Renee. She was going into a dry cleaners. He could see through the windows that there was a man inside with a gun. He tried to scream at Renee to stop. No sound would come out.

He woke up in a cold sweat. He looked at the screen, wondering how he might use the information in front of him. First things first. He hit the print key.

CHAPTER **26**

Jack put down the western he was reading and looked around his apartment. He moved without thinking about it to the window and looked out over Hyde Park Avenue. There was no traffic on the small side street. It wasn't much of a view, but it was home.

He went into the kitchen, and finding he really didn't want anything there, went back to look out the window some more. He was worried about Brad.

His idea to go back over the facts didn't turn up anything useful. If anything, he discovered the reverse since Lisa now declared she never saw Renee that night. There was now no witness putting her with Pierce.

He made the trip by Brad's house. There was nothing telling to be found there. He did find out plenty from Pete, though. Almost too much. Mr. Pierce has quite an enterprise going on and likely killed both a security guard and Renee to protect it.

Jack stood staring at the empty street in front of his apartment. There has to be something more that can be done to help Brad. He looked around his apartment and his gaze fell upon the small stack of newspapers next to his recliner.

Sunday's paper had the article about that snitch at the jail. He went over to the stack of newspaper and retrieved the front page of Sunday's paper. Here's the article. Scanning the article he found the name of the snitch, Derek Pagell.

I might not be able to do anything about Mr. Pagell, but I can at least try, he thought. He grabbed his car keys off the counter that separated the living room from the kitchen and left the apartment.

Driving downtown to the jail, he thought of what a long shot this was going to be. There's a good chance he wouldn't know who to talk to anymore. Even if he found someone he knew, there's a good chance they wouldn't or couldn't help him. Still he couldn't sit by and do nothing if there was a chance.

Jack parked across the street from the jail and sat in the car for a minute. Was he doing the right thing? Of course. It was a crapshoot, but there was nothing to loose in trying.

Jack left his car and crossed the street to the County Jail. Just inside the front door he was confronted with a long counter with bulletproof glass separating him from attendants at the counter. People were milling around, some in lines. Everyone there had a worried look on his face. He got in one of three lines. Soon he reached the front.

"Is Carl Weber still the daytime supervisor?"

"He is."

"I'd like to see him, please. I'm Jack Wilkerson. I used to be a police officer." Jack produced an alumnus card that identified him as a former police officer with the Houston Police Department.

"Take a seat. I'll tell him you're here."

Jack stood next to a wall for about five minutes and

started to wonder if he had been given the runaround when a young officer stepped from behind a door to the back.

"Jack Wilkerson?"

"Right here."

"Come this way, please."

Jack followed the man down a series of hallways until he was shown a door. The young officer knocked on the door.

"Come in."

The officer opened the door and ushered Jack into the office of Carl Weber. Weber rose from behind his desk to shake hands with Jack.

"I don't know if you remember me." Jack said.

"I remember. I wouldn't have remembered your name, but I never forget a face. What can I do for you?"

"You have a Derek Pagell here in custody?"

"We do. I don't know the names of all of our prisoners, but his name is one I recall."

"I'm a friend of Brad Marshall."

"I'm starting to see. Mr. Pagell gained some notoriety with what he claims to have heard Mr. Marshall say." Weber folded his hands on his desk.

"Bradley Marshall would never have admitted committing a murder he didn't commit. I've known the man for some time, and I know he's innocent."

Weber nodded and raised his hands, palm upward. "I understand you standing by your friend, and that's admirable, but what is it you want me to do."

"There was a time, years ago, I'd be asking you to lean on Pagell, to see if you couldn't move him off of his story."

"There was a time when I'd be happy to oblige. But these days if we so much as sneeze on a prisoner, we invite a lawsuit."

Jack leaned forward in his chair. "All I'm asking is for your guards to keep their ears open. If Pagell so much as breathes that he made it up, I want to know about it."

Weber cocked his head to one side slightly. "I don't see a problem with that. I'm not a fan of snitches making up stories to cut their sentence. From what I understand, Pagell is a bit of a celebrity in here for recognizing Marshall and working it into a nice deal for himself. It smells bad, and I don't like it happening in my jail."

Jack smiled. "Pagell may brag about what he's doing. If he does I want him exposed. That's all I'm asking."

Weber took a pad of paper and pen and slid them across the desk toward Jack. "Let me know how I can get ahold of you, and if anything turns up I will."

Jack took the paper and pen. "Thanks. I appreciate it."

"Don't mention it. Sounds to me like the right thing to do. Especially if this Marshall fellow is innocent."

Jack wrote down his name and phone number. "He is."

Leaving the jail, Jack walked with a slight spring in his step. It was a long shot, but sometimes long shots paid off.

Brad smelled fajitas when he entered the Red Lion Tuesday evening. They smelled good. He would think about ordering some later. There were several people in the bar and it seemed noisy; it was busy for a Tuesday.

He went straight to the bar and crawled up on the empty stool to the right of Jack. He placed the manila envelope with the printout of Richard Pierce's finances on the bar in front of him.

"Jack, how are you doing?"

"I'd be doing better if the lingerie show would get started."

Brad eye's got wide. "This place has lingerie shows?" That would explain the crowd.

"You bet. It's a class place."

"How come I've never seen one in here?" Rusty placed a club soda in front of Brad, which he accepted with a nod.

Jack shrugged. "You probably haven't been around long enough to see one. It's been a while."

"Been around long enough? I've been coming here a couple of years."

"Like I said. It's been a while."

"How long a while?"

"Oh I don't know. Rusty, how long has it been since we've had a lingerie show?"

Rusty looked at the ceiling for a moment, his hand on his chin. "Oh, three, maybe four years."

Jack reached for his beer. "Three or four years. See, it's been a while."

"Wow, and they're having one tonight?"

"I don't know about tonight, but we're bound to

have one soon. We're overdue. Rusty, are we having a lingerie show tonight?"

"Not tonight, Jack."

Jack sighed. "Maybe tomorrow night then. I'll wait. I'm a patient man. I've waited three or four years. I can wait another night."

Brad chuckled. "While your waiting, I have something you might find interesting."

Jack looked over at the envelope, one eyebrow raised. "Is that what I think it is?"

Brad nodded. "The illegal finances of one Richard Pierce."

"And it says what we thought it would say?"

"It does. In detail." Brad gave a short explanation of how Pierce takes in cash from various construction companies and launders it though strip joints and dry cleaners.

"It's a lot of money?" Jack asked.

"It's a lot of money."

"You know if Richard Pierce caught you in here with that he'd kill you and take it away from you, in that order."

"I'm thinking I'll see a lingerie show before I see Richard Pierce in here."

"Maybe you're right. I've seen a lingerie show in here. Next question. What are you going to do with this information?"

"I'm not sure yet. I was hoping you'd help me figure out the best way to handle it."

Jack rubbed his chin. "Are you still friendly with that newspaper gal from the Chronicle?"

"I still talk to her from time to time."

"Illegal activities have to be kept secret to stay illegal. Maybe you could get the Chronicle interested in shedding the light of day on Mr. Pierce's activities."

"Okay. But how does that help my situation?"

"Once you bring down Richard Pierce the whole thing should fold like a house of cards. Lisa wouldn't be afraid to testify that Renee was with Richard the night she was killed if Richard is in jail. And keeping Renee silent about the corruption gives Richard motive to kill Renee. I'm just thinking out loud here."

"What if I just took this straight to the police."

Jack shook his head. "They'd never believe you. You're a computer expert. They'd think you made it up to shift the blame away from yourself."

"I guess you're right."

"I might be able to reach them, though. I'm thinking they aren't going to listen to me either, but it's worth a shot. Give me the packet and I'll approach them."

Brad slid the envelope over to Jack. "Hey, I appreciate it. I keep thinking about Renee's jewelry. He has to still have it. If his place gets searched, surely they'll find the jewelry and that would get me out of this jam I'm in."

"If they find the jewelry and Richard Pierce is shut down so that he can no longer push buttons downtown then you're home free. As long as he's walking around with the Mayor's pull in this town, you'll continue to be prosecuted, jewelry or no jewelry."

"I guess you're right. For the charges to be dropped against me, all of Pierce's business, including the corruption and the killings, has to be made public."

228

"That's not going to be as easy as it sounds."

"It would seem like the Chronicle would love a big story like this."

"We'll see. The Mayor is a powerful man." Jack said.

"So, we'll make a two pronged approach then. You take it to the police and I'll take it to the newspaper. That makes sense. You know the guys at the police department better than I do, and I can talk to Jennifer and see where that goes."

Jack nodded. "I assume you can print yourself another copy of this."

"You assume right."

"Be careful with this information. Like I said earlier, it could get you killed."

Brad nodded. "I haven't forgotten what they did to Renee. Besides, they're already trying to take my life away over it, Jack. They're just trying to put me in a cage forever."

"Good point." Jack conceded.

"Are you hungry?"

"Yeah. I haven't eaten yet."

"Me either. I've been smelling fajitas." Brad said, looking around.

"That sounds good." Jack shook his head. "Might as well. They're not having the lingerie show tonight.

CHAPTER **27**

Jennifer placed the bag from the supermarket on the counter in the kitchen of her apartment. She took out apples, walnuts, a lemon and lettuce for the Waldorf salad she planned to make. She also took out a bottle of bubble bath, a magazine and a couple of candles.

With Kevin gone she planned to take it easy and enjoy being alone. No oaf around to bother with. She could do whatever she wanted. Tonight that would be a Waldorf salad, her favorite, and a bubble bath.

Before starting the salad she went into the bedroom. She looked around, checking for anything that might remind her of Kevin. It seemed clear. She opened the closet. There at the bottom of the closet was an old pair of sneakers that belonged to Kevin.

She kicked at a sneaker. I can't call him to tell him he left his shoes. I don't know where he is. He's probably with that tramp. She picked up the sneakers and took them to the kitchen and threw them in the garbage. They were old. They needed to be thrown out anyway. I hope he calls and asks about them so I can tell him I threw them out.

With the last of Kevin's things disposed of, she stood in the kitchen for a moment, her eye's growing moist. Why did he have to do it? Things were pretty good between them. Why did he have to turn out to be such a louse?

She got a tissue from the counter and blew her nose. She needed to stop crying and make the salad. She threw the tissue away and stood washing her hands. She was better off without him. He was never around anyway. He worked nights and she worked days. When he worked. If you could call what he did work. It wasn't really working out between them. Thank God he's gone.

She made the salad and took it with the magazine to the table. She had picked the magazine for it's tantalizing promise of "Seven Ways to Pamper Yourself". She located the article and scanned it. She was already ahead of the game. Number one was fixing your favorite food. Number four was a bubble bath. She thought about number seven: visit a museum. I might do that on my next day off. Houston has several excellent museums and it's been ages since I've been.

She continued to flip through the magazine looking at the advertisements. She stopped for a moment. It seemed so quiet with Kevin gone. Good. I never needed him. He was never here when I wanted him to be, anyway.

She picked at the salad. From now on I can cook only the things I like. I only thought I needed a roommate. He never helped with the rent. Worthless bum. Good riddance.

She finished the salad and continued to look at the magazine. After a while her eyes started to loose their focus on the pages in front of her and her thoughts turned to work.

I really need to try to get another interview with Brad. I'll call him tomorrow and see if I can set that up. I'm sure he likes me, at least a little bit. Plus, he probably liked the last story I did on him.

I almost forgot he tried to ask me out once. I wonder if he will again? He knows I don't have a boyfriend anymore. Brad's nice. I probably would go out with him if he asked.

He probably won't ask. I haven't been exactly friendly to him lately. I'll call him tomorrow and see if I can set up another meeting. I'll have to be ready in case he says yes. What would I wear? She got up from the table to go check her closet.

Jennifer rifled through the clothes in her closet. She wasn't exactly sure what she was looking for. Whatever it was she didn't see it. This was too revealing; that was too conservative. She went back to the table and grabbed the bowl her salad had been in and took it to the sink.

She went back to the closet and took another look. This time she found a couple of outfits and decided to put the final decision off until later. She went back into the kitchen for the bottle of bubble bath and candles. I'll think about it surrounded by bubbles. That will do the trick.

On the way to the bathroom she thought about the interview she planned to get with Brad. Brad didn't kill his wife. Whatever Caruthers thinks about the way the story should be told, it's about time Brad got to tell his side of things. I hope I can convince him to do that. I know he's innocent of these murder charges. It's about time everyone else knew it. Maybe if they did, things would go better for him in court.

Running the water for the bath, Jennifer smiled. Brad would just have to tell her everything he knew so she could help him. No more secrets about 'political implications' or stuff like that. I'll have to convince him I'm on his side. He needs to trust me. She nodded to herself. I can get him to do that.

Shortly after Brad finished the fajitas with Jack he said goodbye and left the Red Lion. Driving back to the Doubletree hotel he thought of how he missed being able to walk home from the bar.

These October nights were great for being outside in Southeast Texas. Jack had said the house was pretty well cleaned up. I wonder if I should move back in?

The thought of the bloodstain on the carpet made Brad shiver. I guess the carpet would have to go. No way I could live there with a red stain in the living room, reminding me of how Renee died. That dark stain would feel cold and wet in my mind from wherever I was in that house, even from the bedroom. The carpet would have to go.

Before the murder, Brad always found some comfort in the memories of Renee that drifted through the house. He missed her not being there, but focused on the positive thoughts about her in that house.

It was just the opposite with Renee. Memories of Brad didn't set well with her. She had said that every time she looked at Brad she thought of their daughter. That was one of the reasons she asked for a divorce.

Brad wondered if those warm memories of Renee

would overcome the pictures in his mind of her lying there in a pool of her own blood. I guess I can't know the answer to that until I go back. I'll do that soon. Not tomorrow. Tomorrow I need to try to get a meeting with Jennifer Hart.

Brad turned into the entrance to the Doubletree and handed his car off to the valet. He went up to his room and got ready for bed.

Before turning in he opened his laptop computer and connected to his server downtown. He had given Jack his copy of Richard's finances. He downloaded a copy of the file to his laptop. Richard Pierce was the man pulling strings to have him convicted of murder; he was convinced of that. And this file was the only thing he had on Mr. Pierce. He felt somehow a little more content with a copy of it in the room with him.

Before he shut down the computer, he took a look at the books again. He shook his head at the corruption and outright theft that he was seeing on the screen. How was it that he could get away with that? How was it that the construction companies would just pay him and not tell someone what was going on?

Brad looked down at the floor. He was sure he knew the answer to that question. The contractors wouldn't mind the game being rigged as long as they thought that they were benefiting in the long run. They don't care how the game is played as long as they get to play.

Percentage wise Pierce's take wasn't that much. The ones that weren't benefiting couldn't prove anything, since they weren't in on it. Brad shook his head. It must be tricky to keep them all happy, but evidence that it could be done was in front of him.

Brad thought again of Renee. How much did she find out? She had only said that she saw something she wasn't supposed to see. She might not have seen that much. Richard Pierce would surely kill to protect a hint of this from becoming public. Not only would it send him to jail, it would ruin his father. His father. I wonder if the Mayor knows about Renee? Maybe, maybe not. There's no way to know.

Brad shut down the computer and climbed in the bed. Tomorrow he would go in to the office and call Jennifer Hart. Brad smiled. She's without a boyfriend now. I wonder if I can talk her into dinner? Brad squirmed around, trying to get comfortable in the bed.

If I'm going to give her this stuff on Richard Pierce I'm going to have to tell her where it's coming from. I'm going to have to tell her what I know about his involvement in Renee's death. I guess you're about to hit the journalistic jackpot, Jennifer.

It also means I'm going to have to enlist her help and be able to trust her. Richard Pierce can't find out about this before the whole thing is blown wide open. He would come after me, or her, if he knew something like this was going to the newspapers.

I've got to tread lightly with Jennifer at first, see how much I can trust her to help me. This is a big story; I would think she would be anxious to be a part of it. But it has to be handled on my terms. Unless he's investigated for murder as well as corruption it won't help me. Wherever he's stashed Renee's jewelry, it has to be found.

Brad thrashed around some more in the bed. He

tried to lie still, and couldn't. Finally he got up and went back to his computer.

One thing that usually worked to help calm him down was to work on his novel. He synced the necessary files with his server and soon was wrapped up in the make-believe world of his own creation. After a couple of hours of building scenes for that world, he was able to go back to bed and sleep in this world.

CHAPTER **28**

Late that Tuesday night Richard parked his car near Tranquility Park in downtown Houston. He had given Duane and Reggie instructions to meet him there. This time of night he was unlikely to be seen at the park.

Richard got out of the car and stole into Tranquility Park from Smith Street where it met Rusk. When he passed the entrance he glanced over to his left at a wall with junk written on it about the park and a bunch of old bastards that claimed to have helped put it here.

He stepped along the dingy brown brick walkway, down three steps and between a couple of pools of stagnant water. Up ahead two big round metal tubes stuck up in the air with water dumping down their sides. He crossed between them to an open area.

It was here he found Duane and Reggie. Behind them was some sort of lame sculpture or fountain thing with three more metal water tubes sitting on tumbled brick pads. They were surrounded by a weak bridge.

Richard looked around. He didn't see anyone else in the park. "Men. How're ya doin?"

"We're fine, Rick. It didn't take us long to get here. We were just down the street at the Hard Rock Cafe." Duane said.

"What I got will just take a minute, and then you two gents can get back to chasing pussy." Richard took a photograph out of his jacket pocket and handed it to Duane. "This guy has been asking questions about us."

Duane took the photograph and looked at it. "You want us to take him out?"

"No. I don't want to attract any attention among the people he's been talking to. I just want you two to persuade him to stop nosing around."

Duane chuckled. "Okay. Reggie here can be real persuasive."

"Don't mess him up. No broken bones are anything like that. Like I said, I don't want to attract attention. I'm sure he doesn't know anything, and I want to keep it that way. If something happens to him, then others might get curious. I don't want any more curiosity. Curiosity is what we're trying to prevent here."

"I think I got it, Rick. We'll just rough him up a little and talk to him. Tell him to keep to himself and stop asking questions."

Richard nodded. "That's what I want."

"Who is he and where can we find him?" Duane asked.

"His name is Jack Wilkerson. I wrote it on the back of the photo. He hangs out at the Red Lion Bar & Grill. I also wrote the address on the back."

"The Red Lion over on Alabama?"

"Yeah. That's it. Don't bother him inside the joint. Remember, I don't want attention here."

"We got it. We'll get right on it."

"Take your time. There's no big hurry. I'd rather you did it right than rush it. Take two or three days if you have to and pick your moment. Get him in the parking lot if you can, without witnesses. You

238

detecting a theme here, fellas?"

"Yeah. You want this done real quiet like."

"You got it. I just want to get the message across and nothing, nothing more."

"We understand. Right Reggie?"

"Uh huh." Reggie nodded.

"Good. I know I can count on you guys." Richard took a wad of bills from his pocket and counted out several for each of the men. "Try not to blow all of this on just one cunt at the Hard Rock."

The two men took the bills and grinned. Richard left them in the park and strode back to his car. Now he had gotten that out of the way. Soon Mr. Jack Wilkerson would get the message that inquiring into my business wasn't a healthy thing to do.

Luis didn't say so when he gave up the information on Jack Wilkerson, but this Wilkerson had to be tied into this Marshall fellow. Who else would be asking questions of Lisa? The police weren't checking into the case anymore. He'd been assured they closed the case with the arrest of Marshall. He was the only one that still had an iron in this fire.

It had to be Marshall. Marshall is the one stirring up trouble. Marshall has to go.

Richard arrived at his car and got in. He sat staring straight ahead. Marshall never should have been let out of jail. Now that he is walking around free there's no way to tell how much trouble he could cause. Tomorrow I'll set something up to take care of Mr. Marshall. I'll get him out of the way for good.

Unlike the situation with Wilkerson, this doesn't have to be kept quiet. He's been stuck in my craw from the beginning, the way the newspaper described him as some kind of local boy made good. I don't like that smart ass rich Marshall prick and I don't care if the whole world knows what happens when I don't like somebody.

Richard started the car and pulled away from the curb. It was late. Whatever to do now? All of this plotting and planning makes me horny.

Richard thought of the tittie joints he did business with and rejected the idea. He wasn't in the mood for a stripper tonight. Those girls sold fantasy so much they started to live in their own make—believe world. It's alright for an afternoon quickie but he was looking for something a little fresher and more substantial.

Richard laughed out loud. Since when is it that pussy might get described as fresher and more substantial? Since when did it matter? Still, the thought of a stripper left him cold.

Richard thought about the Hard Rock Cafe that Duane had mentioned. Not a bad idea. It's been a while since I've graced that joint with my presence. Lots of hot young fruitful things for the plucking in there.

He circled the block and headed back in the direction he had come from, looking for a parking place. In addition to the Hard Rock Cafe, there are several joints within walking distance at The Bayou Place. That's as good a place as any to look for something worthwhile to fuck.

Brad entered his office Wednesday morning. He

was looking forward to contacting Jennifer Hart to set up a meeting. "Good Morning, Rose."

"Good Morning, Mr. Marshall. You only have a couple of messages this morning and neither of them important."

Brad took the message slips and glanced at them. The phone rang and Rose picked it up. "Bradley Marshall's Office. Yes, hold on please." Rose turned to Brad. "Mr. Marshall, Ms. Hart is on line one for you. I wouldn't usually put members of the press through like this, but this woman seems to put an extra spring in your step."

Brad looked down at the floor before returning Rose's gaze. "It shows, does it?"

"I know you pretty well, Mr. Marshall. I'm sure no one else has noticed, least of all her."

Brad grinned. "Thanks Rose." He hurried into his office and shut the door behind him. He collided with the corner of his desk in his haste to get to his chair and pick up the phone.

"Jennifer, I was just going to call you."

"You were going to call me? That's a surprise. I saved you the trouble. What did you want to talk to me about?"

"I'd like to discuss it with you face to face, if that would be possible?"

"When? I'm available this morning unless that's too soon."

Brad took a deep breath. That's quicker than I had imagined. "This morning is fine."

"What's this about? Can I get a hint?"

"Remember you asking me about the political

implications involving my arrest? I'd like to be able to share some of the details with you."

There was silence on the other end of the phone.

"Jennifer?"

"I'm still here. I just had to catch my breath."

"There are some conditions."

"I guess I should have expected that. What kind of conditions?"

"We can discuss that when you get here. If that's alright?"

"Sure Brad. Can I bring a photographer?"

"I'd rather you didn't."

"Alright then, just me by my lonesome. How about I see you in about an hour?"

"That would be fine."

Brad hung up the phone and looked at his watch. It was nine thirty. There were a couple of things to do in order to get ready for her visit.

He logged on to his computer and brought up the financial books of Richard Pierce. He scrolled through them once more, still hardly believing the magnitude and audacity of the scheme they disclosed, and hit the print key.

He listened until his heard the printer making its customary sounds and then got up from his chair to check the output of the printer. It looked fine. There were several pages to print. It would take a few minutes.

Brad went to the door and opened it. "Rose, just to let you know, Ms. Hart will be coming over to meet with me in about an hour."

"Alright, Mr. Marshall."

He thought he detected a faint smile on Rose's face. She must find this quite amusing. I'll get her back for that if I can figure out how.

He went back to his desk and retrieved a bottle of aftershave from the top right drawer. Splashing some on his face he hoped it wouldn't be too obvious a gesture. He replaced the bottle in his desk and wiped his hands on his slacks.

He looked at his watch. Less than ten minutes had passed. This was going to be a long wait. He looked around the office. Everything seemed to be in order. He got up from his desk and rearranged the two visitor's chairs on the other side of the desk from his.

He alternated between pacing in his office and sitting at his desk for the duration of the hour's wait. When he thought he could stand it no more he heard his intercom buzz. "Mr. Marshall, Ms. Hart is here to see you."

Brad jumped up from his chair and tried to walk calmly to the door.

"Ms. Hart. Won't you come in?"

"Thank you, Brad."

Jennifer breezed into the room with a fresh scent that caught Brad by surprise. She was wearing a skirt. Was that the first time he'd seen her in a skirt? He was a bit slow to take his eyes off of her legs and close the door. He finally offered her a seat, which she took. He moved around the desk, careful not to trip over his feet, and eased into his desk chair.

"So, since you've gotten my curiosity peaked with hints that you'll reveal deep secrets, who killed Renee?" Jennifer asked.

"Boy, you get right to it."

"Is that a problem?"

"No. I find you exciting... I mean, I find that particular quality exciting in a woman." Brad took a deep breath. *Slow down here buddy. You've negotiated bigger deals than this one.*

"Good. I like you too, and I'd like to be able to tell your story to our readers."

"There are a couple of conditions."

"You mentioned that on the phone. Alright. I'll at least consider them. What are they?"

"One. You have dinner with me tonight."

Jennifer's eyebrows went up and her chin dropped slightly.

"I don't hear an objection. Do you like steak?" Brad asked.

"Love it. But..."

"Great. I was thinking either Ruth's Chriss or Pappas Bro's. If you have a definite preference I'll leave it up to you. I prefer Pappas Bro's a little myself. They have the piano bar to enjoy while you wait on a table, and I think that tips the scales in their favor. They're also famous for their martinis. I don't drink, but I don't mind if you..."

"Brad." Jennifer shook her head. "I just got out of a relationship that ended badly."

"He was a fool to let you go. I'm not asking you to move in with me, just go to dinner."

Jennifer wrinkled her nose and glanced at the floor. "Alright." She looked up with a slight grin. "Is that the only condition?"

Brad leaned back in his chair. "No, there's one

other. If you print the story, you have to print the whole story. I'm afraid I'll just have to accept your word on that. I want Renee's killer exposed. Unless his entire operation is made public it probably isn't going to help me much."

She leaned forward in her chair. "So you think you know who killed Renee?"

"I don't know who pulled the trigger, but I'm sure I know who was behind her murder, and why she was killed."

"I don't see a problem with that arraignment. Of course I don't know exactly what you have. But since I presume I'm not going to get anything from you if I don't agree then I really have no choice."

"So you agree to both conditions then?"

Jennifer smiled. "Yes, I will have dinner with you, and yes I'll print all the story or none of it."

"And I have your word?"

She sighed. "Yes. You have my word. Now, who killed Renee?"

"Richard Pierce."

Jennifer bolted upright in her chair. "The son of our Mayor?"

"The one and only."

"Political implications my ass. This is a political nuclear bomb. What proof do you have?"

"It's a long story. I'll start at the beginning." Brad told Jennifer of the phone calls with Renee the night she was killed. He told her about Lisa, and Renee leaving the Skybar with Richard Pierce. He told her about the missing jewelry, and his suspicion that Richard Pierce still has it. And he told her that the police had been told to make him the suspect in the case from above, despite their reservations.

"What you've told me is that Richard might have been the one to kill her, but why? Why would the son of our Mayor kill anybody?" Jennifer asked.

Brad got up from the desk and went over to the printer. He took the packet of papers off of the printer and put them on his desk in front of Jennifer. "Here's why. When she called me and said she had seen something she shouldn't have, she evidently had stumbled onto at least a part of this."

Jennifer started looking over the papers Brad had handed her. Brad then told her of the corruption detailed in the financial reports. He told her how cash from the construction companies with contracts through the city was being handed to Richard Pierce and laundered through strip joints and dry cleaners.

"Where did you get this information?" Jennifer asked, referring to the stack of paper.

"I got it from the computer of Richard Pierce, without his knowledge."

Jennifer shook her head. "This is too much. I have to think for a minute. Maybe more than a minute." She put the papers back on Brad's desk.

Brad got up from the desk and went to the window. He wanted to give Jennifer a moment to digest everything he had said. Finally he turned around and addressed her. "Well, will you print it?"

"I'd like to. God, would I ever like to. At this point I'm not sure that I can."

Brad's shoulders slumped. "Why not? It's all true."

"I believe you Brad. This sounds like stuff out of a

Godfather movie going on in our own city, but I believe you. The first problem is substantiating all of it. The only proof that I have that these are the actual files of Richard Pierce is your word, and while I believe you, I'm pretty sure that's not going to get by our legal department."

Brad looked at the floor. "Remember our deal. If you don't print all of it, don't print any of it. You can't just write that I said Richard Pierce killed my wife."

"I know Brad. I'll stand by my word. The thing is, I really want this story. How about this girl that saw them together?"

"Lisa. She's not going to talk as long as she's afraid of Richard Pierce. That's another problem."

"Yes, it is. There's got to be a way. I'm not giving up on this. Now that we know it exists, now that I know what I'm looking for, I may be able to root some of this out on my own." Jennifer's eye's sparkled. "There's got to be a way to print this story. It's the kind of story a reporter dreams about."

Brad wrinkled his nose. "I guess I was being a little naive thinking you could just take it and run with it. Right now it is mostly based on the word of an accused murderer. You think about it. If you need my help, let me know."

"I will. I'll be sure to tell you what I'm finding out as I get it, too."

"I'd appreciate that. Be careful, people die around these animals if they're suspected of knowing too much. There's one other thing."

"What's that?"

"Ruth's Chris or Pappas Bro's? You haven't said."

CHAPTER **29**

"I appreciate your agreeing to see me." Jack said. He was sitting across from Sergeant McNair, the Senior Detective that had investigated Renee Marshall's murder. They were sitting in the noisy squad room with a steel desk between them.

"Not a problem. I'm not sure what I can do for you, though. As I understand it, this has to do with the Marshall case?"

"That's right."

"We closed that case. The husband is being tried for the murder, isn't he?"

Jack adjusted his position in the chair. "He is. I know him. Brad didn't do it."

McNair nodded. "I talked with you before about it. Maybe I said more than I should have. But the facts surrounding the case haven't changed. From what I hear they've gotten worse for Mr. Marshall."

Jack sat forward in his chair. "That doesn't change the fact that he didn't do it, Sergeant. I think you suspect who actually was involved in the murder."

"And who would that be?"

"One Richard Pierce."

McNair leaned back and rubbed his forehead. "His name came up in the investigation."

"Did you pursue it?"

"Are you nuts? And have my badge ripped off me with a chainsaw?" McNair shook his head. "No thanks."

"We think Renee Marshall was killed because of what she found out about the business dealings of Richard Pierce."

"Is that what you have in that envelope there? The business dealings of Mr. Richard Pierce?"

Jack nodded. "It is. It's a printout of his computer files, detailing corruption in the Mayor's office and money laundering." Jack explained the cash payments to Richard Pierce were detailed in the records, along with the laundering of the money through strip joints and dry cleaners.

"Damn. That's some story. I'm pretty sure I know the answer to this, but does Pierce know you have his files?"

"Of course not."

"So that information is stolen property then?"

Jack twisted his mouth into half grin, half smirk. "Are you going to arrest me?"

McNair snorted. "Hell, no. I'm trying to think back over the details of the Marshall murder. That would explain some things, like the phone conversations Mr. Marshall had with his wife shortly before she killed. If she found out about any significant corruption in the Mayor's office it's no wonder she didn't last long."

"I know the last person she was seen with alive was Richard Pierce. And I know he's got some major secrets." Jack patted the envelope in his lap. "It doesn't take a rocket scientist to figure out what happened."

"It also explains the orders from the top to hurry up and make an arrest. If the Mayor's office didn't want us looking into this too closely, then I guess we didn't look too closely."

"You explained the pressure you were under last time we talked. If I were in your shoes I'm not sure I would have acted any differently." Jack looked down at the floor.

"What you're saying makes sense. I'm just not sure what I can do with it. While I believe you, I have no proof that what you have is actually his files. And I can't act on illegally obtained evidence. Even if I busted into Pierce's place and got the actual files, I can't do it based on this. It would get tossed out of court. Fruit of the rotten tree and all of that legal crap."

"I'm offering you the files to do with as you please. I just want to make sure you'll keep in mind who the actual bad guys are here and keep your eyes open for anything that moves in a direction to prove what I'm saying."

McNair nodded. "I hear you. That's fair enough. It's going to take more than what's in that envelope to stop an operation like what you're talking about, but then I'm sure you already knew that."

"I did. We've got a ways to go, but I'm hoping to start stacking some cards in our favor. Brad deserves it. He didn't commit the murder. And besides that, he's my friend."

"Everybody should have a few friends like you. I'll think about it. I don't think I can do much, but whatever I can, I'll let you know."

"I appreciate it." Jack rose from his chair and left the envelope on the desk. He started to leave, then paused and turned back to face McNair. "If you think of any way we can help you put a stop to him and get the right people held accountable for Renee's murder, get in touch, alright?"

"Will do. And I wish I could do more. If I think of anything I'll let you know."

Jack walked away from the desk and shook his head a little. That was about what I expected. I had hoped for more, but deep down I knew he wouldn't be able to do much. It's not McNair's fault. I'm not really giving him much to work with.

Still, it's a start. Maybe if we start stacking some bricks on our pile it will grow into some kind of wall at some point. It better grow quickly. We'll run out of time if it doesn't develop quickly.

Jack turned and looked back at the squad room. There was a day when it would have been a smoke filled room. Things were different back then.

Jack sighed. Some things weren't different. Corruption in the Mayor's office back then would have been just as hard to ferret out. Just as hard to get rid of and just as dangerous. The Mayor's office still had a lot of say so around here. Some things haven't changed at all.

Brad knocked on the door to Jennifer's apartment at eight o'clock sharp Wednesday night. She opened the door and invited Brad inside. After she closed the door behind him, he got a good look at her. Brad's mouth dropped open. She looked stunning in a black dress and the waves of her hair framing her face.

"You look wonderful." Brad said.

"Thanks." Jennifer's smiled beamed. "You look nice, too. Would you like anything to drink?"

"No, I'm fine."

"Let me get my purse then, and I guess we'll go."

Brad watched her glide across the room and disappear in what he took to be the bedroom. He took a deep breath and looked around the room. What he saw was tastefully decorated in earth tones, a flavor of southwest decor. It would have been equally appropriate for Houston or San Diego.

Jennifer appeared with a small black bag in her hands. "Shall we go?"

"Of course. I've been looking forward to this."

"So have I. Did we decide where we were going?" Jennifer asked.

"I think we settled on Pappas Bro's."

"Great. I've never been."

Brad opened the door for them. "Then you're in for a treat. Your place looks nice."

"Thanks. I decorated it myself."

"I got that impression. It looks like someone from San Diego living in Houston."

Jennifer laughed. "Well, duh."

They continued to the car and started on the drive to the restaurant.

"I've been thinking about everything you told me about Richard Pierce and his probable involvement in your wife's murder, not to mention corruption involving
252

city contracts," Jennifer said.

"Oh boy. We're going to talk about the case."

"Well, we don't have to."

Brad smiled at her. "No, I want to get it out of the way. I think we'll wind up talking about it sooner or later and it may as well be sooner. Did I tell you that you look absolutely ravishing tonight?"

Jennifer laughed. "Yes, I think you did. Anyway, I'm going to have another problem when I get ready to write the story."

"Such as?"

"Have you ever seen an article critical of the Mayor, present or past, in the Chronicle?"

Brad sat for a moment, then shook his head. "I can't say that I have."

"There aren't any. They don't criticize the city's administration. It's like an unwritten rule. Generally speaking, this story about corruption would have to be in the New York Times or Washington Post three days running before they would acknowledge it, and then they would try to paint it in a positive light."

"So you're saying that they'll never expose Richard Pierce and his father?"

"If the evidence is there, I think that they will have to. But the evidence will have to be strong. It will have to be irrefutable."

Brad sighed. "Then I'll have to find a way to provide you with irrefutable evidence." Brad looked at her and smiled.

Within minutes they were sitting in a plush booth in the bar of Pappas Bro's Steak House. The hostess had said it would be a fifteen-minute wait for their table.

Jennifer had a gin martini in her hand and Brad had a club soda. The piano was playing 'A Kiss is Just a Kiss', made famous by the movie *Casablanca*. Brad's gaze kept returning to Jennifer.

"How's the novel coming?" Jennifer asked.

"Slowly. It's been great to have, lately. Writing science fiction is one of the few things that can take my mind off of my troubles."

"I need something like that in my life. Although I guess my work does that for me during the day."

Brad looked down at the table. "That doesn't help with the nights, though."

"No, it doesn't."

"I can work on my novel most anytime. It's funny. Renee wasn't around much before the murder. We were, after all, getting a divorce. But I miss her more since she's completely gone. I didn't miss her as much if she was just half way across town. Does that make any sense?"

Jennifer nodded. "I know exactly what you mean. It's weird that I miss Kevin being there at night. He was never there at night when we were together. He was always either playing a gig or practicing. But now that we've split up I miss him being there, even though he wasn't there before."

"Renee had already moved on with her life. I guess I was a little slow to do that myself."

"Did you still love her?"

"In a way I guess I did. You don't spend six years with someone and go through all we did together without loving them. But so much pain had become part of us that not much love was on the surface any more."

254

Jennifer sipped at her drink. "There wasn't much love on the surface, as you put it, left between me and Kevin, either. It was really over between us a long time ago. We were just too lazy to see it."

"So you just grew apart?"

"That, and I caught him in bed with another woman."

Brad shook his head. "Ouch!"

"Yeah. Ouch."

"He was a fool to let you go."

Jennifer smiled at Brad. "You're just being nice. But that's alright. Keep being that way." Jennifer giggled. "These martinis are good. Good and strong. I should be safe if I stop at one."

The hostess appeared and told them that their table was ready. Jennifer followed the hostess and Brad followed her. Watching Jennifer move around in her dress from behind, Brad considered how lucky he was to be in the company of such a beautiful woman.

Sitting at the table Brad looked over at Jennifer. "My attorney would have a fit if he knew I'd asked you out."

Jennifer smiled. "So you're being a naughty boy?"

Brad chuckled. "I don't care. I enjoy being with you. I feel like I can talk to you."

Jennifer's face grew serious. "I feel the same way about you, Brad." Jennifer looked down at the table. "Of course, in my case that could just be the booze talking, you never know."

Brad laughed. "A woman of mystery."

Jennifer smiled at Brad. "I've got to keep you thinking that I'm exciting. You did say you found me exciting, didn't you?"

"I did. I do."

Jennifer's face disappeared behind the menu. Brad smiled to himself, looked at his own menu and tried to concentrate on the selection for his meal. Brad sat with his shoulders back and his chest out. Looking around the room, he felt fortunate to be there with her.

CHAPTER **30**

Jennifer had just logged on to her computer Thursday morning and settled back in her chair. She was trying to keep her mind off of last night with Brad and on her work. She wasn't having a lot of luck.

She noticed yesterday she needed to clean out the inbox of her email. That would be good to kill an hour or so. Then I guess I'll give some thought to what Brad told me yesterday about Richard Pierce. I'm supposed to be an investigative journalist. I should start investigating.

Bill Caruthers appeared at her cubicle. "There's been a huge pile up on the Southwest Freeway near Kirby. It must involve at least eight cars and an eighteen-wheeler. Ambulances everywhere. Get out there and take Bobby with you for some photos."

Jennifer jumped up from her seat and grabbed her bag. "You got it."

She started over toward Bobby's cubicle but met him coming her way in the hallway.

"I just heard. We'll take my car," he said.

In the elevator Jennifer turned to Bobby. "You always insist that we take your car. You don't have some silly problem with women drivers do you?"

"No, I have a silly problem with the sound system in your car. It sucks."

Jennifer looked at the lights blinking the floor numbers as they moved toward the lobby. That jerk Kevin used to complain about the stereo in her car too. "I guess I should get that fixed."

"It's not a problem as long as we take my car."

Jennifer grinned at Bobby. "It's not a problem for me when I sing real loud either. I don't hear it."

Bobby rolled his eyes. Minutes later they were rushing toward the accident on the freeway.

"You seem to be in a terrific mood for a traffic accident." Bobby said. "It's the wrong time of year for a big tax refund, so it must be a fella." Bobby stole a glance in her direction as he drove.

Jennifer blushed. "This is just a normal good mood."

"That's a load of crap. We've worked together too long for you to get away with lying like that."

"Alright. I did have a date last night."

"I knew it. Anybody we know?"

"Yes. But it's none of your business who it was."

"Anybody from the office?"

"No. It's not."

Bobby pursed his lips. "There were a lot of guys at the office hoping it would be them. Your breakup with your boyfriend made quite a stir around the water cooler. The fact that you were available I mean." Bobby grinned at her.

"I don't know whether to be flattered or insulted, that I was discussed like a baseball trading card that had just come up on the market."

"Flattered." Bobby nodded his head. "Look at it this way, if Natalie Wilson became available no one would even notice, much less talk about it."

"Natalie's a wonderful girl! But, I suppose your right. I should be flattered."

"So, who was it last night again? I forgot."

"I didn't tell you. I won't tell you."

Bobby shrugged his shoulders. "I'll find out soon enough."

They were stuck in crawling traffic nearing the site of the accident. With conversation stalled, Jennifer's thoughts returned to the previous night with Brad.

He had been such a gentleman, and easy to talk to. They seem a lot alike, Brad and her. I guess Brad was right about one thing, when either of them sees something they want they tend to work hard to get it.

One goal I'm setting for myself is to help him expose Richard Pierce. Doing that would help Brad, and would help me too. Brad really needs my help. Things look bad for him right now, even though he's innocent.

I don't see how he could even be charged with a crime like that. Anybody that gets to know Brad would know that he could never do anything like that. He would never hurt anyone. I've got to do what I can to make sure he's proved innocent.

Jennifer smiled to herself. Besides that, exposing corruption that big in this city could win me a Pulitzer Prize. Let's not forget that. That's about as big of a prize as it gets in the newspaper business. I could sure use one of those.

Jennifer's thoughts returned to the night before. She thought of how she and Brad <u>had</u> sat at her dining table drinking coffee and talking after dinner. She thought of the brief and tender kiss he had given her before he left. It was a perfect evening.

"This is as close as we're going to get, Jen." Bobby jerked the car off into the emergency lane and slammed it into park. "Wipe that grin off your face and grab your bag. Let's go."

John Cantrinni sat bolt upright in his chair in his office. "You did what?"

Brad shrugged. "I stole his financial records, his files. Richard Pierce's."

"Oh great. Not that theft matters much, what with the murder charges you're facing."

"Relax. He doesn't know I have them."

John relaxed somewhat in his chair. "Well, what do they say?"

"They say that the Mayor is getting hundreds of thousands of dollars in kickbacks from the construction companies doing work downtown. And that money is being laundered through a few strip joints and a bunch of dry cleaners throughout the city."

John whistled. "So this is what Renee bumped into that got her killed?"

"She may not have learned everything. She might have found out about only a part of it. There's no way to know exactly what she found out. But there was plenty that she could have learned that would have gotten her killed."

John nodded his head. "Unfortunately, this doesn't help your case as it stands."

"I know that. I'll get more. I'll get proof. I just

haven't figured out how yet. At least now I know what I'm looking for."

"Be careful, Brad. I don't have to remind you what happened to Renee."

"I'll be careful. Where's that form you said I need?"

"Yes. Here it is." John found a piece of paper from his desk. "Like I said, this is the form you'll need to get the blood test the DA is asking for. There is an address on the second page where you'll need to get it done, along with their hours."

"I'll take care of it." Brad took the paper and rose to leave. "Thanks John."

"Be careful, now. I mean it."

Brad left satisfied that his meeting with John had gone as well as it did. He was afraid John would put up a bigger fuss about what he was doing with regard to Richard Pierce. I guess he realizes my back is against the wall.

I'm glad he didn't ask me about the press. I wouldn't want to have to lie to him, but I wasn't in the mood for a lecture either. My seeing Jennifer can stay a secret for now, and that's good.

Brad chuckled to himself. Not only is it staying a secret good but also seeing Jennifer is definitely good.

In the elevator Brad took the paper out of his pocket and looked at it. Simple form. The address was downtown. He should be able to take care of that next week.

Brad walked back to his office with thoughts of the previous night on his mind and a spring in his step. What a wonderful evening. What a wonderful woman.

He hadn't had such a good time in the company of a woman in a long time.

Sitting at her dining table he'd discovered that they shared a lot of the same views on subjects as diverse as politics and movies. And she was so very beautiful. What a perfect evening.

I hope I didn't press things too fast by kissing her. Probably not. It wasn't that much of a kiss. I guess I'll find out in due time. Jennifer is the kind of woman where you find out real quick where you stand with her.

I probably should give her a call when I get back to the office. I wonder if I should send flowers? That might be a little much. I know, I'll ask her out again. If she yes, I'll send flowers.

Walking down the sidewalk, Brad felt the sun on his shoulders. It felt good. What a beautiful day. I don't feel like a man accused of murdering his wife.

Next to his building Brad noticed a Pyramid Cleaners van parked. He probably wouldn't have noticed it before he had seen Pierce's books, but now the van reminded him of the seriousness of his situation.

Brad took the elevator up and opened the door to his office. Rose was on the phone.

"Oh, he just walked in. Hold a minute please." Rose punched a button on the phone a replaced the receiver. She turned to Brad. "I'm sorry to bother you like this Mr. Marshall, but this man has been calling for you every fifteen minutes. He said his name is Mr. Smith, but he wouldn't state his business."

"That's alright, Rose. I'll take it in my office." Brad started moving toward his office.

"Also you had some dry cleaning delivered, along with those shoes you had repaired. I had them put in your closet."

Brad froze. He hadn't sent out any dry cleaning and he certainly hadn't had any shoes repaired! Mr. Smith! The Pyramid Cleaners van!

Brad turned back toward Rose's desk. "Rose, get up. We have to get out of here."

"What's the matter Mr. Marshall? What's the hurry?"

Brad grabbed Rose's arm with both hands and pulled her out of her chair. They both stumbled toward the door. Brad flung the door open and shoved them both into the hallway. They were only a few feet down the hall when the force of the blast lifted them off their feet.

CHAPTER **31**

Brad lifted his head and looked back in the direction of his office. Instead of an office door there was a huge gaping hole, through which he could see the side of the office building across the street. The hole was framed with jagged edges of steel and concrete. Bits of paper and debris were being whisked around in circles by the stiff breeze buffeting them in the hallway.

He looked down at Rose Abernathy lying beside him. "Rose, are you alright?"

Rose stirred. "Ouch. I think I hurt my wrist." She sat up with some difficulty. "Yes, my wrist hurts, but other than that I'm okay. How about you?"

"I'm fine, Rose. We were lucky to get out of there. The office is gone."

Rose looked back where they had been seconds before. "Oh my God. What happened? Was it a bomb?"

"Yes Rose. It was a bomb. It was meant for me."

"But who would do such a thing?"

"I have an idea. But that doesn't matter right now. What matters is that we're alright."

The sound of sirens reached them from below.

"Emergency vehicles are on their way. I hope no one was hurt." Brad said. "Can you get up? I'd like to move further away from that hole in the side of the building."

"I think I can."

Brad and Rose helped each other up on wobbly legs and moved down the hallway several feet. They stood leaning against each other, looking at the hole in the building that used to be their offices.

The sound of honking horns and sirens came up from the streets below. The wind continued to blow through the opening, adding to the mixture of sounds. Brad saw the silhouette of someone in the building across from them pointing through his own window at them and their damaged building.

"We're so very lucky to have gotten out of there." Rose said, looking up at Brad. "You knew. You dragged me out of there. How did you know there was a bomb?"

"I didn't send out any dry cleaning, Rose, and I didn't have any shoes repaired. Call it a sixth sense. I just knew that whoever made that delivery was trying to harm me."

"Well they would have if you hadn't gotten us out of there. You saved our lives."

"We got lucky, Rose. Is your wrist still hurting you?"

"Yes. It may be broken."

"I'm sure the emergency crews will be here any minute. Let's just wait for them."

Brad and Rose didn't have to wait long. Soon a team of firemen came trudging down the hallway to meet them.

"Are you folks alright?" the fireman in front asked.

"I'm okay. I think Ms. Abernathy here has hurt her

265

wrist." Brad answered.

The fireman stopped next to Rose and examined her arm. "If both of you can walk we need to get you out of here. The building may not be safe."

"Of course. I didn't think of that." Brad said.

The firemen led them down the stairs and out of the building onto the sidewalk. They were on the opposite side of the building from where their offices had been. A fire truck and ambulance were parked beside the building in the street. Rose was taken to the ambulance. A man in a suit with a radio in his hand approached Brad.

"I'm Fire Marshall Higgins. You were in the building when the explosion happened?"

"Yes. The explosion happened in my office. We had just gotten out." Brad answered.

"What is your name?" Higgins asked.

"Marshall. Bradley Marshall."

"Any idea what cause this?"

"I'm sure it was a bomb." Brad answered.

"Not one of yours I take it?"

"No." Brad shook his head. "Certainly not one of mine."

"Sorry. I had to ask. You say you had just gotten out. Did someone call and inform you that there was a bomb on the premises?"

"Not exactly." Brad looked up at the building he had just come from and wondered how much to tell the Fire Marshall. Not much for now, he thought. "We had a series of strange calls and a delivery that couldn't be explained. I had a strange feeling so I got us out just before the explosion. We just got lucky."

"You were very lucky. Who made the delivery you say couldn't be explained."

"A dry cleaners."

"A dry cleaners? Some extra laundry showed up and immediately you thought bomb?"

"I know it's a little hard to understand. Like I said, I just had a sixth sense that turned out to be right."

Higgins scowled at Brad. "You've had quite a shock. Why don't I give you a chance to calm down and think things over and we'll talk later."

"That sounds great. Was anyone hurt?"

"From the report I just got, it doesn't look like anyone was hurt seriously. The floor below the blast was empty, available for lease. The floor above was normally occupied but someone said they were out of town."

"I see. Thank God."

"Yeah. Is there anyone you know of that would want to hurt you?"

"I'm not sure I can think of anyone capable of something like this right now. I guess I'm still a little shaken though."

"Fair enough. Is there some way I can reach you?"

"Its seems my office and office phone are no more. Let me give you my cell phone number."

Higgins wrote down the number Brad gave him, handed him a business card and told Brad he would be in touch. He then disappeared into the building.

Brad looked around at the people gathering on the sidewalk. I wonder what it looks like on the other side? It's got to be a mess. He walked over to the ambulance where Rose was being treated.

"Are they getting you fixed up, Rose?"

"Yes, Mr. Marshall. They're about done putting a bandage on it and then they're taking me to get it x-rayed."

"Good. Do you need to have me follow you and give you a ride home?"

"That would be great of you, if it's not too much trouble. Also, do you have your cell phone on you? I need to call my daughter right away and tell her that I'm alright before she hears something on the news."

"Sure thing, Rose." Brad handed her his cell phone and stepped away to let her call her daughter. After a few moments she held the phone out to Brad.

"She's going to meet me at the hospital and pick me up after the x-rays. So I won't be needing that ride after all. Thanks for offering though."

"Sure thing, Rose."

"Oh, Mr. Marshall. Whatever are we going to do? All of our files and computers, all gone?"

"We didn't loose anything that can't be replaced. All of our files are backed up off site. We'll get new computers. It was about time we got new computers anyway."

Rose smiled. "I guess you're right. This just caught me a little off guard."

"You take a couple of days off. When you feel like it, start looking for new office space for us. This is just a minor setback, Rose. Alright?"

"Alright, Mr. Marshall. I hope they catch whoever did this."

"I'm sure they will. In the meantime, they haven't stopped us. We'll keep going."

Rose smiled and nodded, her chin suddenly firm. "Of course we will."

Brad left Rose and started walking down the sidewalk, picking his way over hoses and around emergency personnel. Someone, a fireman, motioned for him to get off the sidewalk, so he wandered into the street. Barricades had been set up at either end of the block. Policemen kept people away from the area. People crowded around the barricades, some pointing at Brad.

He continued to the corner and around the building to the other side. Again, the street had been cordoned off, with policemen securing the area. Emergency vehicles lined the street except for the area directly under where his office had been. There was surprisingly little debris in the street, mostly glass.

He looked up at the hole in the side of the building eight stories up. A shudder went through his body. A few seconds more and he would be as gone as what was there before the blast.

He moved over to the side of the building and sat down against the corner, his knees up, his face in his hands. Pierce is a madman, he thought. This isn't the end of it either. When he finds out that he missed me, he'll try again.

Brad looked up, the muscles in his neck growing tight. I have to find a way to stop him. This can't go on. Whatever time I thought I had to gather the evidence against him, this changes everything. Who knows what he might try next?

He struggled to his feet and took a few steps in the direction of the wreckage. He turned and walked back to the corner. Back and forth he paced, ten feet either way. His hands were clenched into fists and his mind reeled, struggling for a way to get at the man he knew was responsible for this.

Pacing back and forth on the sidewalk, plans and parts of plans were hatched and discarded. Each time Brad would get an idea he would find a flaw, shake his head in disgust, and start over. What about this? No. Can I do that? No. He shook his fists at the ground, at the air. He glanced up at the hole in the side of the building to remind himself of the seriousness of his challenge, and the evil of the man with which he had to deal.

Brad stopped suddenly and stared ahead through unfocused eyes. The answer, it seemed, was painfully clear. Richard Pierce would have to be confronted, man to man, mano a mano.

He stood for a moment, sweating and shivering despite the warm weather. Meeting Pierce seemed desperate and hopeless. He searched in his mind back over the other ideas he had explored for an alternative. He shook his head. Richard Pierce has to be confronted, and I'm the one to do it.

Brad returned to his pacing. His thoughts flew through his head like a swarm of bees, collecting only briefly on one point or another. He would need to get Pierce to admit to killing Renee. He would need to get him to admit to the bombing of his office. Could he do it? Did he have any choice? I'm going to need some help with this. I know I can count on Jack.

I do have some bait, some leverage to get him to talk to me. He doesn't know all that I know about his business. That can work in my favor. I can use that to get in to see him. I'll have to devise a way to deceive him into telling me everything.

This is going to require a lot more planning, but I don't see another way. I'll get Jack to help me with the planning. I'll need to have everything in order before I attempt this.

Brad looked up one more time at the chasm in the side of the building. He nodded at his own decision. Evil has to be faced head on, and it's time that this man is put out of business.

Brad turned and started back around the building. A calm flowed through him. His face was twisted into a grim smile. Apprehension was slowly being replaced with determination. Brad's jaw grew tight and his eyes narrow. His plans developing, his stride started to show purpose. Richard Pierce will be stopped and held accountable for his deeds.

CHAPTER **32**

Richard Pierce was in his office looking over the accounting on his computer screen when the phone rang.

"Yeah?" he asked.

"It's done."

"Are you sure you got him?"

"The secretary said he'd just walked in."

Richard hung up the phone and smiled. There was one less thorn in his side to worry about. Mr. Brad Marshall was in pieces about now. He laughed. It was his own damn fault, that Marshall. If he had been home waiting for his wife when he was supposed to be, he would have been taken care of then.

He got up from the desk and went to the window. The city looked more orderly to him, more as it should be. He couldn't keep the grin off of his face. Marshall had been an irritant for too long.

Only one thing to do, and that was celebrate. He retrieved his jacket from the back of his chair and after putting it on he checked himself in the mirror behind the closet door. Yes sir, he looked like a winner.

He took the elevators down to the parking garage and headed for the Lincoln. From the distance he heard emergency sirens. That must be the firemen rushing over to pick up the pieces of Marshall, he thought. It's too late to help him now. All the kings' horses and all the kings' men can't put Marshall back together again.

Arriving at the car, he slid into the leather seats. If he'd thought forward to what a special day it was going to be he'd have brought the Porsche. Oh well, we'll just have to make do.

Leaving the parking garage he went only two blocks before getting caught up in a traffic jam. This must be caused by Marshall's demise. Instead of being impatient and irritated I should savor it. What's the hurry anyway? It just turned into a beautiful day! Richard rolled down the windows and listened to the sirens. Sounds like heaven!

It only took about fifteen minutes for Richard to be clear of the traffic and headed south on the Southwest Freeway. Fifteen minutes more and he was taking the Hillcroft exit and parking at the Wichita Bar & Grill. This place was known mostly for its strippers.

A woman sat behind a counter at the entrance, surrounded by red walls and garish decor. "That will be ten dollars, please."

"The owner knows me real well," Richard said as he strode past the counter. Music with a pulsating beat reverberated from the walls. Immediately past the counter, Richard came upon Luke Trevor, the manager, and another man he didn't recognize.

"Hello Luke. How are ya?"

"Richard. Can't say as I'm glad to see you. There's no problem between us, business wise?"

"No, nothing like that. Everything's fine. Everything's more than fine. I just came by your fine establishment for a little celebration."

"Like I need that," Luke scowled. "Go easy on my

273

girls, Richard. The last one you got your hands on you marked up so's she couldn't work for four days."

"That bitch needed a lesson in showing respect."

"What she needed and got was a vacation after tangling with you. I mean it, man. Take it easy."

Richard smirked. "This old lover boy don't want it any other way." He turned and started walking toward the bar. Once there he ordered a Bacardi and coke and took in the sites grinding almost naked on the stage.

Nice, but a little too tall for my taste, he thought. He took his drink and found a booth near the stage. He took off his jacket and put it on the seat before he sat down. A waitress appeared from nowhere.

"I see you've already got a drink," she said.

"That's alright. Bring me another one. I'll be through with this one by the time you get back. Bacardi and coke." Richard took a huge sip of the drink as if to prove his point.

The waitress disappeared and Richard settled back to watch the show. Now there's one I could go for. Look at the ass on that chick. I don't think I've had her before, or have I? Richard's face grew into a smirk. Sometimes it was hard to keep track.

I need to remember to turn on the news later and shed a tear for the loss of my good buddy Marshall. I guess I actually did him a favor. I saved him from getting convicted of murder. Not that I expect to get a thank you card. He laughed.

Richard turned his attention back to the female flesh writhing on the stage. One of these lucky ladies performing this afternoon would be taken later to be introduced to club Richard. He laughed again. Good drinks and entertainment, business is good, problems blown to bits, and sweet looking pussy to be had. Could life get any better?

Richard's cell phone rang. "Yeah?"

"Looks like we missed him."

"I thought you said he was there," Richard spat into the phone.

"I thought he was. But he and the secretary got out just before it went off. Don't ask me how."

The connection went dead. Richard sat for a second and then threw back his head and roared. "No! God Dammit! No!"

The dancer on the stage stopped and looked at him, along with everyone else in the room. Richard sat straining; the blood vessels in his neck were about to burst. He slammed his fist down on the table in front of him.

This is a mess. How could I have been so reckless? Richard pounded at his temples. What was I even thinking? I shouldn't have been so splashy about it. I should have just had him shot. Quick and easy. Now there will be a big investigation of the bombing and for what? For nothing. Marshall is still walking around town causing me heartburn. Well, I'm not going to make that mistake again. Next time will be simple and quiet, with no fuss.

His mouth twisted into a grimace. He barely formed words between his clenched teeth. "You may have gotten away this time, you sonofabitch, but I'll put you in hell, and soon. I don't loose. Next time you're due to die I'll see to it personally."

Brad left the block where his office building was located and headed west on foot. He wanted to get somewhere he could sit and clear his head. He didn't have a clear destination in mind, but it didn't matter. The walk seemed to help. Getting some distance between himself and the bombed out office also helped.

His cell phone rang. He fished it out of his jacket pocket.

"Brad, it's Jennifer. Are you alright?"

"Jennifer. I guess you heard. Yeah, I'm fine. As far as I know no one was seriously hurt. Rose might have a broken wrist."

"Where are you?"

"I'm just walking. I needed to get away from the office, from where the office used to be."

"Can you meet me somewhere?"

"I suppose I can. Sure, I'd like to see you. I'm headed west, what's west? Tranquility Park. I'll meet you in Tranquility Park."

"I'll be right there."

Brad replaced his phone and smiled. It would be good to see Jennifer, a bright spot in a day that hadn't gone very well so far. He continued to walk along the sidewalk.

A pigeon flew down and examined the sidewalk in front of him. He smiled. He had come so close to never seeing a pigeon again. Never had he been so glad to see a bothersome piece of nature in all of his life.

He looked at the faces of the people as he passed them on the sidewalk. He smiled and nodded at some. They didn't realize, he thought, how easily life can be taken from you. They walked along the sidewalk without much appreciation for the fact that they are here to walk along the sidewalk. It was only blind luck that he was here to smile and nod at them. Renee had not been so lucky.

The dark cloud of Pierce hung in the back of Brad's mind, but he refused to let it dampen his mood. He would overcome Pierce. This was a fight he would win, that he had to win.

Soon he found himself at the edges of Tranquility Park where Smith Street met Rusk. He looked around for Jennifer. She wasn't in sight; she probably wasn't there yet.

Over to his left a series of stately plaques memorialized the park's existence. He scanned the words 'Houston, Tranquility Base here. The Eagle has landed.' and nodded in understanding.

He stepped along the warm brick path and veered to the right to the take a seat on a bench. In front of him the left fork of the path went down three steps and continued in front of him between two reflecting pools shimmering with silver ripples in the sun.

To his right two sturdy metal cylinders stood at the edges of the pools with water cascading down their sides.

Further to the right was a plaza, with more of the sturdy tubes standing on an intricate mosaic of brick pads and surrounded by an inviting bridge.

He looked around at the trees and paths of the park as if he were seeing them for the first time. He listened to the sounds of the traffic nearby, and the occasional squawk of a bird, located nearby in the park.

He leaned back on the bench and crossed his legs. There would be time, time to take care of Richard Pierce. Time to avenge the wrong he did to Renee. Right now was not the time. Right now he needed rest and recovery. Right now he just needed to enjoy the fact that he was still alive.

He looked around and saw Jennifer whisking up the path toward him. She looked as if she were almost running. Brad stood up and Jennifer came right up to him and wrapped her arms around him.

"Brad, I'm so glad you're alright, that you're not hurt or worse."

Brad stood there for a moment a bit awkwardly, then returned the hug, putting his arms around Jennifer. A smile crept across his face. She felt good in his arms.

Jennifer pulled back. "What happened? Were you in the office when the explosion happened? What do they think caused it?"

Brad motioned to the bench. "Let's sit down and I'll answer as many of your questions as I can."

They sat next to each other on the bench. Jennifer looked worried.

"Right after I got to the office Rose told me that some dry cleaning had been delivered with some shoes that had been repaired. I hadn't sent any out. She also told me that a Mr. Smith had been calling every fifteen minutes for me, and that he was on the phone. I heard her tell him that I had just walked in. I put two and two together and got us out just before the explosion."

"So it was a bomb? But who would do such a thing?"

Brad's eyebrows rose. "We both know who. But

you can't write that Jennifer. I told the Fire Marshall I didn't have any idea who did it and I don't want Pierce knowing that I'm on to him just yet."

Jennifer wrinkled up her nose. "You're sure it's Pierce?"

"I might have had some question about it except for the dry cleaning. Also I saw a dry cleaning van parked beside the building when I went in. No doubt that's where they were when they set it off."

"Brad, you've got to be careful. When he finds out he didn't get you he might try again."

Brad smiled at Jennifer. "Don't worry. Outside of the office I'm not that easy to find. No one knows where I'm staying."

"I thought I'd loose my mind when I heard that there was an explosion at your office. I was sure something had happened to you. I'm so glad you're alright." Jennifer hugged Bradley again.

"Jennifer, what's going to happen with us?"

Jennifer looked up at Brad. "What do you mean?"

"I care for you a lot. I like you. I like spending time with you."

Jennifer smiled. "I like you too, Brad."

"Right now I have to deal with Pierce. But after I get through with that, maybe we could take a trip. Have you ever been to Europe?"

"Whoa. Europe? I don't know. That's a pretty big step, don't you think?"

"That bomb really woke me up to the fact that we're living life now, without much control over how much we have left. I'd like to enjoy it while I can. I know it's a big thing to spring on you, but give it some thought.

As soon as I finish up with Pierce I'd like to go away for a while, and I'd like to take you with me."

"This would be a big step. We barely know each other."

"I know. But I find you irresistible." Brad took Jennifer's hand in his. "I'm not even sure what I can offer in the way of a relationship. I guess when Renee was killed I still loved her. I suppose all I could offer you would be a leftover heart."

Jennifer nodded her head, and then shook it. "I don't know Brad. I'd like to, but I have a career to think about. I can't just up and leave. At least I don't think I can. I'll think about it, alright? That's the best I can do for now."

Brad smiled and sat back. "That's good enough. There's plenty of time to think about it."

"So what are you going to do about Richard Pierce?"

Brad grimaced. "I can't tell you yet. I don't have all of the details worked out. But one thing is clear: I can't just ignore this. He has to be stopped before more innocent people get hurt or killed."

"Promise me you won't do anything dangerous. My heart can't take any more bombs or worrying if you've been killed."

Brad looked her in the eyes and lied. "Nothing dangerous. I promise."

Sitting together on the bench, Brad felt a warmth erasing the tension of the previous events at his office. This was how it should be. Her companionship gave purpose to his very being on the bench. Life is too short to endure it alone.

CHAPTER **33**

Jack got out of his pickup at the Red Lion Bar & Grill Thursday afternoon and, out of habit, checked to make sure that he had remembered to lock his truck. Turning toward the bar he was approached by two large men walking briskly.

"Hey buddy. Do you know how we can get to the Galleria?" one of the men asked.

"Sure." Jack turned and motioned over his right shoulder. "You go a couple three blocks that way to Westheimer...."

A blow to the back of his neck sent Jack sprawling in the asphalt in front of him. He received two quick kicks to the ribs and felt something crack before he had a chance to respond. Struggling to get back to his feet he felt someone grab him from behind and help him up, holding him with his arms pinned behind him.

The face of one of the men leered closely to his own. "You need to stop asking questions about important people."

Jack felt a blow to his midsection that knocked the air out. Struggling to breathe, the man was back in his face. "You understand me?"

Jack nodded. He felt something cold and hard that he took to be a gun barrel against his cheek.

"Tell me that you understand me."

"I understand you," Jack managed to say, gasping for breath.

"Make sure that you do," the man said.

Jack felt a blow to the side of his face. He was released from the back and he went down to his hands and knees, his head down. Instinctively he kept his head down to allow the thugs to leave. He didn't want any more argument with either of them.

Jack raised his head. They were gone. He struggled to his feet and felt the side of his face where he had been hit. His hand came away wet and he confirmed that he was bleeding from the corner of his mouth.

He took a deep breath. Ouch. He grabbed his left side. Probably a broken rib or two. Well it wasn't the first time. I'm getting old enough though, at some point we hope it's going to be the last. Jack shook the cobwebs from his head and started for the door of the bar. His feet obeyed him, if barely.

Entering the bar he kept his head down and went straight through the bar to the men's room. There he started some water flowing and looked in the mirror. Not bad. I'm not pretty, but then I never was. He got a paper towel, wet it, and applied it to the cut at the corner of his mouth. The cheek above it was badly bruised and tender.

He looked down at his clothes. They were dusty. With one hand holding the paper towel, he used the other one to try to knock the dirt off of his knees. That will have to do.

He looked at himself in the mirror. I should have seen this coming. Not just when those men walked up, but I should have been looking for them. I should have seen this coming days ago.

He shook his head. Next time I'll be smarter. How many times have I told myself that? He chuckled. Ouch, that hurt. I need to lay off of the laughter for a couple of days.

He went back out to the bar and took a stool. "Give me a beer, Rusty." Jack looked down and continued to hold the paper towel against his face.

Rusty poured a draft beer and put the mug in front of Jack. "You look a little put upon. What happened, Jack?"

"Funniest thing. I ran into a stray door in your parking lot."

Rusty nodded. "Just one? I wouldn't figure that a single door could get the better of you."

"Actually it was two doors. You know how they like to travel in pairs."

"You weren't robbed were you?"

"No. They didn't want money."

"Want me to call someone? Police?"

"Naw. What are they going to do? Ain't no law against being as dumb as a door."

"Still, I don't like my customers being threatened."

"Did I say I was threatened? I just ran across some swinging doors and didn't have sense enough to step out of the way. Really Rusty, everything is fine."

Rusty shook his head and left Jack to his beer, which he raised to his lips. The cold wet liquid felt good at his mouth. He tried to smile. That didn't hurt too bad.

Jack gave some thought to what had just happened.

Did it change anything? No, not that he could see. He wasn't about to be scared off from helping his friend just because a couple of goons came around to visit.

If anything, it was a lucky thing they came by. It was a reminder Mr. Pierce plays for keeps. We need to be careful. From now on, I don't step out into the parking lot when big ugly guys are hanging around like they're looking for someone. This could have been a lot worse. If Pierce knew what all we have on him it would have been a lot worse. It's a good thing they showed up to remind us how delicate this situation is.

Jack sat nursing his beer and the corner of his mouth. Whatever we do from here, we'd better be careful.

A middle aged portly woman sat down on the stool next to him. "Hi Jack."

"Hello Judy." Jack nodded to her.

"You look like you got roughed up."

"I just fell down."

"Where did you do this falling down?"

"Right out there in the parking lot. Stupid of me."

Judy nodded. "If you say so. But it seems to me a big healthy man like you would need some help falling down. A couple of big guys poked their noses in here just before you showed up. You didn't happen to run into them out there did you?"

"Big guys? Oh yeah. They wanted directions to the Galleria. They probably want to get an early start on their Christmas shopping." Jack replied. He took a long drink from his beer.

"Yeah. They looked like early shoppers to me. They were looking for something. I didn't stop to think that it might be a mall. Hey, if I buy you a beer will you tell me the real story?"

"If you buy me a beer, I'll tell you a story. I don't make any promises about how real it will be."

Judy emitted a deep rolling laugh and slapped the bar. "Good enough. I see they didn't damage your spirit any. Rusty, we'll have another round here."

Brad drove to the Red Lion thinking about his decision to confront Richard Pierce face to face. He needed some help with the planning of it. This would not be a time for mistakes. Jack had experience in planning operations that dealt with the criminal element. He should be of some help, besides being a second mind off which to bounce ideas.

Brad strode into the bar and saw Jack sitting on a stool. Approaching him, he noticed Jack seemed to be laughing at something with Judy, sitting next to him.

"Jack, I need to talk to you."

"Alright partner. Let's find a booth."

Judy chimed in. "Jack, if young Brad here starts getting rough with you, give us a holler. Maybe between the both of us we can take him. One lickin' a day is all a fellow ought to have to endure."

Jack chuckled. "Will do, Judy. Will do." He moved off his stool and motioned for Brad to follow him. He wandered over to a booth and sat down with Brad close behind.

"What was that all about?" Brad looked up at Jack's face for the first time. "Damn. What happened to you?"

"Aw hell, I've already told the story so many ways I can't remember which one is the truth. It's nothing." Jack held a paper towel up to the side of his face, partially obscuring the damage.

Brad shook his head. "It doesn't look like nothing. Does this have anything to do with our friend in high places?"

"The terminology they used was 'important people'."

Brad nodded. "I got a little message delivered from them myself today. My office is gone."

Jack dropped his hand, his eyes wide. "What do you mean it's gone?"

"I mean as in blown up. Destroyed. Rose and I barely got out of there before the blast took out the whole office."

Jack whistled. "Looks like the stakes got raised a bit. That guy is a madman."

Brad leaned back. "That's the way I see it. I can't sit by and let this sort of thing continue."

Jack's eyebrows went up. "All of the sudden I'm not real comfortable where it looks like this conversation is headed. What do you have in mind?"

"I think I need to confront Mr. Richard Pierce, face to face."

Jack leaned back and studied Brad's face. "You have lost your mind. That man will kill you and dispose of you in the nearest dumpster."

"Not if I play it right. Not if I don't give him any reason to kill me. Not if I give him reasons he thinks he shouldn't kill me."

"You think you can do that? Tell me. I'm listening."

286

"What does he want most? Why did he kill Renee, and why is he coming after us? It's to protect his organization, right? To keep it secret and functional."

Jack nodded. "That's the name of his game, sure."

"I show him the records I got from his computer. I tell him my attorney has a copy and if anything happens to me he'll take them to the cops and to the press."

"We're not having any luck getting the cops or the press interested in those records."

"Right. But he doesn't know that. He would be terrified of those records being spread around town," Brad said.

"Alright. Suppose he doesn't kill you. What do you tell him you want from him? Why does he think you're coming to him at all instead of just going to the police and the press?"

"I'll tell him that I just want to be left alone. That I don't care what he does, that I don't have any interest at all in his politics or what happens downtown. That's his business, not mine. That I just want my life back the way it was, and for him to call off the DA."

"Won't he assume you're a little irritated that he killed your wife?"

"That's easily explained. We were getting divorced. I'll tell him he did me a favor."

Jack looked at him quizzically. "Is that all you want to get from him, to be left alone?"

"Of course not. I want him to admit that he killed Renee, and for that matter that he bombed my office. Mainly that he killed Renee. If I can get him to tell me where her jewelry is that would be perfect."

"Suppose he tells you that. It's your word

against his."

"I'll record it."

Jack slapped at the table. "Here we go again. That boy is gonna kill you. You walk in there set up to record the conversation and he's bound to swat you like a gnat."

"Not if I do it right. I'll need your help. These days you can get transmitters that look like a pen, for instance. They're very discreet; they can't be detected. You'll be nearby recording what's said between us. That is if I can count on you."

Jack sat for a second, rubbing his chin. "Oh, you can count on me. You can count on me to sit down there and record you being shot, and I'll even hang around and record the sound of your body being thrown in the dumpster."

Brad threw up his hands. "Do you have a better idea?"

"No I don't, and that pisses me off."

"Are you saying that it won't work?"

"No, I'm not saying that either. It might work. As a first pass at a plan it's not bad. A lot of details still need to be worked out. You need to be prepared for every contingency. But the overall framework, you might be able to get away with it."

"I've been racking my brain and I don't see that I have a lot of choice. I can't just sit around and wait for them to build another bomb, or decide to use a sniper next time. Richard Pierce has put a target on my back. I've got to respond."

"One thing that bothers me is he'll want to know why you haven't just taken those records to the cops and to the press already. What do you tell him?"

"I tell him that doing that doesn't help my murder case. That I need his help there. I need him to call off the DA. The records get exposed only if something happens to me, or he doesn't help me with the murder case against me. I'll tell him that I know it was him that set me up there in the first place."

"This is looking better all of the time. Still, I wish we had better luck getting some interest paid to those records. But then we could sit around wishing all day until one or both of us wind up dead because of this gangster."

"Exactly. And that's not my style."

Jack paused. "I suppose you want my help with the surveillance gear?"

Brad's mouth turned into a half grin. "Well, you do have more experience with that sort of thing, don't you?"

Jack snorted. "Barely. But I know where to go to tap into all of the experience we need. Alright. Let me take care of that. Right now lets got over this plan and flesh it out into something where you walk out of this little operation alive."

Brad nodded. "That is the primary objective."

"Primary objective. Yeah. And a damn good idea."

CHAPTER **34**

Jennifer pushed back from her computer Friday morning and sat staring at the screen. What was supposed to be in front of her was the beginning of a follow up piece on the explosion at Brad's office. What was there was a single sentence that she had rewritten seven times, and she still wasn't happy with it.

She couldn't get her mind off her conversation with Brad the day before. It had kept her up half of the night and now was getting in the way of her work. Maybe if she wrote a second sentence and came back to the first one later?

Going away with Brad would be a huge step. I don't have the vacation to do that. I'd have to quit my job. But would that be so bad? I'm getting tired of this anyway. How often does a girl get a chance to go away with someone like Brad? Jennifer shook her head. I don't know what I should do.

She imagined herself with Brad walking hand in hand on the streets of Paris, under the shadow of the Eiffel Tower. Paris, the City of Light. They would have coffee together, laugh and talk about life. She smiled at the image playing in her head.

Or they would be together in Venice. That would be something like a dream, floating along the canals of Venice together in a gondola. She imagined Brad's arm around her as they drifted along, her head on his shoulder. The images were too pure and fantastic. Where else might they go, what else might they see and do in Europe together? Castles? The Alps?

The smile left Jennifer's face for a moment. What if it doesn't work out? What then? Jennifer shook her head. That's silly. We would be happy together, I'm sure of that. Just him and me, traveling Europe, together. Sounds perfect. Let's see, I could travel Europe with a wonderful guy, or I could sit here and pound out copy for the local rag. Such a hard decision!

Jennifer hid the fact that she was sitting grinning at her own thoughts with her hand over her mouth. Brad is so sweet to have asked me, I can't believe it. Her smile vanished when she looked again at the computer screen and was reminded of the bomb yesterday. Someone is trying to kill him, and it must be Richard Pierce. Brad didn't mention his name, but he's right. We both know who wants to kill him. I wouldn't have believed Richard Pierce would do such a stupid thing, would risk everything to kill Brad that way. He must be crazy. What if he tries again?

Brad better be careful. I know he will be but it's just scary, knowing that someone is trying to kill him. I don't know what I'd do if something happened to Brad. I probably should call him a little later and make sure he's alright. I wonder if he'll think I'm silly for doing that? Too bad. I'm calling him right after I finish this article.

Jennifer threw herself into the follow up article and forced words onto the screen. For the next half of an hour she worked and then sat back and looked over what she had written. She frowned. It wasn't her best work, but it would do.

She submitted the article and then reached for her phone. No, I'm not going to call him just yet. I'm going to wait a little while. I'll call later in the day. It won't seem so silly then.

Jerry appeared at her cubicle and sat down in her visitor's chair. "Hi Jen. What are you up to?"

"I'm trying to decide what to do with my life."

"Oh good. A weighty issue where I might have an opinion. If you were trying to decide on a nail polish color I'd be of no help."

"So what is your opinion?"

"I think you should cure world hunger." Jerry nodded.

"I'm talking about in the next few weeks."

"Oh. In a hurry, are we?"

"I've received an invitation to travel, in Europe."

"That's a real dilemma. I hear Europe is scary this time of year."

"Real funny. I'd have to quit my job. I don't have that kind of vacation."

"I take it this invite came from a fella?"

"It did."

"Do you like the fella?"

"I do."

"You must care about him a lot if you're thinking about quitting your job to go off traveling with him. I'd say forget about the job. You can always find a job. Finding a special fella isn't always so easy."

Jennifer smiled. "That was the way I was leaning. Thanks Jerry."

"One other thing. I wouldn't burn any bridges here if I were you."

"I wasn't thinking of doing anything like that."

"What I mean is, this paper likes your work. They may buy freelance stuff from you regardless of where you're writing from."

"I didn't think of that. It would be great if I could continue to write."

"They don't do it often, but it's not unheard of. It's probably worth talking to them about it, before you just up and quit. That is if you'd be interested in something like that."

"I would. Thanks again, Jerry."

"Don't leave without saying goodbye."

"I'm not leaving yet. There are still some things that have to be cleared up here first. It may be months." Jennifer sighed. "I've got to say though, you've gotten me even more excited about the idea. Even if I didn't write for this paper, I wouldn't have to stop writing. Heck, I might even start a novel." Jennifer beamed her excitement.

Jerry threw up his hands. "You've gotten me excited about the idea. I don't suppose the two of you could use a valet? I work cheap."

"I don't think so. This trip would be just the two of us."

"Yeah. I was afraid of that." Jerry formed his mouth into a pout. "Later." He got up from the chair and disappeared around the corner.

Brad entered his hotel room that same Friday

morning, back from his workout at the gym. Without an office he thought he might work on his novel there in the hotel room. There wasn't any other business. His servers were gone and with it any email that might be floating around out there on the Internet looking for him or his office.

He needed to wait to hear from Jack before his business with Richard Pierce could move forward. He didn't mind the wait. Making the decision to confront Pierce caused a lot of the anxiety over the situation to magically disappear.

He had just set up his laptop when his cell phone rang. He didn't recognize the number.

"Hello?"

"Mr. Marshall? This is Rose."

"Rose, how are you doing? Did they get your arm fixed up yesterday?"

"Yes. It wasn't broken, just a bad sprain. I have a bandage on it. It should be good as new very soon."

"I'm glad to hear that, Rose."

"I took the liberty of calling a realtor, Mr. Marshall. I thought you might want to get started right away on deciding on some new office space."

Brad chuckled. "This is quick. Nothing stops you, Rose. I'll bet you called them from the hospital yesterday didn't you?"

"Well I.... is that alright?"

"Sure. I don't mind."

"I set up a meeting for ten o'clock this morning, if you can make it. The lady said she had a couple of places you might be interested in."

Brad looked at his watch. It was only nine. "That's

fine, Rose. What's her name and where am I suppose to meet her?"

Brad took down the information. "Thanks Rose. You're on top of things as usual. I'll get back to you with what I decide."

Brad shook his head. Nothing stops that woman. He closed the laptop. No point in getting involved in his novel with so little time before he should leave.

He looked around the room and his eyes fell on the Houston Chronicle lying on the bed. I wonder what Jennifer is doing right now? He imagined her sitting at her computer, her cute face twisted into a scowl as she searched for the right words to put in the article she was writing. He smiled.

I wonder if I should call her? No, I don't want to look like an impatient schoolboy. Flowers, now that might work. Couldn't hurt. He opened his laptop back up and used it to get the address of the Houston Chronicle. Then he visited another website and ordered roses to be delivered at the Houston Chronicle address for a Ms. Jennifer Hart. He typed out 'Thinking of you. Brad' for the card, gave them his credit card information and he was done.

He leaned back in his chair with his hands behind his head looking at the confirmation screen for his order. Bradley, sometimes you're a thoughtful devil. He closed his laptop back up for a second time.

He looked at his watch and decided it wasn't too early to start downtown for his meeting with the realtor. Walking to his car, he tried to imagine the look on Jennifer's face when the roses arrived. He wondered how long it would take for them to be delivered.

Probably not long. Early this afternoon is a good guess.

He managed to find a parking place on the street next to the address that Rose had given him and went inside. He was supposed to meet a Ms. Baxter on the tenth floor. He took the elevator up and got out to find a woman standing there to one side of the elevators looking as if she were waiting on someone.

"Ms. Baxter?"

"Yes. You must be Mr. Marshall."

"I am. Nice to meet you."

She turned and put keys in the locks of the doors behind her. "The first place I wanted to show you is right here. It was previously occupied by two attorneys. Of course if the layout doesn't suit you you're free to have it redone."

She opened the doors and entered the offices with Brad behind her. Brad wandered around the elegant but empty office space while the agent prattled on about square footage and lease terms and the like. There was plenty of light. There was room for Brad and Rose and the servers.

He found the electrical room and checked the panels to make sure that they would handle the load and there seemed to be communication access. The latter would probably have to be increased for his commercial Internet connection.

Brad went back into the room that would be his office. He imagined his desk. Yes, this would work. He stood at the window and looked out at the beautiful sunshine of the day. It put a smile on his face.

He walked to the door and turned around to look at the room once more. There was something about it.

The way the sun came in the window. The window faced south, the same as his bay window in the living room of his home. The sun gleaming through reminded him that he'd not been back to his house in a long time.

He stood there looking at the sun through the window. A memory came to him and he saw Renee standing in the sunlight by the living room window, smiling at him. He shivered, and shook his head to clear the image. I need to go back to the house. The last thing I need is to start getting visits from ghosts. I need to keep them buried. It's time I went back where Renee died.

He found the agent near the front of the office, looking like she was trying not to look impatient. "This looks fine Ms. Baxter. Tell Rose I'm satisfied with this."

"Don't you want to see the other place?"

"Oh, I don't know. Is it as nice as this?"

"Well, no. It's not quite as nice, but it's more affordable."

"I assumed you would show me the best of the two first. This will do. Get with Rose, she's empowered to handle the details."

Ms. Baxter held out her hand with a smile on her face. "Very well. Nice doing business with you, Mr. Marshall."

Brad shook her hand. "Likewise."

Brad left the tenth floor and started for his car. Now to visit his old house, and see what ghosts may have to say.

CHAPTER **35**

Richard pulled into the circular drive of his father's palatial estate Friday afternoon. He had called for his father at his office and been told he was at home. His father was planning a party that evening, and no doubt was seeing to some of the arrangements.

Richard entered the house and called out to his father. "Dad!" No answer. He went through the house and stepped through the patio doors to the deck overlooking the pool. "Dad?"

"Over here, Son," his father answered. His father was standing beside a line of tables being covered with tablecloths. "We thought we'd set up the buffet here. What do you think?"

"That's fine, Dad. You worry too much about little details, not just like this, but in business too. Where's Clara? Why isn't she handling this?"

"She was here earlier. She's getting her hair done. It was her idea to put the buffet here, actually."

"This is fine. Don't worry about it." Richard said.

"Yeah. I wished I could have had this little shindig tomorrow. But people are so busy on the weekends this time of year."

"Tonight's fine, Dad. You've had parties on Friday nights before."

"I know. Everybody says they'll be here. You're

coming, right?"

"Sure, Dad. I'll be here."

"Good. There should be a lot of nice girls here for you to talk to. Clara has seen to that."

Richard wrinkled his face. "Geeze, you know I don't need any help there."

"That's Clara's doing, not mine. Getting you hitched is starting to look like some sort of mission she's on."

"With all due respect, and I like Clara a lot, Dad, I don't want her getting too involved in my personal life."

"I know. But I can't stop her from inviting cute young things to the party for you to talk to," Leonard chuckled. "I wouldn't stop her from inviting cute young things anyway. They do dress up the place real nice."

Richard raised an eyebrow. "Yeah. Don't let Clara catch you saying that, or admiring those women she invited for my benefit."

"Not a chance. Hey, what do you know about that bomb downtown yesterday?" The Mayor looked up at Richard.

"I don't know nothing about it. Why would I?"

"Oh I don't know. I just thought maybe you'd heard something, something on the street."

"No, I haven't heard a thing."

"I wished I knew who it was, bombing our city. I'd have 'em fried in oil. I hope they catch the bastards."

Richard swallowed hard. "I'm sure they will."

"You know who I think it was?"

"No Dad, who?"

"Terrorists. New York and Washington get all of

the attention, but we're on the terrorists' list too, you know. We supply a fourth of the nation's energy. It's a wonder they didn't hit one of our refineries."

Richard stood with his hands in his pockets and nodded at his father. "Yeah. It's a wonder."

"Well, whoever did it, I just hope they catch 'em so I can have the pleasure of seeing them hang. Maybe we'll bring back public hangings."

"You know, it might not have been terrorists. Wasn't it the office of that Marshall fellow that got bombed? The guy whose wife was killed? Maybe someone is trying to take out the whole family. Maybe they were into drugs or something."

"I didn't think of that. So that's what you're hearing, that it's some kind of drug thing?"

"I'm not hearing anything. I'm just thinking out loud here. I read that it was his office that got bombed and that his wife had been killed. He's been charged with her murder. Maybe it was someone that was getting him back for killing her? I don't know," Richard shrugged.

"Messy business. If it's not terrorists then obviously that Marshall fellow has gotten mixed up in some messy business, what with people sending him bombs."

"I agree." Richard said. "I think if it was terrorists, they'd hit a refinery or chemical plant like you said. This seems personal to me, like Marshall got himself mixed up in something ugly. He is going on trial for murder you know."

The Mayor nodded. "You're probably right. I'll call a few people Monday about this bomb and remind them that Marshall isn't too lily white. Who knows, maybe he planted the bomb himself just to get potential jurors to have sympathy for him. He wasn't hurt you know. Got out just in time. Doesn't that sound fishy to you?"

"Sure does. Sounds real fishy."

The Mayor raised one hand and shook his fist in the air. "Whoever did this, I want 'em found and staked out naked in a fire ant bed. I can't have bombs going off in my city, no sir. One thing I can't have is bombs going off. It's bad for business."

"I hear you, Dad. Well I just dropped by to see if you needed any help. Do you need me to do anything?"

"No. Everything is taken care of, I think. The caterers are setting up here, and the pool guy is supposed to come by and give it a last minute check this afternoon. I wish he would go ahead and show up. The liquor has already been delivered. The band should be here in a couple hours to set up."

"I'll see you later, then."

"Okay, yeah. See you later, Son."

Richard left his father and went back through the house toward his car. Damn, Dad was sure mad about that bomb. I've never seen him so worked up about anything, except maybe an election.

That bomb was stupid of me. Reckless! I should have picked something quieter. Well, what's done is done. There's no way they'll trace it back to me. No one even knows I'm out to get Marshall. He'll be dead before anyone has a chance to put the two of us together. I just have to figure out how, and this time, quietly. This next time, I'll choose my method carefully.

The first thing Brad noticed when he pulled up to his house that Friday afternoon was that the yard had been mowed recently. Carlos must believe in his innocence, at least to the extent that he believed he would eventually get paid for continuing to care for the yard.

Brad sat for a moment staring at the front of the house. There was no real reason to hesitate; yet he did. Ghosts, after all, do exist in our minds. He opened the door to the car. He had come here to visit the house. It was time to do that.

Brad eased up the walkway looking at the bricks and windows that he used to call home. The house looked asleep, as if it were taking a nap this afternoon.

He opened the door with the familiar creak and let it swing wide. His gaze sought out the space on the floor where Renee had fallen to die.

Only a small stain, barely visible, remained. Jack was right. Tina had done an excellent job of cleaning up. His jaw drew tight. No one should be put through that.

He entered the house and went to the window in the front of the living room. He drew open the blinds, letting sunlight pour into the room. Looking back at the stain on the floor, it was even less visible than before.

He imagined Renee lying there as he saw her the last time he was in the house. A shiver ran through his body as he saw the marks on her back where the bullets had entered her, and the pool of blood around her. He shook his head. There was no reason to go there. I'll take care of the man responsible for your death very soon, very soon now, Renee.

He walked into the kitchen, almost on reflex, and looked into the refrigerator. Nothing growing in there. Again, Tina had been taking good care of the place. He looked around the kitchen. Everything was remarkably in order. It seemed he could move back in, if he was ready.

He went upstairs, first to the guest bedroom. Nothing had changed in there. Then he opened the door to the master bedroom. He stood for a moment looking at the bed that he had shared with Renee.

When Renee had left he had been hurt and angry with her, and had slept in that bed as an act of defiance. He did it to prove that he didn't need her. Now, that was no longer necessary. Now the bed looked to him like a reminder of the love they shared over the good times. The bed would have to go.

Brad closed the door to the bedroom and went back downstairs. He sat down on the sofa and looked at the sun coming in through the window.

Could I move back here? Yes, I suppose I could. Do I want to? Brad put his head down on his knees in the palms of his hands. I don't know.

Memory fragments of life with Renee and their daughter in the house played through his mind. He saw them both, laughing and happy. He saw his daughter as she got ill, and Renee's tears. He raised his head up to try to stop the visions, and when that didn't work, shook his head and tried to focus on the upcoming task with Richard Pierce.

Brad smiled. I should have had the courage and

foresight to take Pierce head-on right away. I suppose I didn't have all of the material I needed until recently, though. It's going to be a sweet piece of work to put that ugly monster away for what he did to Renee.

Brad checked his cell phone battery. Jack should be making the surveillance arrangements. I need to be patient. When Jack gets the equipment, I'll get with him and we'll be ready to move.

Brad looked over at the small stain, all that was left of Renee's blood on the floor. He shook his head. I'll get him for you, Renee, I promise.

He got up and moved with a purposeful stride to the front door. With a quick glance over his shoulder, he left the house.

CHAPTER **36**

Jack entered the small shop and looked around. Shelves were filled with small electronic appliances, and at the back of the store a round man with black glasses stood behind a glass case.

Above the man a thirteen-inch television set displayed a skewed picture of Jack standing in the middle of the store.

"Can I help you with something?" the man asked.

"I'm sure you can. I need some equipment."

"Surveillance gear?"

"Right."

"Overt or clandestine?"

"Uh, clandestine."

"I see. We sell that stuff only for entertainment purposes you understand. Not for anything illegal."

Jack approached the counter. "Yeah, right. I don't want to cause you any trouble, I just want to help keep my buddy alive."

The man studied Jack for a moment. "The name is Gary. Gary Mason."

Jack took his hand in a firm handshake. "Jack Wilkerson."

"You're Marine."

Jack grinned. "I was in the Corps once. Does it

show?"

"The way you carry yourself, the way you talk. I notice details."

Jack nodded. "I noticed you taking my picture. I don't see a camera."

"You won't. It's in my glasses."

Jack's chin dropped. "You mean you have a little bitty television camera in your glasses there?"

"Yeah." Gary took the glasses off and held them out to Jack. "They aren't real glasses."

Jack took the glasses and looked them over. On the front he could see a small dot he took to be the lens. "This is incredible."

"So, you say your friend is going someplace dangerous and you want to keep an eye on him?"

"Well, yeah. Eyes or ears. I didn't realize until now just how easily it might be to actually keep an eye on him."

"We have all sorts of cameras like this, tie tacks, pins. And some for sound too, of course."

"How far do these transmit?"

"About a quarter of a mile, or less depending on the environment."

Jack looked up at Gary in amazement. "This is going to be fun."

"Most of my little toys are."

"Yeah. I don't think eyeglasses would work. My guy doesn't wear glasses and we don't want the target to get suspicious."

"I hear you. If your target, as you call him, wasn't camera shy and the nervous type, then you wouldn't be in here talking to me."

Jack chucked. "You know your business. Okay. Lets see what all I need. Let's wire him up for video and sound. And I want him carrying backups. And then I'll need the equipment for me to listen in while I'm in my truck."

"And record it."

"And record it. We have to record it."

Gary nodded, grinning. "I knew when I woke up this morning that it was going to be a good day."

A few minutes later, Gary helped Jack carry a case containing radio receivers and two small television screens out to his pickup truck. He showed Jack how to plug it in to the cigarette lighter and how everything functioned. In a plastic bag Jack had the transmitters for Brad to wear, the two television cameras, one tie-tack and one lapel pin in the form of an American Flag, the camera being hidden in the blue field, and the two sound microphones.

Gary pointed to the tiny sound microphones. "You can pin those most anywhere, but you don't want them to be too muffled. Under the flag is good for one of them. Under a shirt collar is good for the other, maybe."

Jack nodded. "I feel better. It's like he has someone covering his back all the way while he's in there. Thanks."

Gary grinned. "Don't mention it. I really get a kick out of my job. So, who are you going to record? Do I know him?"

"You know of him, and you know I can't tell you."

Gary look dejected. "Alright. I figured as much, the kind of money you spent."

"Tell you what, after it's hit the papers, I'll send you a copy of the tape, how about that? You've been a big help to me."

Gary rubbed his hands together excitedly. "Can't ask for more than that. I can't wait."

Jack drove off still amazed at the scope of what he was able to purchase. Surveillance gear had really come a long way since he was a cop, and that wasn't very long ago.

Still, Brad was headed straight for trouble. It was going to take all this and all our wits to keep him from winding up dead. Pierce doesn't mess around with his enemies, and he's decided Brad is in the enemy category. He's not too happy with me either.

Jack shook his head. I wish I could think of another way. Looks like a good friend would come up with a way to save Brad from walking into Pierce's office and declaring himself straight out. Looks like it, but I can't. The best I can do is be there and at least with all of these toys, keep an eye on the situation.

Jack's hands gripped the steering wheel tightly. What if this turns south? What if Brad winds up in trouble? What do I do then? Jack shook his head. For one thing, it was time to get out his old service revolver and make sure it was clean. For another, if I need help at the last minute I better figure out ahead of time how I'm going to get it.

Jack drove toward home lost in his plans. One thing was certain. When my friend Brad goes in to battle Pierce, I will not let him down.

The Red Lion was busy when Brad entered Friday night looking for Jack. He'd received a call earlier. Jack had told him that he'd had success in finding the electronics they would need for Brad's meeting with Richard Pierce, but he had not gone into details. Brad was anxious to hear more. Brad ran a hand through his hair. He was anxious, period.

Jack was up at the bar in a group of four or five that seemed to be talking and laughing. Brad went up the bar next to them, not wanting to join in. "Give me a club soda, Rusty."

The bartender put a glass in front of Brad at about the same time that Jack appeared at his shoulder.

"I noticed you come in. Let's see if we can find a booth. It's pretty crowded in here." Jack peered out over the room. "There's a table over there." Jack pointed in the direction of an empty table.

Brad took his drink and nodded. He followed Jack to the table. As soon as they sat down, a waitress was at the table checking on them.

"We don't need anything right now. We'll signal if we do." Jack said to the waitress.

"So, you had some luck today?" Brad asked.

"Boy, did I ever. You won't believe what kind of toys you can buy these days. I spent a bunch of your money, too. I'll give you the bill later."

"I don't care what it costs. You know that."

"Yeah, I forgot. I should have had a look at fishing boats while I was on your dime."

"Funny. Actually, if this works I might buy you one. Now, what did you get?"

"Get this, not only are you going to be wired for

sound, but I'm going to get a video of the whole thing."

"Get out of here. You got video cameras that small?"

"You can't see them. One is a tie tack, the other is a lapel pin of an American flag."

"I like the flag. I'm not crazy about wearing a tie, but I suppose I should anyway." Brad said.

"You don't have to wear both, I just figured you should have backup."

Brad nodded. "That's good. And you have the equipment to pick up the signal?"

"It's in my truck. It runs off of the truck battery. And it will record the whole event."

"You did good, partner."

"I'll be parked in the truck right outside of your meeting. Oh, I got a cell phone, too."

Brad grinned at Jack. "You did what?"

"I got a cell phone. I wasn't sure why, but I thought it might come in handy. Here, I wrote the number down for you." Jack took a piece of paper out of his shirt pocket and slid it across the table to Brad.

Brad took the paper and chuckled. "I can see it now. I'm meeting with Pierce and my cell phone rings. It's you telling me to point camera two a little more left." Brad broke into laughter, slapping his knee with his hand.

"More likely I'd ask you if he had a television on up there tuned to the football game. I'm glad to see you relaxed about this whole thing."

"I'm scared to death. That's nervous laughter you just heard."

"I understand that."

"But I'm more scared of failure than anything else. I need to get Pierce to admit to killing Renee. If I can't do that then this is all futile, and he goes on killing or trying to kill... I have to get this right."

"You will. Appeal to his vanity. Tell him you admire his operation. Make him proud of it. Make him want to tell you what a smart man he is. Men like him like to talk about themselves. That's my experience anyway."

"Men like him?"

"He's got a reputation with the ladies. I use the term ladies very loosely. I'm sorry if I'm stepping on any toes here. But it's obvious from the way he conducts himself around town he's got quite an ego. You can use that."

"I got you. I'll try to keep that in mind when I meet with him."

Jack sat back in his chair with his palms face down on the table. "When do we want to do this?"

"I'm going to call him tomorrow morning and try to set up a meeting for the afternoon."

"I didn't think you'd wait around."

"I can't wait around. It's too dangerous to give him a chance to take me out before I get the chance to expose him."

"I knew you'd see it that way. So give me a call in the morning. Let me know as soon as you know when the meeting is on. I'll get with you before the meeting and show you the little toys I have and how they work."

Brad grinned. "I'm looking forward to that."

"Yeah, they're fun. Where are you planning to meet him?"

"His place if he'll agree to meet me there. He'll be more comfortable, more at ease at his place."

"That's good thinking."

"Also, and I didn't think of this until you told me, there would be video, but it's more compelling that it is actually him on the video if it's shot at his apartment."

"If he won't see you at his apartment?"

"I'll ask to see him at his office. Same things apply to his office that apply to his apartment."

Jack nodded in agreement. "Let's go over what you're going to say to him again. Also, we need a code word or phrase. If things start to go badly, you need to be able to notify me without alarming Mr. Pierce."

"I didn't think of that."

"Well it needs to be something innocent sounding."

"I know. If things turn south I'll get religion. I'll say something like 'Oh God'."

"I got it. Hell, if you make any reference God then I'm calling in the reserves."

"The reserves?"

Jack leaned forward in his chair. "The cops."

"Oh yeah. Let's hope the conversation doesn't go that way."

"I'm sure it won't. Let's talk about what you want to be saying."

Brad and Jack went over the things they wanted to get Pierce to admit, and difference ways to approach the subjects with him. They practiced parts of conversation, with Jack playing the part of Pierce. At the end of their preparation both of them were satisfied Brad was ready for Pierce.

CHAPTER **37**

Richard opened his eyes to find sunlight and a slight pain in his head. He moved, and that made the pain worse. He rubbed his head. Champagne last night. That was the problem.

He sat up in his bed. He shouldn't have had the champagne at his Dad's party last night. It always gave him a headache.

Nice party, though. Two phone numbers, and a blow job in the bathroom. Not bad. Not bad at all. Richard slapped his legs and threw them over the side of the bed. A little ibuprofen will cure this head thing and I'll be set to find out what the day will bring.

He got up from the bed and went to the window. Down below there was very little traffic, it being Saturday downtown. I probably should make a stop by Dad's and see if anything needs to be done after the party. That won't take long.

Such a bright day, there must be something for a bright boy to get into. Richard scratched his ass and thought for a moment. Coffee. I'll make coffee.

He went into the kitchen and started the coffee pot. Then he went back to the bedroom and dressed in his customary black jeans and shirt. He pulled on some black boots, as he felt a little rugged today.

He retrieved a morning Chronicle and sat down at

his table with newspaper and coffee. He had just started on the headlines when the phone rang.

"This is Brad Marshall for Mr. Richard Pierce."

Richard froze. He gripped the phone, aware that he was in danger of dropping it. After a pause he answered.

"Hello Mr. Marshall. This is Richard Pierce speaking."

"I would like to meet with you."

Richard turned the information over in his mind. This was too good to be true. Here I am racking my brain trying to figure out how to get rid of this guy, and he drops into my lap. Better play this cool, though. "What is it we have to talk about?"

"I have some information, and a proposition. I'm sure you'd find the meeting beneficial to you."

"Alright. When and where?"

"This afternoon? I could drop by your apartment. This won't take long."

"Would you be alone?"

"Yes. I would be alone."

Richard paused. He couldn't help but grin into the phone. He would need to make sure that everything was set up. "I have an appointment that I would need to cancel. Can I call you right back?"

"Sure. I'll give you my number."

Richard copied down the number and hung up. This was sweet. Careful now. This has to be done quietly. First to arrange for backup and security.

He called Duane. "Duane, I need you to be at my apartment at one o'clock this afternoon... good. Bring Reggie."

That took care of the backup. Now for security. He punched more numbers on the phone.

"Louis. This is Pierce. I need some help this afternoon. Your kind of help."

"Sure thing. What exactly do you need and where?" came the voice over the phone.

"I've got a meeting going on at my apartment. I want to make sure this guy coming isn't wired or anything like that."

"You got it. When?"

"Be here at one o'clock. I'll set up the meeting for two."

"You got it."

That takes care of security. Richard called Marshall back.

"Marshall. How about two o'clock?"

"You're sure that won't be any inconvenience?"

"No. Not at all. Although I can't imagine what we have to talk about. Still, if it won't take long, and you say I might benefit, then I'm up for a least listening to your spiel."

"I thank you."

"See you then."

Richard hung up and started laughing. This was too rich, too good to be true. Careful now, Richard. Don't let giddiness allow any mistakes to be made this time. It's time to plan the demise of one Mr. Marshall. By tonight he'll be out of my way forever.

He scratched his cheek, a frown forming on his face. Could this be a trap? What was Marshall really up to?

If it is a trap, it would have to be something lame.

I'm going to have him outnumbered. This game will be played by my rules. It's going to be a trap alright. But I'm going to be the one setting it. In the end, it will look like Marshall was so overcome with grief and remorse he took his own life. Poor sap. Richard laughed.

Richard went over to the window and looked out over the town he felt as if he ruled. When will they ever learn? When you play without fear of losing you don't lose. He laughed and stretched his arms out wide.

———————————

"It's on for two o'clock'" Brad said to Jack into the phone.

"Alright. I'll be in position around one. Don't you dare go in there until you hear from me."

"I won't, believe me." Brad hung up the phone and went over to the table in his hotel room. On the table was a printer he'd picked up the afternoon before. With a few strokes of a pocket knife, he had the box open and the printer set up. It took less than five minutes to start the process of printing Pierce's financial data for the meeting.

Brad stood with his hands on his hips watching the sheets of paper being extruded from the printer. He smiled. This would be quite a surprise for Mr. Richard Pierce. I'm sure he doesn't think anyone else has been looking at his little secrets.

Brad looked around the room. This part of his life would soon be coming to a close, he thought. Part of what kept him from returning to his own house was the guilt he felt at not being there when Renee needed him.

316

When he finishes exposing Richard Pierce for Renee's murder that debt will be repaid.

He thought of Renee's voice on the phone when she called him, told him she was in trouble. His head hung down, his eyes moist. It's too late to stop him, Renee. But I can make him pay.

His cell phone interrupted his thoughts.

"Brad, it's Jennifer. Are you busy?"

"Not right now. I have something this afternoon. Why?"

"Oh, I don't know. I just thought I'd like to see you. If that's alright?"

Brad smiled into the phone. "Of course it's alright. I'm in room five eighteen at the Doubletree."

"I'll be there in half an hour."

Brad put away his phone and went to the mirror. He felt silly, but his reaction to her call was to brush his hair. Satisfied that his hair looked fine, he went back and checked the printer. It was almost finished.

Brad tried to picture his upcoming meeting with Pierce, but his imagination failed him. He'd never met the man before. He'd seen a picture from the newspaper, so he knew approximately how the man looked.

There would be others there at the meeting, no doubt. I'm wanted for murder, Brad smiled to himself. He wouldn't take the chance to meet me alone.

Brad shivered. I'm walking right into the underbelly of this corrupt city enterprise armed with nothing more than proof of their misdeeds. Have I lost my mind? God, if there's any other way, please show me now.

He started to pace across the room. This is just stage fright. I'll be alright once this is put into action. I can do this. I know I can do it.

The printer quit spitting out pages, but Brad continued to pace. Slowly at times, but always moving, lost in thought, playing out the coming meeting in his mind.

Some minutes later came a knock at the door.

"Jennifer. Come in."

Jennifer stepped into the room. "Brad, you look worried. You're sweating. Do you feel alright? Maybe you're coming down with something." She wiped his brow and looked up into his eyes.

"No, I'm alright. I've just been going over some things in my mind. I'm fine."

"You don't look fine." Jennifer looked over at the printer. "What's going on, Brad? Does this have anything to do with what you said you had going on this afternoon?"

"Well, I... well yes."

Jennifer stood with her hands on her hips. "I knew it. What is it? What are you up to?"

"I'm meeting Pierce at two."

Jennifer's mouth flew open. "You're not! He'll kill you!"

"No he won't. I'll convince him that it's not in his best interest to harm me in any way."

Jennifer shook her head. "I don't like it. I don't like it one bit."

"You don't have a say. He's out of control and he has to be stopped. This is the only way."

"Let me go with you."

Brad laughed. "Not on your life, little lady. No, this is a job for me alone. Well, almost alone. Jack is going to be recording the event from down on the street."

Jennifer looked puzzled for a moment. "Oh, I get it. You're going to be wired, as they say. That's smart. What if he finds out?"

"Then I'm messed up real good. He won't find out. The electronics are too small for him to notice."

Jennifer stood looking at him, shaking her head. She moved up close to him. "Hold me?"

Brad put his arms around her and held her close, a look of surprise on his face. Her head was on his shoulder. He rocked her gently back and forth. The smell of her perfume was sweet.

"I don't want to loose you," she said.

"I'll be alright."

"Promise?"

"I promise." he said.

She looked up at him and kissed him intensely. He felt her body moving against his. "What time is your meeting?"

"Two o'clock."

"That's plenty of time."

CHAPTER **38**

Jennifer bounced out of the hotel and headed for her car. She smiled up at the sunshine on the roof of the parking garage where her car was parked.

Behind the wheel, her shoulders sagged. What a mess, to feel this good and not have something to do. Brad said to meet him later tonight at someplace called the Red Lion Bar & Grill, over on Alabama Street. I guess I can drive by there and make sure I can find it.

She perked back up and started the car. After that I'll go shopping. I'll need new clothes to carry with me to Europe!

She left the parking garage and started east on Westheimer, moving south to Alabama after a couple of blocks. She continued east on Alabama. She saw the Red Lion on her right. Looks alright, I guess. It looks fairly small.

She turned around and went to the Galleria, parked and went inside.

This was going to be fun. I've never shopped for a trip to Europe before. Somehow I'm sure I'll manage. She looked at the people she passed in the store and wondered if they noticed her happiness.

An hour later, she had purchased two outfits and sat down on a bench to decide what to do next. She looked at her watch. It was almost one o'clock. Brad would be leaving soon, if he hadn't already.

She crossed her legs, her foot dangling nervously in the air. She propped her chin up with one hand and tried not to think of the danger that Brad was walking into.

She jumped up and gathered her bags. It's best not to think about it. Brad will be fine. He's smart and he knows what he's doing. He'll come out of this alright. He has to.

Walking back to the car she felt her eyes grow moist. She could almost cry with worry. Searching in her purse for a tissue, she tried to get control of herself. She took a couple of deep breaths and told herself that everything was going to work out fine.

At her car, she put the bags in the trunk and got behind the wheel. She didn't know what else to do except go home and wait until it was time to meet Brad later. Maybe he would call when everything was finished. I'm sure he will. I need to be home to answer when he calls.

She started the car and headed home. She sighed. If I can just get through this day, just get through today, everything will be great.

At home, she tried on the outfits that she had bought and looked at herself in the mirror. She imagined how they would look on the trip, and wondered what Brad would think of them. I don't know his tastes that well, except that he's a man.

She smiled to herself. Yep, he's a man alright. Satisfied that she had made the right decisions with her purchases, she put the clothes away.

She went into the kitchen to prepare a late lunch.

Staring at the shelves of her pantry, she wrinkled her nose. She should eat, whether she felt like it or not. She got a can of tuna out of the cabinet and put it back. She got it back out. Making tuna salad would give her something to do, even if she didn't eat it, she thought.

She put a couple of eggs on to boil and looked at her watch. It was almost two. She was almost panting as she waited for the eggs to boil. Please Brad, please make this go okay.

At exactly one twenty, Brad put away his cell phone. He looked in the mirror. He adjusted his tie, noting that the tie tack with the video camera within was placed just right. He checked the lapel pin with the other camera. His hands went to the two microphones, just under his collar.

Jack had just called and said that he was in position on the street beside the loft apartments of the old Rice Hotel. He went over to the table in his hotel room and picked up the folder containing the financial records of Richard Pierce. He was ready.

Driving downtown he went over the meeting in his mind, and how he expected it to go. He had to get Pierce off his guard. He had to appear friendly with him. He had to convince Pierce that he was glad that Pierce had killed Renee, that Pierce had done him a favor. Otherwise, that bastard would never admit it.

Brad gripped the steering wheel tightly. Could he do it? He had to. He didn't have any other options.

He circled by the old Rice Hotel. There was Jack's truck, with Jack sitting inside of it. It being Saturday, there were places on the street to park. He picked one, and looked at his watch. It was ten minutes until two.

He looked up at the loft apartments. Somewhere up there was his opponent. Would he be alone? I doubt it. Time to test the gear.

"Testing. One. Two. Three. Testing. Do you read me Jack?"

Brad's phone rang. "Jack?"

"Yeah. Everything's working great. I hear you loud and clear, and I've got two pictures of your dashboard up on my screen."

"Alright then. I guess we're ready."

"Go get 'em, buddy. I got your back."

Brad picked up the folder and got out of his car. He crossed the street to the Rice Lofts apartments and went inside. He found himself in a spacious lobby, lushly decorated with plants. His insides trembled a little as he was waiting for the elevator.

In the elevator, he took several deep breaths. Calm down, he told himself. You've got to appear calm.

The door opened and he stepped into a hallway with thick rich carpet and dark paneled walls. Finding some numbers on a couple of doors, he searched out and found room 314. He knocked on the door.

The door opened to reveal a large man dressed in a black knit shirt and black sport jacket. Brad thought he showed a hint of a gun under the jacket.

"Come in. Mr. Pierce is expecting you."

Brad nodded and stepped into the room. It had high ceilings and was very spacious. The floors were wood. The wall opposite him was covered in windows. In front of the windows was another large man dressed the same as the first. Between him and the second man were two couches, facing each other and sitting on a rug, with a coffee table between them. Off to the right there appeared to be a kitchen.

To the left were a door and a desk. Two chairs were in front of the desk. Behind the desk a man was standing. Brad recognized the man to be Richard Pierce. He wore a gray knit shirt, and like the other men, a black sport jacket.

The man in front of him pushed Brad's arms out and ran his hands down his sides, obviously checking for a weapon. "He's clean, Rick."

"Of course he is. Come in, Mr. Marshall. Welcome to my home," Pierce said, gesturing with his hand. Pierce stood smiling at him.

Brad moved over to the desk. "So, we finally meet."

"Finally? I'm not sure what business we have with each other. But your message was intriguing. You alluded to some sort of proposition. I'm always open to new business."

"I hope you'll find my proposition irresistible."

Richard cocked his head to one side and gestured with one hand. "Is that what you're carrying? The proposal? A little show and tell presentation?"

"Not exactly. I'll show you what I have in a minute. Perhaps if I explain what it is that I'm looking for here. I want to be left alone. I want you to stop threatening me."

Richard leaned forward in his chair with raised eyebrows. His smile was gone. "I'm not engaging you in any way. It is you that is here engaging me."

"Look," Brad said, smiling. "You're a powerful and intelligent man with a lot of influence. Someone is making my life difficult. I'm convinced it's you. I thought that you might be reasonable and that we might reach an understanding."

"My influence is not an issue where you are concerned."

Brad's fingers curled until he made fists. He struggled to maintain control, forcing a smile to remain on his lips. "I know you killed my wife. You did me a favor. Let's just leave it at that, and you call off the District Attorney?"

Richard snarled at Brad. "I don't know what you're talking about. And frankly, this discussion is beginning to bore me. Is there anything else?"

Brad shook a fist at Pierce, his voice breaking. "I know you killed Renee. You had my friend Jack roughed up. And you blew up my office."

"I did no such thing. Those are some pretty outrageous accusations." Richard turned to his right. "Louis!"

CHAPTER **39**

A short man with a mustache came out of the door to the left. He carried a short wand type instrument in his hand.

"I'm afraid I'll have to ask you to stand up, Mr. Marshall," Richard said.

Brad stood up and placed the folder on the desk. The man with the wand walked straight to Brad and started waving the wand over his back. When he got to his mid-section there was a series of beeps. The man fished around in Brad's pockets and came out with his phone, which he placed on the desk.

A detector for electronic circuits! Of course. Brad had read about such things being used to sniff out bugs in foreign embassies.

"Oh God," Brad said, forcing a smile.

"God can't help you now," Richard said.

The man then started moving the wand across the front of Brad. It beeped at his tie. The man jerked the tie tack out, verified that it made the wand beep, and placed it on the desk. The lapel pin was next. It took a few more seconds for the man to find the two microphones, but the result was all of Brad's electronics were soon on the desk.

The small man with the mustache raked the smaller electronics off of the desk and into his hand. He left

Brad's cell phone on the desk. He closed his hand tightly and held it up to Richard. "He's clean on this end. Give us another minute."

Richard nodded. They all stood there in silence. What were they waiting for? Another series of beeps came from the direction of the short man called Louis. He took out a cell phone.

"Alright." he said into the phone. He turned to Richard. "We've got the other end of this little broadcasting station. It's in a pickup truck on the street. Just one old man, by himself. What do you want us to do?"

Richard nodded slightly, his gaze fixed upon Brad. "This must be your friend Jack as you called him," Richard said to Brad. "Tell him to hold him for ten minutes and then let him go. Make sure you get the tape."

"Get the tape, hold him for ten, then turn him loose," Louis said into the phone. He disappeared back behind the door.

Richard reached for the folder on the desk. "Now, lets see what you brought me." Opening the folder, Richard's face turned white. He took a deep breath. "Oh my. I see that you've been snooping where you shouldn't have been."

"A copy of that file is with my lawyer. If anything happens to me he has instructions to give it to the police and to the Houston Chronicle."

Richard's eyebrows were raised. He studied Brad's face. "Bullshit."

"No. Really. . ."

"Bullshit. You've already shopped these around the

police and newspaper. That's how your type operates. They told you this was nothing. This is just words and numbers on paper. You could have made this stuff up. You have plenty of reason to fabricate this, anything to divert attention away from the murder you committed."

Brad's knees turned weak. He wanted to sit down, but he didn't want to show his weakness. He gathered himself up and stood straight. "I didn't kill Renee. You did."

Richard opened a drawer to his desk and took out a .38 revolver. He pointed it at Brad. "Actually, I didn't kill her. I had a couple of my boys do it."

"I knew it," Brad said.

"Pity too. I kind of miss the way her ass thrashed around while she bellowed my name," Richard said.

Snickers came from the large men in the room. Brad's fists clenched tightly and his jaw was firm. He thought about trying to run for the door. There was no way he would make it out alive.

"Put your keys on the desk," Richard said.

Brad reached into his pocket put his keys on the desk. Richard reached out and picked them up.

"Now we go for a little ride, Mr. Marshall."

"You know, there are plenty of people that know I came to see you."

Richard laughed. "I haven't seen you! Don't you understand by now how things work little man? I run this town. You call 9-1-1 and the police take you downtown and question you all night. The police call me and I say I never saw the man and that's that. Besides, look around you at all of the witnesses that I was somewhere else. Now move it." Richard gestured toward the door with the gun.

Walking out into the hallway, Brad looked behind him to see that Pierce had put the gun into his jacket pocket, but it was still leveled at him. The two large men followed. He walked down to the elevator and stood. One of the larger men reached around and pushed the button for the elevator. It opened immediately.

Once in the elevator Brad saw the button for the garage was pushed. He rode down trying to think of a way out of this. There had to be something he could do. He obviously couldn't overpower them. There were too many of them and at least two of them were armed, probably all three.

The elevator door opened and Brad felt the barrel of the gun poke him in the back.

"Move along," Richard said. "Nice and easy. Don't get any ideas. I'll kill you here if I have to."

Brad peered around the garage as he walked slowly forward. If someone, anyone else would show up he could make a break for it. Surely these madmen wouldn't open fire if there were other witnesses. He saw no one. They were alone in the parking garage.

"It's this Lincoln here. Duane, you drive," Richard said.

The back door was held open for Brad.

"Move over," Richard said, and got in beside Brad.

Soon they were leaving the parking garage and going out onto the streets of Houston.

They came to a stop almost immediately at the first traffic signal, beside the old Rice Hotel. Brad craned his neck to see if he could see Jack. He saw Jack's truck and someone appeared to be standing beside it. He shook his head. Jack had his own troubles right now.

Richard sat beside him with the gun in plain view now. A curious smile had crept over his lips.

"You're not worried about what Jack will say to the police?" Brad asked.

Richard chuckled. "You just don't get it. Didn't I explain this to you? Who are they going to believe? Some old man whose main hobby is drinking beer, or the son of the Mayor?"

Brad's shoulders slumped. Richard was right. Throughout this whole ordeal he had been up against the power and might that this man wielded. I probably wouldn't even have been charged with murder had it not been for him pulling the strings.

"You forgot to lock the doors, Duane," Richard said.

"Sorry." The door locks clicked in unison.

There went that idea before I even had it, Brad thought. He looked at the gun pointed at him. This is no time to give up.

"So, you did kill my wife? Why?"

"She saw some things she shouldn't have. Had to do with another killing. I couldn't have her running around town spreading rumors."

"What did you do with her jewelry?"

"Her what? Oh. I'd forgotten about that. I remember now. It's in the drawer of my nightstand. I thought they might make some nice baubles to throw away on some other whore."

Brad's face flushed and his muscles grew tight. He

330

resisted the urge to lash out at Richard.

"Surely you're not bothered by her passing?" Richard said. "I got the impression you were no longer that close."

"What gave you that impression?"

"It was obvious she hadn't been getting any at home. Man, was her pussy grateful."

Brad jerked in the direction of Richard, but caught himself.

"Careful now, cowboy. Settle down. It won't be long now."

"Where are you taking me?"

"Home. I'm taking you home. You're going to get real sad over the murder you committed. You're going to kill yourself."

"I see," Brad said. He looked out at the buildings flowing by the window of the car. Think. There has to be a way out of this. Think.

There's too many of them, he thought. I need to separate them. I need to get them to turn on each other.

"You boys up there, you know whatever Pierce here pays you, I can afford to pay you four times as much. I'm a very rich man."

Duane laughed. His face peered over the back of the seat in front of Brad. "Rick takes real good care of us. It's like we get anything in the whole city that we want. Like we have the keys to it. No thanks. We're real happy with Rick. He takes care of us."

Brad's shoulder's slumped. Well, he had to try. He went back to watching the buildings slide by the window. There has to be something else he can try. He can't just give up.

I'm so close. I know where Renee's jewelry is. If I could just get free and get the police interested. With Jack's help I know I could get the police on him if I could just get free. Damn him for locking the doors. Maybe some of my neighbors will be outside when we get to the house. That's going to be a long shot.

He looked over at Richard with the gun. His stomach felt sick with the revulsion he felt over that man. Here was a man that used his talents and power to destroy lives and line his own pockets. He would have hated Richard Pierce if he had never met him. Now that he'd met the filthy pig it turned his stomach.

"Once last chance fellas. I can make you rich men," Brad called out to the men in front.

"No thanks. Like I said, Rick takes real good care of us," came the reply.

Richard laughed. "You just don't get it. I'm the big man. You're just a sad little guy that's about to end it all. You were too sad and too weak to face the miserable life you had in front of you. That's what they'll say about you." He laughed again.

Brad seethed with nowhere to go. His gaze crawled over the inside of the car, looking for something that would help him. He found nothing. He watched as the gun swayed while Richard laughed. He sat tensed, and waited for a moment, a second, when the gun was pointed away from him so that he might grab it. The opportunity never came. Richard calmed back down quickly, the gun still leveled at Brad.

"I can tell by the way you're looking at it that you would like to try to grab the gun. I assure you I will not hesitate to shoot you here."

"Won't that mess up your plans?"

"Not much. I have the gun pointed at your head. We'll just drag your body out and put it in your house. No bother to us, really."

Brad turned back to the window. Is this how it was to end? He thought about Jennifer, recalling the feeling of her against him earlier that day. This can't be. I can't let this happen. I still have plans for my life.

CHAPTER **40**

"There's a cop behind us, Rick," Duane said from behind the wheel.

"Has he been following us or did he just get here?" Richard asked.

"He just showed up."

"Then don't pay any attention to him. He doesn't even know we're here."

Brad started to look behind them.

"No. Don't do that," Richard said. "If I have to shoot you here I will. And he won't see it."

Brad settled back down in the seat. His mind raced, trying to think of something to do, some way to get the cops attention.

"Rick, he turned on his lights," Duane said.

Richard looked at his watch. "That old man in the truck is still back there. Nobody knows we're here. I wonder what he wants? Well pull over, Duane. It must be some sort of mistake."

Duane pulled the car over to the curb. Richard peered out the back window at the patrol car parked behind them; it's lights still flashing.

A booming voice came from the loudspeaker of the patrol car. "Everybody out of the car with your hands in the air."

Duane and Reggie stared at each other. Richard

looked down at the gun in his hand, then at Brad.

"Use your juice and get us out of here, Rick," Duane said.

"Keep a gun pointed at this guy," Richard said to Duane. As soon as Duane had his gun out and pointed at Brad, Richard put his own in his pocket. "They must have us confused with somebody else." He opened the car door.

"Yeah. Rick will just show 'em who he is, like before," Duane said to Reggie.

Richard opened the car door.

"Richard Pierce, we know you're in there. Get out of the car with your hands in the air. Everybody out with your hands in the air."

Richard slammed the car door shut, his face white. "Get out of here!" he screamed.

The tires screeching, Brad and Richard were thrown back deep into the seat. The car accelerated and swerved back and forth as Duane weaved through the light traffic. Horns blared. They paid no attention to stop lights. Brad looked out and saw the scenery flying by. Behind them sirens wailed.

Looking over at Pierce, he saw he had the gun back out. Again he was facing the barrel end of the pistol. The car swerved, and Brad struggled to remain stationary in his seat.

"Well, what are you going to do now, Pierce?" Brad asked.

"Shut up."

Brad looked out the window. They were entering the Southwest Freeway, and they were traveling fast. The car continued to swerve back and forth as Duane made his way through the traffic.

The car jerked to the left and threw him up against the window. He saw that they barely missed the back end of an eighteen-wheeler.

Was this how it was going to end, in a car crash? Am I going to be shot and mangled? Brad looked at the gun and then back out the window. He saw the cars flying by them and held on to the armrest for support. The tires squealing, they ricocheted back and forth.

"I need some direction up here, Rick. What do you want me to do?" Duane asked.

"I'm thinking. Alright. Move over to the right. Get ready to take the next exit," Richard said. He peered out of the back of the car.

"Next exit is Kirby," Duane said.

"Right. Take the Kirby exit. The cops are a ways back. Right after we get off of the freeway, stop and let me out," Richard said.

"I got it." Duane said.

Brad looked at Duane. He saw his opening. He hollered up to the front seat. "You see what he's doing, Duane? He getting out and leaving you to the cops."

"Shut up," Richard said through his teeth.

"You should have taken me up on my offer, Duane. This is how old Rick takes care of you. He's going to hang you out to dry with the cops while he disappears."

The tires started screeching, Richard and Brad were thrown hard up against the back of the seat in front of them. The car came to a halt in the middle of the freeway. Duane's face leered over the back of the seat at Richard.

"What the fuck, Rick?" Duane asked. "Is he right?

What the fuck do you mean you're getting out and leaving us?"

"You imbecile! Get moving!" Richard screamed.

"Why don't you just use your juice to get us all out of this? Like before? You want to get out? Get out now!"

The sirens closed in on them, surrounding them in the middle of the freeway. The doors opened on the police cars and again the voice was heard over the loudspeakers. "Everybody out of the car with your hands in the air."

"You moron," Richard said to Duane. He placed the gun on the seat and opened the car door. Looking over at Brad, he said, "This isn't over."

"Oh yes it is," Brad replied.

"So the whole time I was sweating blood in that car, thinking that you hadn't had a chance to call the cops, you'd already called them?" Brad asked Jack.

They were sitting together at a booth at the Red Lion. Brad had to go looking for him, after the police had dropped him back at his car. But he knew where to look.

"Right. I called Sergeant McNair yesterday and told him what you were up to. Called him again when I was set up on the street."

"Why didn't you tell me?" asked Brad.

"I didn't want you to rely on the police. I really didn't know how much help they would be," Jack shrugged. "They hadn't been much help so far."

"I guess they finally got the hint."

"McNair told me when things went bad that he figured if Pierce was dirty he'd do something stupid when you showed up with those financials."

"So you talked to him later today?" Brad asked.

"Right after you came out of the garage in Pierce's car, he came walking up to the truck and scared off that little punk with a gun on me."

"You did see me come out of the garage, then?"

"Yeah. They did too. They had an unmarked car on you when you came out. The patrol car must have showed up later when they decided to bring it to a close."

"I'm glad they finally got around to it. I damn near got clipped in the car."

"I'll bet you were surprised when they showed up," Jack chuckled.

"Was I ever. When I got out of the car they made us all lie down on the ground and put everybody in handcuffs. Then I heard McNair's voice saying 'Not that one, he's okay.' I got up and there he was."

"Well they have him for kidnapping you. McNair says that they'll get a search warrant and since they know what they're looking for they'll find those financial records on their own now. Mr. Pierce and his friends are in a lot of trouble, including his Daddy."

"I told McNair where to look for Renee's jewelry."

"Pierce told you where that was? Good." Jack nodded and took a sip of his beer. "They should have enough to make him the subject of the murder charge instead of you."

"McNair said he would recommend that to the DA.

Said it might take a week to straighten everything out."

"Is that wonderful looking woman headed this way looking for you? Sure seems like it," Jack said, his gaze pointed toward the door.

Brad turned around in his seat to see Jennifer bouncing toward him.

"Oh sweetie, you're here!" she said, kissing him lightly.

"Hi. Jennifer Hart, I'd like you to meet Jack Wilkerson."

Jennifer and Jack exchanged a handshake.

"God, am I glad you're alright. I knew you would be. I was worried sick, though," Jennifer said.

"I'm sorry I couldn't call you. Pierce took my phone."

Jennifer formed her mouth into a pout. "Why didn't you tell him you needed it to call an important woman in your life?"

Brad chuckled. "Somehow I don't think it would have mattered to him at all."

"So tell me, what happened?" Jennifer asked. "Don't leave anything out."

Brad gave Jennifer a brief description of the afternoon's activities. He tried to downplay the danger.

"So Richard Pierce is in a lot of trouble. And what happens with your murder case?" she asked.

"That should get dropped this week," Brad said.

"Yippee!" Jennifer threw her arms around Brad. "I knew you could do it."

"You'll be busy for at least a week anyway, writing this up for the Chronicle," Brad said.

"Oh, I didn't think of that! This is going to be my

exclusive. I'll win a Pulitzer! Not to mention all of those long interviews I'll need to have with you." She threw her head on Brad's shoulder.

"I'd leave you two alone, but I claim this joint as my office," Jack said.

"Oh we'll be alone soon enough. Brad is taking me to Europe."

"Europe!" Jack's eyebrows went up, a big smile creeping across his face. "I'm a little jealous. How come I don't get a trip to Europe?"

Brad turned to Jack, his arms around Jennifer. "I figured, what with all of the help you've been to me, you'd rather have a new fishing boat."

Jennifer kissed Brad on the cheek, then rubbed her nose against him and smiled.

Jack sat back and put his hands palm down on the table. His face took on a serious tone. "I just might let you do that. I just might." He winked.